HOW TO SLEEP AT NIGHT

HOW TO SLEEP AT NIGHT

A NOVEL

ELIZABETH HARRIS

WM

WILLIAM MORROW

An Imprint of HarperCollinsPublishers

HarperCollins books may be purchased for educational, business, or sales promotional use. For information, please email the Special Markets Department at SPsales @harpercollins.com.

FIRST EDITION

Designed by Michele Cameron

Library of Congress Cataloging-in-Publication Data

Names: Harris, Elizabeth, 1983– author.
Title: How to sleep at night : a novel / Elizabeth Harris.
Description: First edition. | New York, NY : William Morrow, 2025. |
Identifiers: LCCN 2024011420 | ISBN 9780063353237 (hardcover) | ISBN
   9780063353251 (ebk)
Subjects: LCGFT: Queer fiction. | Political fiction. | Novels.
Classification: LCC PS3608.A7828 H69 2025 | DDC 813/.6—dc23/eng/20240612
LC record available at https://lccn.loc.gov/2024011420

ISBN 978-0-06-335323-7

24 25 26 27 28 LBC 5 4 3 2 1

For Kelly

HOW TO SLEEP AT NIGHT

1

ETHAN SAT DOWN next to his husband at their dining room table, took his hand, and then told him something terrible.

"Gabe," he said, "I want to run for Congress."

"That's great, angel," Gabe replied. He was grading a stack of tenth-grade history papers, and he wasn't sure how seriously to take this.

Ethan had been interested in politics since they met, back when they were still routinely carded buying alcohol. Ethan was twenty-four at the time, working in the office of the New York State attorney general, a vicious thug from a dynastic Democratic family. Gabe was a twenty-one-year-old college student, and he fully believed that Ethan could become president of the United States one day, the way he believed the most beautiful theater major at his small liberal arts school would eventually win an Oscar. But life marched along. Ethan went to law school. They got married. They had a kid.

"There's an open seat," Ethan continued, his gaze steady. "And I had a call today with a political consultant."

Oh. Maybe this was serious. Gabe could feel a ribbon of panic rising in the back of his throat.

"Okay," Gabe said, drumming his thumb against the table.

"The guy who's held the seat for twenty-eight years is retiring," Ethan said. "It's a little south of us, but you don't have to live in the district to run for Congress, only in the state."

Gabe tried to breathe while counting to ten.

"The candidates who are going to run hold useless local offices, and most people in the district have never heard of them. So if I come in with a bunch of advertising, really flood the zone, it sounds like I've got a shot."

Twenty. Maybe he should count to twenty.

"It's a reliably Republican district," Ethan said, standing up from his chair to pace the room. "And it's going to stay that way."

There it was.

Ethan had always been to Gabe's right politically, and twenty years ago, when they started dating, that was fine. Gabe was so liberal there wasn't much room on his left anyway. And even when they disagreed in theory, they still rooted for the same team: They both voted for Democrats. Ethan *worked* for a Democrat.

But over time, Ethan's views had shifted. Slowly at first, like a shadow tilting in the afternoon sun. As he became more conservative, the overlapping ground between them narrowed. Today, there was almost nothing left.

"And I'd be an interesting story," Ethan continued, striding from one end of their dining room to the other. He was six foot four, and his long legs carried him across the space in just a few quick steps. "At least a couple of news outlets will be curious about a gay Republican who used to be a Democrat. It's the future of the conservative movement, with Black conservatives and gay conservatives and immigrant conservatives. This is what the Republican Party should be!" He was gesticulating now with his long fingers spread wide. Was he giving a stump speech in their dining room?

Ethan noticed that Gabe wasn't speaking.

"Honey?" Ethan sat back down at the table. "What do you think?"

Gabe felt like he was trying to breathe into a plastic bag. "I'm—I'm not sure," he said slowly.

"Look, I won't do this if you don't want me to," Ethan said firmly. "It's not just my life, I recognize that. It's also going to put you in the spotlight."

Gabe gave him a smile, the muscles of his face drawn more tightly than he would have liked.

"Do you have any questions?" Ethan asked. "What can I tell you about how this would work?"

Gabe's mind was frozen. He'd lost the ability to process language.

"Think about it. I know it's a lot to absorb." Ethan stood up and kissed the top of Gabe's head. "I'm going to go do a little work." He disappeared into the kitchen, where Gabe heard him putting water in the kettle, readying mugs for tea.

Gabe sat at their dining room table, still and silent, panicking. He took off his glasses to polish away a smudge with his shirt, and rubbed until one of the lenses popped out in his hand.

2

NICOLE WAS STANDING in her kitchen making peanut butter and jelly sandwiches for her kids. One required crunchy peanut butter and the other smooth, one liked orange marmalade and the other raspberry jam. Not even the bread was the same. She was battling with the lid of the crunchy jar when she heard a familiar voice coming from the television.

"The governor did say that, but I haven't found any record of it happening," said the woman on TV. "He's a real challenge to cover."

Nicole startled and felt the jar slip from her hand. It dropped onto the cold tile of her kitchen floor, cracking the foundation of her daughter's lunch into shards of glass suspended in goo.

She took the lonely top of the peanut butter jar with her into the next room, stepping carefully over her mess with bare feet. She couldn't possibly recognize that voice after so long, she thought. It had easily been fifteen years.

But she did. Nicole arrived in front of the television to find Kate Keller staring back at her from the Global Satellite News Network, opposite a morning anchor with his serious face on. Kate Keller. Her hair was different, shorter now, hitting just below her chin, and the intervening years had left her with a more angular face, sharper cheekbones. But it was her, beaming into Nicole's living room, fucking up her morning.

"What was that?" Austin asked as he trotted down the stairs, fastening the final buttons on his shirt. She pulled her eyes away from the TV and tried to make them focus on her husband. What had he just said?

He tried again: "Hey. You okay?"

"What? Yeah. I broke one of those glass jars of peanut butter," she said. She looked down and saw that she'd trailed dribbles of oil in from the kitchen.

"Why don't you just buy Jif?" He slid past her to rejoin the mug of coffee he'd left in the living room. He took a sip and dropped onto the couch to put on his leather oxfords.

What do I do? Nicole thought. What would I normally do? Normally she would rush back to the kitchen before the kids tracked peanut butter all over the house. But normally a woman she'd repeatedly seen naked wasn't on TV in her living room.

Austin looked at Kate Keller over his coffee mug and Nicole felt herself stop breathing. Then he found a spot on his khakis and started scratching at it with his fingernail.

"He repeats misinformation so many times that people start believing it," Kate told Nicole's husband as the morning anchor nodded along. "We can't be a conduit for that."

The last time Nicole saw Kate, they had staggered through a near silent breakfast, hangovers blazing, at a diner on Ninth Avenue in Manhattan. It was the kind of place that was once everywhere in New York City, with pleather booths and six-page menus, where the bacon was almost liquid with grease and the coffee tasted faintly of a house fire.

Nicole and Kate had known one another for years at that point, and they had clawed each other's clothes off the night before. But over eggs and toast that morning, as conversations ricocheted fast and loud around them, they could think of nothing to say. They chewed mostly in silence, dropping occasional observations about their breakfast or the topography of their headaches. They couldn't find a rhythm, and maybe were too tired to really try. Nicole was relieved when the check materialized before they'd finished their food.

Outside on the street, they hovered opposite one another awkwardly before Nicole moved in for a quick kiss, touching their lips lifelessly together. She pulled back again before Kate could reciprocate. They said they'd talk soon, which they didn't, and turned away.

"We're forced to become filters in a way a lot of journalists really aren't comfortable doing," Kate said from the TV screen. "It scares us to say that someone is lying."

3

KATE ALWAYS DREADED doing TV. She was afraid her nerves would make her slow on her feet, or that she'd misspeak in the moment and step in some shitstorm that would drag her for days on social media. She was a print reporter. She liked that her thoughts had to sit for a minute before they went out into the world. And of all things, talking off the cuff about politics was the worst. Shitstorms aplenty even when you chose your words with precision and a dictionary.

"We'll be right back," the handsome anchor said, peering intently into the camera. He paused, looking purposeful for a few silent moments, then his veil of televised professionalism abruptly fell away. His brow unfurled, his posture loosened, and as he complained to a producer about a new teleprompter he disliked, Kate heard the cadence of his voice become more natural, no longer hitting periodic words with excessive emphasis. He was like some sort of Pinocchio marionette in an expensive blue suit becoming a real boy.

"Thanks, Patrick," Kate said, unpinning her microphone. A producer popped up behind her and unwound a cord from inside her jacket.

"You going to the newsroom today?" he asked, staring at his phone.

She watched him for a second or two, wondering if he'd look up at her. He didn't.

"Going there now," she replied. She gave a quick smile and a "thanks" to the producer who untrussed her.

"That was a good story on the front page today about Brett Cooper," Patrick said.

Kate had no idea what story he was talking about. She hadn't written it, so she hadn't read it. Political reporters were expected to live and breathe the details of voter sentiments and poll numbers, of who was up, who was down, and who was about to be indicted. She should have ingested as much coverage as possible from all her main competitors by the time she finished her instant oatmeal that morning, sucking it down while hunched over her kitchen counter. She played a word scramble game on her phone instead. Kate hadn't even read her own newspaper.

She could guess what the Brett Cooper story said anyway. He was running for reelection as the Republican governor of Georgia and as the telegenic brand ambassador for the hard right. He gave a great speech and somehow looked athletic and vigorous in a suit, his dark blond hair gelled into submission, but the man had gained a national following by whittling away at the edges of American democracy. Kate had just been talking about him on the air, his enthusiasm for banning books and his disdain for things like facts. He was among the most popular politicians in the country, certainly the most discussed, and he was clearly readying himself to run for president in the next election.

"Yeah, great story," Kate said of the article she hadn't seen. She rose from behind the blue lacquered anchor desk, ready to make her escape. "These are crazy times. Fifteen years ago, nobody would have believed this."

"Keeps us in a job, though," Patrick said with a grin. "Am I right?"

He was. Lunatic behavior made for better stories. And Kate was sick of it. It made her want to toss her expensive, work-issued laptop out her living room window and watch it shatter against the sidewalk.

KATE STEPPED OFF the elevator and swiped her ID badge at the bulletproof glass doors, which relinquished a muffled "pop" as they unlocked. She walked through the *Herald Ledger* newsroom, a big open rectangle of space. Newsrooms were designed this way so different departments could be within shouting distance if they needed to collaborate on news, a comfortable approach for what had traditionally been a business of yellers.

Kate powered past the Business Desk, where reporters tended to look more put together than their compatriots, pulling on the occasional suit for meetings with Wall Street types. She hung a left at the Metro Desk, where many of the youngest reporters could be found, sitting straight and eager in their mesh swivel chairs, along with a clutch of veterans who had spent their adult lives in that department, obsessed by New York or preferring a life with minimal travel. She continued past the International Desk, where there were no reporters because they were all based overseas. Editors in that corner vibrated with anxiety and caffeine.

She reached her desk, which had an unobstructed view of a multi-story parking garage, and dropped her jacket over the wall of her cubicle. There were few political reporters in the newsroom at any given time because the beat generally required lots of travel or a station in DC. But the editors were always there. They became fixtures, like water fountains or spiky office plants.

The LED lights overhead exposed fingerprints and oily streaks on her laptop screen, but she made no move to clean it, instead taking out her phone while the computer booted up. She scrolled through her emails, which were mostly PR pitches ("Are remote Fridays effective against teacher burnout?") and blasts from political candidates taking gleeful shots at their rivals ("Don't let Kickback Kathy get to Congress!"). Then she checked Instagram. She often picked up followers when she did a national TV show, but she was sure to disappoint them. Kate rarely posted anything, mainly using the app to watch cooking videos, though she hardly ever cooked herself. It was difficult to make an elaborate meal for one person, so she ate a lot of runny scrambled eggs, sourdough toast, and raw vegetables straight out of a colander.

She had eleven new followers today. There was a dermatologist named Dr. Mitch, whose teeth were white like halogen bulbs shining from his face, a woman whose profile description said she was "here for the English Bulldog content," which made the follow a peculiar choice, and—wait.

Her third follower was "Nicole H." She had curly hair, a thick upper lip, and a wide smile. The account was private, but the profile picture, small as it was, looked like it could be Nicole Harmon. Kate brought the phone within inches of her face and examined the tiny photo.

It was her.

God, she had been in love with that woman. Nicole had been fearless, intimidated by no one, certain she was a match for any situation. She was always the first to dance at a party, always trying to make a regular day into an event. In college, where everyone was in love with Nicole, people used to say she had *Pretty Woman* hair. The red came out of a bottle, but she did have big curls riding down her back that looked like they belonged on a young Julia Roberts.

Kate and Nicole dated for a while in their early twenties, and almost immediately, Kate saw a future for them together. In her eyes, Nicole was the sexiest, the funniest, the smartest, someone with whom she could build a whole life. Except she treated Kate like garbage. Why they hadn't worked, why Nicole hadn't given them a real try, was an excruciating puzzle box Kate could never solve. For years, she'd been furious about their dynamic, which cast her in the role of the besotted, accepting scraps of attention in secret. She blamed herself as much as she blamed Nicole. Now, she recognized that they had both been young and they didn't know what the hell they were doing. There had been something powerful between them, even if it was kind of shitty, too.

Nicole had never had much of a presence on social media, as far as Kate could tell, and she stopped updating her profiles altogether around the time she left New York and moved to Louisville, Kentucky. Her Facebook picture was of her in a red dress and sunglasses on the roof of what looked like the Metropolitan Museum of Art. It was probably taken fifteen years ago. Kate couldn't imagine leaving New York City for Louisville, which she knew made her sort of an asshole. She understood that it was a lot more affordable, and that it was what people described as a "manageable" city, which Kate took to mean it was an easy place to have a car. But Nicole's family lived in Cincinnati, which was just a few hours away, and New York had not gone for her as she'd planned.

After Nicole left, her online trail ran dry pretty quickly. Kate had never been able to figure out what she did professionally, but she did find Nicole's husband, Austin Moore. He worked at a pharmaceutical company, had gone to high school and college in Lexington, and had an MBA from a major university in Pittsburgh. He was a lot older than Nicole, and was either extremely photogenic or lamentably handsome.

One time, Kate had fallen down a bit of a rabbit hole, putting her reporting skills to unwholesome use. She figured out where they lived and how much they paid for their four-bedroom, three-thousand-square-foot house ($495,000!). But that was years ago, probably around the time Kate and her now ex-wife, Shirin, were planning their wedding, and it made her feel pathetic. She hadn't done it since.

But no time like the present! "Nicole Harmon," she googled on her laptop. Not much came up: A bio from when Nicole was getting her master's in art history at Columbia. An obituary for her grandmother, dead at age ninety-seven, that listed Nicole as a survivor. And there were some useless hits on "ourphonebook.com," which offered the false promise of information in exchange for a real credit card number. That was about it.

So Kate switched to the husband. He was still at the same company, Paxol Pharmaceuticals, according to the internet. He had a fancy title now, senior vice president of national corporate affairs, and worked in—Halifax, New Jersey.

She looked them up in Louisville public records, found their address, and searched for the house. It sold more than a year ago for $670,000.

They had moved back.

She picked up her phone and studied the bio of her new Instagram follower. "Nicole H. Don't post pictures of your dinner." Kate took a screenshot and texted it to her brother, Ethan, and his husband, Gabe. The four of them had spent a couple of late nights together in their twenties, drinking too much in Williamsburg bars. That was during a brief flash of time when things between Kate and Nicole felt simple and clear.

"Recognize my new follower?" she texted them. "I'll give you a hint: she was not your favorite."

It was Gabe who texted back first.

Gabe: Is that Nicole Harmon?? Wow—it's been 100 years and I still hate her! Block her! Block her!

Kate smiled, and followed her back instead.

G ABE PAWED THROUGH his backpack looking for ibu-profen. It felt like there was a small animal trapped in his head, trying to burrow its way out through his left temple. He found the bottle buried in his bag, next to a pair of tiny red socks and a collection of dusty pebbles his daughter must have stored there for later use. He put three pills in his mouth and swallowed them without water.

He was in the teachers' lounge waiting to make copies, a room that filled his nose with the astringent sourness of cheap coffee. The Xerox in the main office was usually broken, so there was often a line to use this machine. Never in the mood to stand around and wait, Gabe would put off his photocopying until the last possible moment, like the one in which he found himself that morning. He needed packets with readings and essay questions on World War II for sixty-seven students. He was sixty-six copies short. A math teacher was running off worksheets in front of him, which allowed Gabe time to focus on his fretting.

Gabe's parents loved Ethan, but it had taken them years to get over the fact that he wasn't Jewish—and they were barely observant. Their real religion was the Democratic Party. They lived in Bennett, Long Island, a purple town with just a hint more blue to it than red, kind of like a bruise, and they were proud of the fact that unlike progressives in New York City, their votes actually mattered. Gabe had grown up in that town, around liberals and conservatives, but his parents had retreated into a more clearly defined bubble as they'd grown older, no longer forced through their children or their jobs to spend time with people they disagreed with.

After a few strained conversations about voter ID laws, they stopped asking Ethan about his preferred candidates. They were aware he was conservative, but they settled into the delusion that he still supported Democrats when it was time to cast his ballot, or at least in elections that mattered. Ethan had been kind enough to allow them their fantasy. Learning he'd become a Republican would be much worse than knowing he was nominally Protestant.

The math teacher finished her copies and Gabe stepped up to make his packets.

"Morning!" a voice boomed behind him. Michael Lyman, the AP Government teacher, materialized at his side.

"Hi, Michael," Gabe said.

"Making a lot of copies?"

"Yeah, sorry. It's going to be a couple minutes."

"No problem," Lyman said, leaning against the cinder block wall to wait. "Hey, how old is your daughter now?"

"She's five. How far along is your wife?"

"Thirty-seven weeks! She could go any day. I've done my research, read all the important parenting books, but man, I've barely held a baby before! I don't know what the hell I'm going to be doing."

"You'll figure it out," Gabe told him. Lyman was among the most condescending people on the planet and Gabe found it momentarily charming that he'd admitted ignorance on any subject. "Babies have very few needs at the beginning. They eat, they sleep, they poop. You'll get a handle on that, and then they'll grow new tricks. But it happens slowly, so you'll be fine. More tired than you've ever been, but fine."

Lyman chuckled approvingly. "I'm sure you're right."

The printer made a crunching sound, and its rumbles and whirls abruptly stopped. Gabe got down on one knee to try to find the problem.

"It's so crazy," Lyman said. "I can't believe they're going to let me walk out of the hospital with an infant."

"It's crazier than you can imagine," Gabe replied into the bowels of the printer. He found a crumpled piece of paper sandwiched between some rollers and yanked it out.

"I hate this machine," Lyman said. "You ever think about having another kid?"

"Not really."

"It's got to be expensive for you. Surrogates and all that."

Gabe nodded.

"I want two kids," Lyman continued. "My wife wants three or four, but no way. No idea how we'd afford that."

"Kids aren't cheap," Gabe said, rising from the floor as the machine spun back to life.

"How'd you guys do it?" Lyman asked with blank curiosity. "Did you have a surrogate or did you adopt?"

Gabe blinked at him as he wondered: What the hell is wrong with people?

The first time Gabe got a question like this, he had just told his assistant principal he was going to be a father and would need to take paternity leave. "Do you know the genetic mother?" she wondered, in a tone like she was asking if they'd selected a stroller. He was so shocked by the question that he answered in elaborate detail. (We had an egg donor, he told her, who we interviewed but don't keep in regular touch with, and a surrogate who we talk to all the time. Also, the baby is due in May so I'll need help finishing out the school year.) Once he parted with that information, he felt like a curiosity. Like he needed a shower.

When Chloe was a baby, those questions came every few months. But as she grew into a kid, people thought less about her gestation. Once in a while, though, when Gabe was trapped at the copy machine, for example, someone would ask. Gabe's favorite response was a reciprocal question, which he considered to be an inelegant but necessary fuck you. "How about you?" he'd ask those strangers. "Did you do IVF?"

The embarrassment wafted over his targets in waves, first at being asked such a rude and personal question, then when they realized they had done the same.

It did backfire on occasion, like the time he was trailed around a party for two hours by a woman who wouldn't stop apologizing. She reappeared by his side at periodic intervals to beg forgiveness, rehashing their exchange in front of whoever Gabe was speaking to at that moment. He didn't want the equivalent to happen at school, where he was trapped with Lyman not for an evening, but for years. It was best to remove himself from the situation before he said something he'd come to regret.

"I didn't realize how late it was." Gabe snatched a stack of copies off the machine. It wasn't all of them, but it was enough for his next class. "I've got to get going. I've got a meeting with a student," he lied.

"Your copies aren't done," Lyman said.

"I'll come back for them later," Gabe called over his shoulder as he pulled open the door.

Gabe's phone buzzed. It was Kate, texting about some woman she dated a few lifetimes ago. Ethan must not have told her yet.

MOM," HENRY SAID, climbing into the back seat of Nicole's bright white SUV. "Sarah's bringing a bag of dirt into the car."

"It's not dirt," Sarah protested. "My teacher said it's soil."

"That's great, sweetie," Nicole replied. "Oh, does that bag have a hole in it?"

"I don't know." Sarah struggled to unfurl her seat belt while clutching the plastic baggie in one hand. Her tightly curled hair, which had been in a pouf at the top of her head that morning, was loose around her face, the hair tie never to be seen again.

"Let me hold that while you get in your booster." Nicole reached over and took hold of Sarah's prize. It was indeed a bag of dirt. Fluffy dirt, the color of dark chocolate. At least the upholstery inside the car was black.

"She's going to get dirt all over the car, Mom." Henry, her eight-year-old, was a rule-bound child who felt compelled to point out when others misbehaved. He liked to tell Nicole who in his class had to stay inside for recess because they'd been disruptive, or which kids brought candy to school even though it was forbidden. There was, of course, an extra twinkle in his eye when he tattled on his little sister.

"It's okay, honey," Nicole assured him, handing the bag back to Sarah. "If it spills, we can vacuum. Sarah, why do you have dirt? Soil, I mean."

Henry pouted. "I was helping."

"We're composting at school," Sarah said proudly, nestling the bag into the purple tulle of her dress. She insisted on going through life exclusively in what she described as princess outfits. "I'm going to put the soil in our garden," she explained. "Or I'll sell it and get rich!"

Nicole nodded. No one had warned her that so much of parenthood was trying not to laugh at one's children. "Good to have a backup plan," she said. She pushed the start button on her car, allowing it to rumble quietly to life.

Sarah was a confident kid. If she caught a ball one time, she declared herself an amazing baseball player, and when she sounded out her first word, she said she was the best at reading. Nicole encouraged this outlook, aware that the world would mostly question the abilities of her little girl. Henry, on the other hand, was always more aware of the things he couldn't do. His insecurity was only getting more pronounced as he got older.

"Henry, honey," Nicole said, "how was your day?"

No response. She turned to look at him as he stretched his legs, which were long enough now to rest on the floor while he was wearing his seat belt. He was getting tall, like his father, but he still looked like Nicole. He had her unruly curls and her thick upper lip, a dimple like hers on only one cheek. Sarah also had the curls, but her face was more of a mix.

"Henry?"

Still no response.

"HENRY!"

"What?"

"Please don't ignore me. How was your day?"

"I don't remember," he said. "Can I play Candy Cart on your phone?"

"No, honey." Nicole put the car in drive and rolled it gently out of the parking lot to ferry the children to their weekly art class. In the rearview mirror she looked at her kids, who were bathed in slanted afternoon light—just as Sarah dug a booger out of her nose and popped it into her mouth.

Nicole gagged quietly in the front seat, and pretended she hadn't seen a thing.

O KAY, WE'VE GOT them," said the kids' art teacher, a recent college graduate whose tangled ponytail stretched between his shoulder blades. "We'll see you at pickup, Mom."

God, she hated that. She understood that teachers and coaches were not going to remember the name of every parent. But did they have to call her "Mom"? They all did it, even educators who were weeks away from retirement, but it made her feel worse when the twenty-two-year-olds said it, because she was old enough now for that to be true.

Her phone buzzed in the side pocket of her leggings as she crossed the parking lot.

> Dana (Oliver's mom): Hi Nicole! I'm taking Oliver to the playground this afternoon. Is Henry available?

> Nicole: No, sorry. He has art class.

> Dana (Oliver's mom): Oh, too bad!! They had so much fun there on Monday!

> Nicole: They did. Henry scrounged at least ten water balloons from Oliver—next it'll be cigarettes.

> Dana (Oliver's mom): OH MY GOD is Henry smoking??? That is so scary!!

> Nicole: What?

> Nicole: Oh, no. That was a joke.

> Dana (Oliver's mom): Ohhhhh! Haha! That's funny!

Jesus, Nicole thought as she stuffed her phone into her pocket. She hoped Oliver was more interesting than his mother.

She climbed back into her SUV, an enormous hybrid that had felt like a perfectly reasonable choice in Kentucky, but here in Wickham, New Jersey, just a quick drive from Manhattan, it seemed out of place. Louisville school parking lots were filled with four-door pickup trucks, with flatbeds that were used for hauling rolling luggage and coolers. Wickham was definitely the suburbs, but it was more of a Volvo town. And forget trying to drive her car into the city. She was an excellent parallel parker, but she could never find a spot that was big enough.

She knew she should leave the art studio parking lot, but she didn't have anywhere to go. Both kids were inside and she had one hour until pickup, which was not long enough to do anything other than go to the grocery store or stare at her phone. She could have squeezed in a quick coffee with a friend, but the reservoir of people in town she knew and actually liked was shallow.

She took out her phone and opened Instagram for at least the third time that day, a new habit she was forming, and searched for Kate's profile. Her face popped up in what looked like a professional headshot that highlighted the sharpness of her jaw. Nicole wondered if she'd been instructed not to smile for the camera. A picture pinned at the top of Kate's page was of her deep in conversation out in the desert some-where, a long, narrow notebook in her hand.

Nicole clicked on the photo of Kate in the desert and zoomed in on her angular face. It wasn't as if she had never googled Kate. Anyone who says they haven't looked up their exes is lying. She knew that Kate was a journalist, that she worked at the *Herald Ledger*, that she had a lot of social media followers. That was all fine. But there was something different about seeing "Kate Keller" on TV that morning, an echo of the person she'd known, that made her face more difficult to shake. It felt as though the universe was taunting Nicole with this woman she had refused to take seriously as a romantic partner when they were younger. At the time, Kate didn't seem sufficiently driven or together, and Nicole had been an ambitious and arrogant little shit. Kate was on TV now, while the high-water mark of Nicole's day was buying natu-rally sweetened gum at Whole Foods.

Kate had been the year behind Nicole at Skidmore College, in up-state New York, and they ran in overlapping circles. Kate was from New York City, which seemed impossibly cool to Nicole at the time. Nicole was from Cincinnati, which was far less sexy, but at least she had a car in college, a nine-year-old Ford Festiva she could use to ferry herself and friends outside of their campus bubble.

Kate had chestnut-colored hair and wide-set hazel eyes. Her right iris had a smudge of brown cut through it, as though a few drops of ink had leaked from a pen, blocking out the flecks of green and gold under-neath. She used to joke that she was a female version of her brother, too tall and with shared features that looked better on him—she was almost five foot eleven but chose to round down when asked her height. On their small college campus, however, she said her stock had been ele-vated and she wasn't going to waste it. An out lesbian from the moment she arrived at school, she went home with a rotating array of college girls in a way that always struck Nicole as daring. Their female class-mates who did the same with guys found themselves sneered at, but Kate's love life was never seen as somebody else's conquest. If anything, it made her more appealing, the way it did for handsome boys in col-lege bands. Nicole had quietly dated a girl in high school, but she wasn't out at Skidmore until her junior year.

She and Kate must live very different lives now, Nicole thought, but they were in the same city, more or less. Perhaps they could reconnect. Nicole wouldn't be thrilled if Austin was scrolling through the internet looking for ex-girlfriends he could meet for a drink, but he had other outlets, both social and professional, that Nicole did not.

"Fuck it," she said aloud.

Nicole opened up a direct message and started tapping at her phone.

"Hi! It's been a long time!" she wrote. "I saw you on TV the other day. You looked great."

Before she could think better of it, Nicole hit send, then dropped her phone like it had become suddenly hot in her hand.

6

GABE STEPPED OUTSIDE into a cold, prickly rain. He scurried away from Manhattan Arts High School, where he taught history, and headed toward the subway to start his commute home to New Jersey. When he reached Broadway, which would shield him with the noise of pedestrians and passing cars, he pulled out his phone and called Kate.

"Your brother wants to run for Congress!"

"What?" Kate said.

"Congress! Ethan wants to run for Congress!" Gabe had kept this information bottled up all day, and he was yelling now. But this was New York City. He passed two kids on brightly colored scooters, a man with a soggy goldendoodle, and a woman in a business suit and trench coat whose eyes were fixed on her phone. No one looked at him.

"Are you serious?" Kate asked.

"Do I sound serious?"

"I don't know. You sound hysterical."

"Great," Gabe replied. "Because that is the appropriate response!"

"Oh my God," she said. "You are serious. Holy shit."

Gabe stepped in a puddle and felt cold water seep into the toe box of his right shoe, a tan suede boot he should not have worn that day.

"Hang on," Kate said. "I'm in my cubicle. Let me go find a room with a door."

Kate was Gabe's sister-in-law, but she had also been his best friend since college, and she too had watched Ethan drift to the right as he aged. She was the only person who would understand the waking nightmare that was taking form around him.

"Okay, I'm back," she said. "It's been years since Ethan said anything to me about wanting to run for office. Have you guys been talking about this?"

"We have not. I thought this dream died on the rocks of middle age."

"Those are some pointy rocks," Kate said.

"We almost never talk about politics anymore. Whenever it comes up, Ethan stays perfectly calm and I feel like my brain is going to explode out of my ears. It always ends with me screaming, 'You need to stop, you need to stop, you need to stop,' while Ethan just looks at me, totally unflustered."

"He's really the worst person to fight with," Kate said.

Gabe removed his glasses and used his shirt to wipe pinpricks of rain off the lenses. When he returned the tortoiseshell frames to his face, the lenses were smudged. He'd made them worse.

Gabe hated the idea that there was something he and Ethan *couldn't* talk about, and he would look sometimes for points where they might overlap. He tried serving up the far left as a peace offering a few times, hoping he and his husband could ridicule the same people for a change, poking fun at a clownish devotion to sixteen-letter acronyms and an eagerness to be offended by everything. But all that did was show how much of their common ground had melted away. Ethan insisted the "Democrat Party" was beholden to the very people Gabe thought were nuts.

"I can't believe he's finally going to do this," Kate said.

"Well, he's not necessarily going to do anything. I have to say yes first."

Gabe looked for cars in the direction of oncoming traffic then stepped into the street, where he was nearly hammered by a guy on a bike going the wrong way down Eighty-Second. "Asshole!" Gabe shouted at full volume. This was not his customary response to violations of his right of way, but it felt good to scream into the ambient hostility of Manhattan traffic.

"So what are you going to do?" Kate ignored that Gabe had shrieked an obscenity into the phone. "Are you going to let him run?"

"I have no idea," Gabe said. "I really preferred pretending this part of him didn't exist. I've always just focused on the way he lived his life—who he was with me, what he's like as a father. He supports these awful policies, but he has no power over them. His politics didn't mean anything in the real world."

"I get it," Kate replied. "I've always thought he should run for office, but some of the stuff he believes now, I just can't understand it."

"That's because it doesn't make any sense!" Gabe cried. "How can this wonderful person—*my* wonderful person—how can he believe this shit?" Gabe wanted to kick over a garbage can and watch it roll into the street.

"The man hates his job, though," Kate said.

Ethan worked at a big law firm handling transactions for financial companies, spending sixty hours a week buried in paper so his clients could spin money into more money. He said it was like being shackled to an ergonomic chair while watching his life trickle by one grain of sand at a time—frustrating, dull, and yet somehow comfortable. He would tell this to people while laughing, but Gabe never found it funny.

"But why should we subject ourselves to this disaster?" Gabe said. "There's no way he could actually win."

"Why can't he win?"

"Because he's a gay Republican and this is America."

"This is the Northeast."

"This is New Jersey!" Gabe hollered. "How much time have you spent in New Jersey?"

"It's not disqualifying anymore. Besides, he reads as straight. If people want to forget he's gay, they can probably do that."

"Oh, Jesus," Gabe groaned.

"You didn't talk about this at all before you moved to New Jersey?"

"No! We moved to the suburbs so we could have a backyard and join a town pool, not so Ethan could become the next Newt Gingrich. Honestly, this didn't even occur to me as a possibility. We live in Longbourne, for Christ's sake. Most of my neighbors would rather blow up the town than elect a Republican."

"You don't have to live in the district to run for a congressional seat," Kate said. "You just have to live in the state."

"So I've learned. But I don't think Ethan was expecting this, either. Some congressman is retiring in the district next to ours. Ethan says it's a reliably Republican area and—"

"Joe Bucco's seat!" Kate said. "Is that where Ethan wants to run?"

Gabe scraped around in his brain for the specifics. "I think so, yeah. That sounds right."

"Wow. Gabe, you're not going to want to hear this, but that is a serious opportunity," she said. "Bucco has no obvious successor, and the people running have zero name recognition and not a lot of money. Whoever wins that Republican primary *will* become a member of Congress and—"

"I know, I know." Gabe pulled off his glasses again and wiped frantically at the lenses with his shirt.

"Okay," Kate said gently. "Let's game this out. What happens if you say yes?"

Gabe thought of his friends, his colleagues, his students. The things people would assume about him were detestable. Inconceivable. He reached his subway stop and stood at the top of the stairs to finish his conversation in the rain. He noticed that his jacket, his hair, and his phone were all soaked.

"If I say yes," Gabe said, "then issues we can't even talk about will become the center of our lives. And his politics, which I hate, will become the most prominent thing about either of us."

"That's all true," Kate said. "And what if you say no?"

Gabe felt a drop of cold water roll down his neck. "If I say no, then I will be taking this thing from him that he's always wanted. I'll be saying, 'Sorry, forget about your dream, let's just live the life *I* want.'" Kate was quiet on the other end of the phone. "And I don't think he'd admit it, but part of him will always resent me if I don't let him do this."

"I don't know if that's true," she said.

"How could it not be? It doesn't say anything bad about him. But this could be a once-in-a-lifetime chance, and if I say no, this won't be a dream that just died. *I* will have killed it."

The world looked bent and warped, obscured by the rain on Gabe's glasses. He and Ethan disagreed about many things, but in the day-to-day of their private life together, they took beautiful care of one another. Their daughter, Chloe, was five years old and still prone to waking up in the middle of the night, and it was always Ethan who got her settled back in bed so that Gabe, who got headaches when he was overtired, could get enough sleep. Ethan had been skeptical about suburbia, but Gabe had grown up with a house and a yard and he felt strongly it would be better for their family and an easier place to raise a kid. So Ethan, who had lived almost his entire life in New York City, agreed to move. And every night, for at least a few minutes, they would come together to focus on each other. They could have work to do after Chloe went to bed or a show they wanted to watch, but first, they would sit down, just the two of them, and they would talk, performing this ritual at the dining room table or on the living room sofa or over a mug of hot tea. They adhered to their rule never to go to bed angry.

It occurred to Gabe in that moment that if their roles were reversed, there was no question that Ethan would support him. Ethan would say yes. And Gabe could not be the reason for his husband's regret.

Gabe closed his eyes and quietly made his decision. He would give Ethan his blessing. For his husband, he would say yes. He could see no other way.

7

STANDING IN THEIR walk-in closet, before his collection of khaki, denim, and plaid, Gabe wondered what kind of outfit would announce "Republican!" Should he wear boat shoes? A soft-collar shirt made of an American flag? Something with a gun on it? More important, should he wear such an outfit this morning, or should he wear the opposite? Maybe a mesh tank top and a thong. Because this afternoon, Ethan, Chloe, and Gabe were getting their picture taken for Ethan's campaign website.

He kept these thoughts to himself and put on khakis and a windowpane button-down shirt. Ethan didn't ask him to wear long sleeves to cover his most visible tattoo, but he did it anyway. Gabe had the word "Together" written horizontally above his left wrist. It was a decision he made at twenty-four that he would not have made at forty, inspired by the slogan of a magnetic progressive politician who promised a national transformation that never materialized. It was not a great tattoo—he had his wedding anniversary and Chloe's birth date on his right shoulder blade, and he much preferred those—but he'd made peace with it as a monument to a particular time in his life.

Andrew, Ethan's newly hired campaign manager, had insisted they be photographed in the town square of Wickham, New Jersey, which was manicured and suburban, its sugar maples and pin oaks turning crimson in the cool fall air. It was in the district where Ethan was running, and Gabe had never set foot there before.

"I'm so glad to hear we've piqued your interest," Ethan boomed into the phone from the passenger seat of Gabe's Subaru, which was heading south on the highway toward Wickham. "I'm really looking forward to that lunch. Yep, you have a great weekend. See you then."

He hung up. "Scott from work connected me to a mentor of his who might be interested in contributing, and this guy is *very* plugged in with donors in the tristate area," Ethan said, drumming his hands on his long thighs. "This is good!"

"Great," Gabe said, glancing over from the traffic on the turnpike to look at his husband. Since he'd decided to run, Ethan had an energy about him Gabe hadn't seen in years, a pulsing determination. It was sexy.

Ethan drained the last of a Diet Coke and returned it to his cup holder. The man's blood was probably two-thirds artificial sweetener. He had quit drinking years ago, never touched a cigarette or a drug again, but he decided that Diet Coke was an acceptable long-term vice. He usually drank between four and six cans a day.

"I talked to Kate about trying to land a profile somewhere," Ethan said.

"Oh yeah?"

"A congressional primary in New Jersey isn't going to be front-page news, but I feel like I've got an interesting enough biography for at least one good story, right? Gay man. Former Democrat. We are the future of the Republican Party right here!" he said, sweeping his hands around the Subaru.

"Please keep the future of the Republican Party on your side of the car, thank you," Gabe said, shooing the words back toward Ethan with a flap of his hand.

Ethan gave one low bark of laughter. "Excuse me. Anyway, Kate suggested a couple of reporters we should target, someone at the *Ledger*, someone at the *Recorder*, reporters at a few of the tabloids that have a big readership in North Jersey. And Andrew is working on a bunch of conservative websites."

"Daniel says Republicans are bad people," Chloe chimed in from the back seat.

"What?" Ethan squawked. "Sorry, what was that, sweetie? Who's Daniel?"

"Daniel sits at her table at school," Gabe said.

"Daniel's my friend. He says Republicans are bad people. Are we Republicans? Are we bad people?"

"God, no, sweetie," Ethan said. "I mean, no, we're not bad people. I'm a Republican, yes, and Abba is a Democrat." He put a hand on Gabe's shoulder. "But Republicans aren't bad people. Most Republicans, just like most Democrats and most people everywhere, are good people just trying to do their best. They tend to be more conservative than a lot of the people we know from school, but they're not any better or worse than anyone else. Do you know what conservative means, honey? Honey?" He was losing her to the trees passing outside the window. "Do you know what conservative means?"

"No."

"Conservatives are careful. We believe there is wisdom in history and that we have to be very cautious before we make changes, no matter how good our intentions are," he said. "Conservatives also believe that individuals, like you and me, are the best people to make decisions about our own lives. Do you think it makes sense for Daddy and Abba to make decisions for you, or should it be someone who's never met you but has done a lot of studies? Should they decide what's best? I don't think so."

"And Democrats know that times change," Gabe added. God help her if she started spouting Ethan's talking points at school. "We want to make sure that *all* people are protected, which hasn't always been the case throughout history. We want to make sure that everybody can be safe and happy, and that *everybody's* rights are protected." He shot Ethan a look. "Does that all make sense, sweetie?"

"Abba, did you ever meet a dinosaur in real life?" Chloe asked.

"They've been extinct for a very long time, honey. I'm not quite that old," Gabe said. "But today I feel like I am."

"Daniel, huh?" Ethan said to Gabe, an exaggerated scowl scrunching up his face.

Gabe shrugged. "Daniel's mom works for the governor."

"Huh. Maybe I should meet her."

I THOUGHT SHE WAS going to wear a dress." Andrew, Ethan's campaign manager, was standing in Wickham's tidy town square, a large rectangle of grass and carefully pruned bushes with an oddly proportioned stone gazebo at one end. His arms were crossed over his chest. "She's not wearing a dress."

Chloe, who tended to run hot, was climbing a tree nearby. She was wearing purple leggings and a striped T-shirt while the adults around her were tucked into fleeces and midweight jackets.

"I have her dress," Gabe said, waving the bright blue fabric in the air. "I am working on it."

She loved that dress. That morning, she had been thrilled about the prospect of parading around in it with the new red sneakers Gabe bought for the occasion, her first shoes that fastened with laces instead of Velcro. But when it came time to leave the house, she refused to change out of her leggings, and she refused again when they got out of the car. On the drive down, they had struck a deal, which some might ungenerously call a bribe: If she had her listening ears on during the photo shoot, she could have pizza for dinner and ice cream for dessert. Gabe didn't want to blow his leverage before she was even out of the car, so he said she could play for a few minutes before getting into her picture outfit.

Ethan was crisscrossing the grass with Robin, his communications lead, and a photographer who was carrying two cameras, one slung over each shoulder. They were looking for a spot that would be recognizable to locals as this particular town square without including its hideous gazebo, which had a fake thatch roof molded out of brown plastic.

"Chloe, two-minute warning," Gabe said. "I'm going to need you to get down in two minutes, do you hear me?"

"Okay, Abba." Chloe was hanging upside down from a low branch, her red sneakers kicking around at his eye level and her chestnut hair streaming toward the brittle grass. Gabe walked a few paces away to give her space. Chloe was a tornado of physical energy, but she was a serious kid. She asked exacting questions and preferred the company of grown-ups, maybe because she didn't have siblings. Gabe was an only child and he had turned out fine, but he wondered if a brother or sister would have helped her take the world more lightly. Well, too bad. Surrogates were a fortune and that kitchen was closed.

"So, why exactly isn't she wearing the dress?" Andrew asked.

Gabe turned to face him.

"Andrew, do you have kids?"

"No."

No shit, Gabe thought to himself.

"She is not wearing the dress because she is five years old and because there is a tree she wants to climb and because, at this moment, we all want her to wear the dress." Gabe forced himself to smile. "Just give me a minute, and I will get her changed." He turned to Chloe. "One-minute warning. Finish up in the tree."

"You should really send those listings to Gabe," Ethan told Robin as they returned to the rest of the group. "He's the board chairman of our household."

"What listings?"

"I sent Ethan a couple of listings for some great houses in the district," Robin said, a pair of cat-eye glasses resting on the top of her head. Her affect was completely flat. "If you started looking now—"

"Whoa, whoa, whoa, whoa, whoa!" Gabe said, raising his hands in front of him as a barrier to the nonsense. "Nobody is moving. We just moved like a year and a half ago. We love our house. Chloe is settled in her school. We are not moving." He looked at Ethan, silently demanding his support.

"It would be a lot to move again so soon," Ethan said.

"I love you," Gabe said to his husband. Then he turned to Robin: "You seem very nice." She didn't, particularly. "But no."

"If we're not moving today, can we please get back to the dress?" Andrew said. "We want to get started while the light's still good."

"No one is moving!" Gabe replied. "But yes, I will handle it." He walked toward Chloe, who was perched happily on her branch orchestrating a conversation between two sticks. "Time's up," he said. "Down, please."

"Whyyy?"

"Because we're going to start taking pictures very soon so we need you to get dressed."

"I am dressed."

"We need you to put on your blue dress."

"No, thank you."

"Thank you for being polite, but Chloe, we had an agreement," he said, trying to wrestle his voice into a tone that was firm rather than pissed off. It wasn't her fault he felt like the blood vessels at his temples might burst. "As soon as this is over, we can go have pizza and ice cream. So the sooner you put on that dress, the sooner we get to do those things."

She ignored him.

"And if you are not on your way to the car to get dressed by the time I count to five, then we are not having ice cream today." He'd save the pizza in his arsenal so he could get her to hold still for the camera.

"One." No movement.

"Two." She kept her eyes fixed on the branch.

"Three." He let a warning creep into the word.

"Fou—" She dropped out of the tree and started running toward the car.

She sat in the back seat as Gabe helped her fasten her dress and retie her shoes.

"You look great, honey," he said. "Go give Daddy a hug and tell him you're ready."

Chloe ran across the grass to Ethan and jumped as high on his body as she could reach. He caught her and lifted her up, then held her with one arm while he continued his conversation with Robin. Chloe rested her head on Ethan's shoulder, their matching faces side by side, high above the other grown-ups. She had Ethan's coloring, his chestnut hair and pale skin. The same wide-set hazel eyes. The angular jaw. Gabe, with his narrow face, dark curls, and olive complexion, didn't look like them at all.

Technically, they didn't know if Chloe was genetically related to Ethan or to Gabe. She'd been born with the help of a surrogate and an egg donor, and the fertility clinic had created some embryos with Gabe's sperm and some with Ethan's. Their doctor asked if they wanted to decide whose embryos to try first, or if the clinic should pick at random among the healthiest-looking contenders. They opted for healthy-random, and their surrogate got pregnant on the first try. That was Chloe.

When she was a baby, people saw what they wanted to see—Gabe's toes, Ethan's mouth. But over time, it became obvious whose DNA was marching around inside her jawline. When Kate and Chloe were together, most people assumed they were mother and daughter, with their shared coloring and matching eyes embroidered with green and gold. Ethan once admitted he'd been worried Chloe's resemblance to him might upset Gabe. But it didn't. Chloe was Gabe's child, a piece of his heart that trotted around in the world in tiny mismatched socks. Her genes did nothing to change that.

Standing in that town square, it occurred to Gabe that thousands of strangers would be looking at photographs of his family, and he wondered what they would see. People who didn't know them. People who didn't know anyone who was gay, at least as far as they were aware. Would they look at pictures of Gabe's family and think that he didn't belong? Gabe felt a tightness in his throat as Robin called him over to be photographed.

8

"GOD, IT'S AWFUL in here." Kate leaned against a wall of blue tiles that felt damp on the back of her shirt. She had come with Ethan and Gabe to watch Chloe's Saturday morning swim lesson at an indoor pool in Wickham, New Jersey, which they would follow with pancakes and waffles at a diner. The air around the pool deck was thick and heavy, almost viscous. "Is it always like this?" Kate asked. "This room feels like the inside of somebody's mouth."

"Gross," Gabe said.

"But evocative!" Ethan teased. "Are you a writer?" Kate gave him the finger before remembering she was in a room full of children. She quickly flattened her hand against her lap.

Chloe was in the pool in a bright red bathing suit stamped with stars. She was at that phase of learning to swim where she flailed around wildly with her arms and legs while an instructor propped her up by the belly. Chloe swam like she was drowning, much in the way toddlers walked as if they were drunk.

"Have you told Dad yet?" Kate asked.

"I have," Ethan replied. He pulled a can of Diet Coke out of his bag and cracked it open. He preferred cans, even when out and about, because they had more bubbles. He finished them so quickly it didn't matter that once they were open, he couldn't close them again.

"What'd he say?"

"He said, 'It would have killed your mother.'"

This was absolutely correct. Their mother had considered Ethan's politics to be her greatest personal failing. But she died of pancreatic cancer six years earlier, so she would be spared this particular humiliation.

Their father was a conservative Democrat who would be considered a Republican in New York, but he'd moved to Santa Fe when Kate and Ethan were in middle school, right after their parents divorced. He and Ethan naturally thought about the world in similar ways, but he quickly remarried and made minimal effort with his children from across the country. As adults, Ethan and Kate spoke with their father only on the occasion of major life events, birthdays, and Christmas Eve. They were not close.

"Kate, I want your opinion on something," Ethan said. He waved to Chloe, who had returned to the side of the pool. She ignored him.

"Sure." Kate put her canvas tote bag directly into a chlorinated puddle on the white tile floor. "Shit," she said as she hauled it dripping into the air.

"Oh yeah, don't put your bag down," Ethan said.

"Thanks for the tip."

"I'd like your help with a messaging challenge," he continued. "I think most conservatives around here will vote for a gay candidate, at least the right gay candidate."

"That's probably true," she said.

"But my real problem is that I used to be a Democrat. In a lot of circles, that's not to be trusted."

"Certainly not these days," she replied.

"Exactly. It's genuine, though. I am not a Democrat anymore. Conservative voters can trust me, I just have to explain it to them, so I need to have a good answer ready for when people ask."

Gabe fanned himself with his T-shirt. His loose curls were getting puffy in the humidity, stray hairs rebelling to strike out on their own.

"So what's the real answer?" Kate asked.

"Well, I grew up in New York City, the center of the Democrat universe, right? I wanted to get involved in politics, so I worked for the attorney general, but I didn't believe in what he was doing. I didn't like his policies or his approach."

"How about the criminal behavior?" Kate said brightly. A few years after Ethan left the AG's office, his former employer, Willard Keyes,

was arrested and sent to prison for funneling payoffs through his epony-
mous law firm.

"Also not a good look." Ethan laughed. "But seriously, I saw how
the government can involve itself way too much in people's lives, and
how dangerous that can be. Once I started paying attention to conservative ideas, I realized they made more sense."

"Hmm," Kate mused. "You're not going to be able to run away from
your biography, so I actually think you need to lean into it."

"What do you mean?"

"I mean you shouldn't just have an answer in your pocket in case
somebody asks you about it, I think you should lead with it. How about
this: You aren't a Republican because you were raised a Republican,
you came to these ideas on your own. You thought for yourself, and
now here you are, a true believer. You're not a default Republican,
you're a strong Republican. Or something like that. Try to turn it into
a good thing."

"Huh," he said quietly. "I like that."

"Gabe, you asleep over there?" Kate asked.

"Awake, unfortunately," he said. "But I love my husband."

"Aww." Ethan kissed Gabe on the cheek.

"Do you think anyone would mind if I go drown myself in the
pool?" Gabe asked.

Kate and Ethan laughed with the same staccato rhythm as Ethan put
his arm around Gabe's shoulders. "That's my ray of sunshine."

"Oh good, she's getting out of the pool," Kate said. "Let's go eat
pancakes before I die of heatstroke."

9

THE KIDS WERE in their bedrooms, and as long as they stayed there, Nicole didn't care if they were sleeping. She hadn't spoken to an adult without a child present all day, so she went to the living room to find her husband.

It was Friday night, and Austin was watching golf. He had DVRed a tournament and was sitting on their living room sofa, squinting his eyes in concentration. Austin loved the grace of the sport, the incredible precision it took to curve a ball just so, to master the physics of the open air. To him, it was an art form.

When Nicole watched golf, she saw a bunch of men in ill-fitting polo shirts standing around in the grass. Then they walked in the grass. Then they stood again. Sometimes, people clapped. Occasionally, somebody would swing their club and the camera lens would shoot toward the sky, tracking a ball that was too tiny to see clearly on television. Usually, when golf was on, she went elsewhere, but tonight she was desperate to talk to a grown-up.

"Hey." She dropped down on the sofa and curled her feet underneath her. Austin was still in the outfit he'd worn to work, slate-gray pants with creases in the thighs from his day spent sitting at a desk and a made-to-measure dress shirt the color of a blue jay. He liked wearing blue because it brought out his pale eyes, which were the color of the ocean in an ad for a tropical beach. They popped even more now that his hair had gone fully white. Austin had always been a good-looking man, but he was sixteen years older than Nicole, and the lines of his square jaw, which had been so appealingly chiseled, were beginning to slacken with age.

"Hey, babe." He gave her knee two quick squeezes, then put his hand back in his own lap. He had a tumbler of bourbon on the coffee table in front of him and a spoon he'd already licked clean. He allowed himself a single bite of chocolate ice cream every night after Henry and Sarah went to bed.

"How was your day?" Nicole asked.

"It was crazy. All week it was like that, just back to back to back." His eyes did not move from the television. "This is exactly what I need to be doing right now."

The golf tournament was on their DVR. He could pause it.

"My day was fine, thanks," she said.

"What, honey?" He took a sip of his bourbon.

"Austin."

"Sweetheart, I'm just watching this round right now."

"The only adults I interacted with today were fictional characters in a book."

"Mmm."

"A book about a sex cult in Nevada." There was nothing Nicole hated more than feeling invisible.

"It's so great you have your books." He wasn't listening.

"Austin?"

"Your books and the kids."

"Seriously?" She fantasized about grabbing Austin's bourbon tumbler and throwing it as hard as she could into the television. She imagined it cracking the glass, making the flat screen splinter and smoke. She pictured him jumping off the couch, yelping in alarm. But she didn't do it. She'd be the one who had to deal with buying a new TV and getting the rug cleaned.

"Austin, turn it off."

"God, that was a great shot!" He launched forward and slapped one hand against his thigh. "Did you see the ball twist around that tree? Wow. I'm sorry, honey, what did you say?"

The crowd on their TV was shouting and cheering. They did that now in golf.

"Pause it, please," she said forcefully. He lifted the remote as if it were heavy in his hand and stopped the tournament.

"Okay, honey." Austin sighed. "What's up?"

"Nothing, I just—" Nicole closed her eyes to regain her composure. "I'm going out for a drink next week."

"Oh." He sounded surprised, which was fair. Nicole never went out. "That's a great idea, doll. You should go out more. Who are you meeting?"

"A friend from college," she said. "No one you know. Do you remember Kate Keller?"

He thought for a moment. "Is that the Kate who drank too much?"

"That's the one. I followed her on Instagram recently and we started talking. I really need to expand my social circle beyond swim classes and birthday parties."

Nicole took a sip of Austin's bourbon. If forced to choose, she would say she was more attracted to women than she was to men, and Austin would offer freely that this made men less of a threat because it was rare for one to pique her interest. The inverse of this concept—that if she were more attracted to women, they should be considered *more* of a threat—never seemed to occur to him. She had been so young when she was with women, and now she was with him. This struck her as a symptom of something beyond his healthy sense of self. It felt like he didn't take her relationships with women all that seriously. But she found jealousy in a partner both inconvenient and unbecoming, so she didn't belabor the point.

"It's been hard for me to find my people here," she said.

"I know it has." He rested a hand briefly on her back. "Absolutely. You should reconnect with old friends."

"Yeah." She took another sip and set his drink back on the table.

Austin had been unfaithful to his first wife. He'd had a one-night stand while in Chicago on business and another after a marathon night of drinking on the Lower East Side, and for their first few years together, this worried Nicole. It made her vigilant about his female friends, suspicious of women colleagues. He was a bit of a flirt, but so was she, and over the course of many years, he'd never done anything to arouse her suspicion. Gradually, her jealousy had faded away, though she wondered if that was a sign of her growing detachment as much as it was a building of trust. She never thought he'd be capable of managing a full-blown affair, however; it would have required too much effort on his part.

"Does it work for you if I go into the city on Thursday night?"

"Please," he said. "Go have a drink. Have one for me."

He smiled at her, then turned back to the television. He switched the golf back on, concluding their conversation, and Nicole felt herself recede into the furniture.

"Mom?" Henry appeared in the living room wearing rainbow-striped pajamas.

"What are you doing up, sweetheart?" Nicole asked.

"Can I have another hug?"

"Sure, honey." Nicole pulled herself off the couch to walk him upstairs.

"Good night, Henry," Austin called from the sofa. His eyes were still on the game.

10

KATE WAS ALREADY drunk when she showed up at her favorite East Village gay bar for her twenty-second birthday. It was winter break during their senior year, and Gabe had organized a party, invited all her friends, and tracked the important ones down for their RSVPs. He arrived early to claim a cluster of tables at the back and tied a balloon in the shape of a beer can to one of the chairs. When Kate walked in, she was hanging off the neck of a girl Gabe had never seen before who had a large phoenix tattooed on her back. As the guests rolled in, Gabe kept an eye on the door and jumped up to welcome friends he recognized. Kate thanked him profusely, always en español—she'd spent the previous year studying abroad in Mexico City, and she insisted on speaking to everyone in Spanish that night, regardless of their level of understanding. Mostly, she spent the evening ignoring her guests in favor of her beautiful new friend with the bird tattoo.

It was clear to Gabe the moment he saw Ethan, who was tall and cute and basically walking around wearing Kate's face, that the two of them must be related. Ethan was Kate's big brother, three years older. Gabe got up from his chair as Ethan approached the table.

"Hi," Gabe said. "You're Ethan, aren't you? I'm Gabe."

"Gabe." Ethan smiled. His eyelids were heavy and the cleft in his chin was covered in light brown stubble. He glanced at his sister, who had not noticed him come in. "It's good to finally meet you. Looks like you're playing host tonight. Can I buy the host a drink?"

Ethan bought him many drinks, in fact, and they shut down the bar that night. Long after Kate and her friends had left the party, Ethan continued to suck down a stream of vodka sodas with two limes each, while Gabe alternated between beer and water. Around 4:00 a.m., when the bartender turned on the fluorescent lights overhead, they fumbled their way outside to hail a taxi. When the cool air hit them, Ethan excused himself.

"Just one sec," he said. Gabe watched as Ethan turned around, bent over, and threw up between two parked cars. It splattered a bit on the dented bumper of a minivan.

"Oh my God, are you okay?" Gabe asked.

Ethan was only sick for a few seconds. When he was finished, he spit and wiped his lips with a tissue he pulled from his pocket, and then he was fine.

"I'm good," he said. He popped a stick of gum into his mouth to clear up his breath and offered the pack to Gabe with a mischievous smile. "Want some?" he asked.

They took a cab back to Ethan's apartment.

For years, Gabe thought this story about the night they met was hilarious, a great line to be shared at parties. "He puked on a minivan, and I went home with him anyway!" But as Ethan's drinking slid increasingly out of control, Gabe told the story less and less, until he stopped telling it altogether.

THE SUMMER AFTER Kate graduated from college, she and Nicole tried to date. Kate was flailing around in the world without any real direction or structure for the first time, living with her mother while applying haphazardly for jobs at newspapers, magazines, and, incongruously, law firms. Nicole, who graduated the year before, had a head start. She was working at an art gallery in Chelsea, a job she hated, but she was gaining experience in her field while sharing an apartment in Park Slope with a roommate and two tabby cats, Duck and Turtle, actual animals they were keeping alive. Nicole had her shit together, and for Kate, this was both enormously attractive and desperately intimidating. Kate relied on drinking to quiet her jitters when they were together, which often didn't work, and had its drawbacks even when it did, but she considered it a temporary fix. Kate felt certain they would find their footing.

"I'll walk you to the train," Nicole said one morning. Kate was sitting on the floor tying her Converse sneakers, while Turtle, the friendlier of the two cats, assisted by rubbing up against her arm.

"Okay," she said, because it would've been uncool to jump up and shout: "Yes! Come with me everywhere!"

When they reached the subway, they weren't ready to say goodbye, and Nicole suggested they keep walking. "Let's see how far we get," she said.

They made it more than nine miles, all the way to the Upper East Side, where Kate was staying with her mother. They passed stoop sales in brownstone Brooklyn, where passersby could pick up old rain boots, chipped dishes, or a hookah. They crossed the Manhattan Bridge, which rumbled under their feet when a D train rolled by. Then they walked north along the East Side, past tenements laced with fire escapes, glass office towers, and boxy, white-brick co-ops that looked like wedding cakes. They made stops along the way for coffee, tacos, and beer.

"Did you know I had a crush on you in college?" Nicole asked as she slid a nacho piled with jalapeños into her mouth.

"No, you didn't," Kate said.

"I did! I even asked you out one time."

"I'm sorry, where was I when this happened?"

"You were a freshman and I was a sophomore, and I asked you to go to the movies with me."

"You mean that comedy about that family of undertakers? That was supposed to be a date?"

"Yes! We went, and you were totally clueless. I wanted to make a move on you in the theater, but I couldn't get you to look at me. Then when I dropped you off, by the time I put the car in park, you were already out the door saying 'Thanks for the ride!'" Nicole mocked Kate's former self with an exaggerated wave.

"That was not a date!"

"No, it wasn't." Nicole ran a finger along the line of Kate's jaw. "But I wanted it to be."

Nicole had a habit in college of making out with girls at parties, but Kate didn't take it seriously. She assumed Nicole was doing it for the benefit of the guys who swayed around watching her with wide eyes and Solo cups filled with beer. Kate realized she might be misreading the situation only when word spread during Nicole's junior year that she'd gotten herself a girlfriend while studying abroad in London. But they were never on campus together after that. When Nicole was back at Skidmore as a senior, Kate was studying in Mexico. They didn't reconnect until they both found their way to New York City after graduating.

They finished their nachos and pilsners and continued their walk north. When they reached Kate's apartment building (her mom's apartment building), they were exhausted, but they still didn't want to say goodbye. Kate ran upstairs to change while Nicole sat on a stoop across the street, her aching legs splayed out in front of her.

They split a cab back to Nicole's place in Brooklyn and somehow found the energy to tear each other's clothes off when they arrived.

IT DIDN'T LAST, because Nicole dropped her. She just stopped texting back. They were not technically girlfriends, but they'd been sleeping together for two months and Kate felt she at least deserved a phone call. She never received one, and hadn't heard from Nicole since.

Kate thought about this while she dumped the contents of her closet onto her bed. She was going to a party thrown by a friend from Skidmore, a party where Nicole was likely to be, so Kate needed a hot outfit. She settled on her tightest black jeans, heavy black boots, and a blue plaid shirt with only a few buttons fastened. It hung open in a way that made her clavicle part of the conversation.

She arrived at the party by herself, armed with only a twelve-dollar bottle of pinot grigio. It was late enough in the evening that the discarded dishware and layer of filth could have been attributed to the forty-odd guests ambling through the apartment, but Kate knew better. The host, Cassie, was a slob, and the place always looked like someone had detonated a bomb of takeout containers and shoes.

Kate made her way through the musty garden apartment to deposit her wine in the fridge, and there, in the kitchen, she saw Nicole. Her curls, which had reverted from store-bought red to their natural brown, were loose around her face, and she wore a boxy gray dress that stopped at her upper thighs. A guy with aggressive sideburns was trying hard to hold her interest, which hopefully meant she was at the party alone. Thank God. Kate had heard that Nicole had a girlfriend already, a woman named Jenna who was a few years older and an actual lawyer. Kate had almost stayed home that night because she didn't want to watch them parade around the party together.

Kate looked away and headed for the first person she recognized, a woman named Suz who had been in her senior seminar on early-twentieth-century modernism. Suz was talking to a very skinny, very tall man who towered over her and had to hunch to hear her speak. Kate didn't care if they were flirting, she was going in. The three of them were just settling into a conversation about illegally downloading movies off the internet when Kate felt a gentle touch on her upper arm.

"Hi," Nicole said, her eyes drifting around Kate's body. "It's good to see you."

"Yeah, hi. It's good to see you, too." Shit, Kate thought. She hadn't meant to say that.

"Do you have a drink yet?"

"Nope." Kate looked in Nicole's direction but did not invite her to join the conversation with Suz and the tall guy.

"Let's get you one." Nicole nodded toward a table crowded with jugs of bottom-shelf liquor, soda, and juice.

The conversation wasn't terribly memorable, a superficial catching up about their nascent professional lives. In the months since they'd last spoken, Kate had started a job covering housing at a local paper in Hoboken called the *Daily Tribune*, and she liked it more than she expected. Nicole was applying to master's programs in art history while working for the gallery trolls.

What Kate remembered most clearly was not what they said to one another, but the strain it took to project indifference, like she was trying to look relaxed while lifting one end of a heavy sofa into the air. She crossed her arms so she wouldn't grab Nicole and shake her, demanding to know why she'd given up on them. She wanted to climb into the woman's brain, to claw around for a reason.

After a few minutes, Cassie, the party's host, joined Kate and Nicole with a smile on her face that seemed to be putting pressure on her neck muscles. Kate had gotten drunk and cried to Cassie when Nicole ghosted her, and she wondered if Cassie was expecting a scene.

"Hey!" she said, a bit too loudly. "Kate, I need to steal you for a minute. There's a guy here who is a reporter for the *New London Post*. You should meet him. You ladies can talk later, okay?" She tripped as she pulled Kate away by the arm. "Say byeee!"

A few hours and who knows how many drinks later, Kate was waiting in line for the bathroom while trying to focus her eyes on a subway map that was pinned to the opposite wall. The bathroom door opened and she leaned back to let a beautiful woman with straight black hair squeeze by. Kate smiled, then looked down at the floor as she passed.

"Hey," Nicole said, appearing in front of her as if she'd dropped from the ceiling. She put her hand on the bathroom door so Kate couldn't close it. "Can I talk to you?"

"Uhh." Kate caught herself staring at Nicole's thick upper lip. "I guess."

Nicole walked into the bathroom behind Kate and locked the door. "Hi," she said.

"H—" Kate started to answer, but Nicole grabbed her and pulled their mouths together.

They kissed with their lips and their tongues and their hips and their thighs until Kate felt Nicole push her up against the tiled wall and unbutton her jeans. They breathed into each other's mouth as Nicole slid her flattened hand past the band of Kate's underwear. She put her other hand over Kate's mouth to keep her quiet.

The whole thing only took a few minutes. Nicole waited for Kate to put herself back together, then unlocked the door. They walked out without a word.

There were only two people waiting in line outside the bathroom, neither of whom they recognized. Kate felt disappointed, and realized she hoped they would be seen. As they walked together down a narrow, windowless hallway toward the kitchen, she felt a bubble of anger form and expand in her chest.

"So, is your girlfriend here?" Kate asked as they reached the drink table. She had been watching Nicole, and she knew she was there alone. "I don't think I've seen her."

Nicole paused. "You haven't," she said. "I do have a girlfriend, though. I'm an asshole."

"Heyyy!" Cassie appeared. "What are we talking about?"

"We were just saying goodbye," Kate said. "I'm going home."

A few days later, Nicole asked Kate to meet her at a bar in Williamsburg. Kate waited hours to respond, but she was always going to say yes. When Kate arrived at the bar, Nicole was tucked into a dim booth, a stream of blue Christmas lights strung on the wall behind her, illuminating her curls. Two foggy glasses of beer rested on the table.

"They only had one IPA on tap," Nicole said. "So I took the liberty. Otherwise I wasn't sure you'd let me buy you a drink."

This was Kate's third drink of the evening. She'd been nervous and had some wine at home before she left.

"Look, Kate," Nicole said, taking a breath. "I owe you an apology."

"Oh?" Kate allowed a sharpness to lace the edge of the word.

"For disappearing on you. That was just . . . I fucked up. You deserved better than that," she said to her beer. "And I'm sorry."

Of all the things Kate thought might happen over drinks, this was not on the list. Nicole had fucked up and Kate did deserve better, *they* deserved better. She loved that Nicole admitted this. But Kate waved it off, desperate to resuscitate some of her dignity.

"It was no big deal," she lied.

They finished their drinks and moved on to a gay bar nearby, which was dominated by handsome twenty-five-year-old men in tight pants who didn't care that Kate and Nicole were making out in the corner. Kate gripped Nicole's face in her hands while they kissed, terrified Nicole might slip away again and leave her panting at the bar.

They went back to Kate's new apartment, a tiny studio up four flights of stairs in Hell's Kitchen. In the morning, Nicole stayed long enough to swallow half a cup of coffee and an ibuprofen, and then she left.

2008

Gabe was startled awake at 3:00 a.m. by a banging on his front door. He stretched out his hand to the other side of the bed, hoping Ethan would be the one to go investigate, but the sheets were empty and cold. That, more than the banging, jolted Gabe awake. Ethan was supposed to have been home hours ago.

Gabe rushed to the front door and found his neighbor Dave on the other side.

"He's breathing, so I didn't call 911." Dave motioned behind him to where Ethan lay, face down, in a puddle of his own vomit. He was splayed out on the terrazzo floor, his long limbs reaching almost from one end of the vestibule to the other.

"Oh my God. Ethan!" Gabe got down on the floor and tried to shake Ethan awake. "Ethan!"

"What? Hey, angel." Ethan smiled groggily. A chunk of drying vomit was crusted into the cleft of his chin. "I'm fine. I'm totally fine. I'm just really tired." Their neighbor was still standing above them, watching. Gabe wanted to cover Ethan with his body, to protect him from the man's judgment.

"Good, he's talking," Dave said. He opened the door to his apartment, then turned back to Gabe. "You're going to clean this up, right?"

Gabe wanted to reach into the vomit and throw a handful of it into his neighbor's face.

"Yes, I'm going to clean it up, but have some compassion, asshole. Good night."

Ethan was six inches taller than Gabe, and Gabe groaned as he lifted his giant boyfriend off the ground. They got in the shower together and he held Ethan upright as he washed the stink off his body.

Once Ethan was in bed and the hallway was reasonably clean, Gabe layered two trash bags together, one inside the other so they wouldn't rip, and filled them with bottles of vodka, tequila, and whiskey, half a case of beer, and a box of cheap red wine. It was all the alcohol they had in the apartment. The morning sky was tinged pink and purple when Gabe took the bag outside and dropped it on the curb.

NICOLE CLIMBED THE narrow staircase to Kate's apartment with a box of cannoli in one hand. She liked to bring gifts, to let Kate know she'd been thinking of her, especially since she rarely saw the woman outside the four walls of her studio apartment.

She brought a bottle of prosecco sometimes, a slice of strawberry shortcake, or a miniature apple pie from the bodega for them to share. This time, Nicole wanted to do something special.

Kate had won an award earlier that month for a series of articles about terrible landlords, and Nicole told her she'd take her out to celebrate. But at the last minute, Jenna called. Her mother had given her two tickets to the ballet that night that would otherwise go unused, and Nicole couldn't think of a plausible excuse to skip it. She canceled on Kate, who was probably standing on the subway platform on her way to the restaurant when Nicole's text came through.

Nicole researched the best cannoli in the city and traveled across town to pick them up before heading to Kate's apartment. Kate didn't particularly like chocolate, which Nicole found inconceivable, even after years of knowing her.

"Hi," Kate said when she opened the door. Her chestnut hair was in a messy bun at the top of her head. She wore jeans and a white shirt, which had just a few buttons fastened at its center.

Nicole pushed the box of cannoli into Kate's hands and reached her face up to kiss her. She unfastened the remaining buttons on Kate's shirt before they'd fully closed the door.

The next day, Nicole went to her girlfriend's house for dinner.

Jenna had roasted a whole chicken for the two of them, made rice and a salad, lit candles at the center of the table. When Nicole sat down to eat, she noticed a brass key sitting on her cloth napkin.

"What's this?" she asked.

Jenna took Nicole's hand in both of hers. She was wearing a blue dress shirt and slacks, protected by a large apron with a muffin on the front.

"That's a key to my apartment," Jenna said. "Anytime you want to be here, I want you here. So that key is yours now." She leaned over and pecked Nicole lightly on the lips. "Can I get you some chicken?"

The key felt heavy pressed into Nicole's palm, but she wanted to keep things moving forward with Jenna, who was attentive and kind, if a little earnest. Nicole loved walking into a room with this dykey woman whose hair was cut high and tight. Jenna wore nicely tailored suits, which her mother, a partner at a white-shoe law firm, helped her purchase. Nicole preferred tight pants and how she looked in a sundress. On her own, she read as straight, but when she held Jenna's hand, her sexuality was made visible.

And Nicole could not afford to take risks with her future. When she'd moved to New York after college, she assumed she would quickly ascend in the gallery world, where she would elevate overlooked artists and help redraw the boundaries of photography and painting, all from behind her boldly patterned clothing and statement glasses. Instead, she worked at a Chelsea gallery where her bosses were different shades of verbally abusive and she was so poorly paid she nearly qualified for food stamps. She picked up a second job at a cocktail bar, where the tips were good but customers preferred to order their drinks with a hand somewhere on her body.

So she moved on to plan B. She was getting her master's in art history, on her way to becoming a curator or a professor, but she had no family money or connections to fall back on. Her father worked for a local utility in Cincinnati and her mother was an administrative assistant at a middle school. Nicole needed every advantage she could find. She wanted a partner on a similar trajectory, whose accomplishments and drive would match her own, whose success would reflect light back on her. Jenna was two years out of law school, working as a prosecutor in the Manhattan district attorney's office, living on her own in a prewar apartment in Prospect Heights. In her bearing, she seemed older than her twenty-seven years and settled into adulthood; at least it looked that way to a twenty-four-year-old Nicole.

Kate and Nicole had been friends for years, and once they started touching each other, it felt impossible to stop. But when they tried to date after Kate graduated from college, their dynamic was strained. Kate seemed lost and jumpy, as if someone were forever dropping a heavy book right behind her. And she drank too much. Nicole found it embarrassing to be out with someone who would slur and lose the thread of conversation. They didn't even last through the summer, so Nicole told herself she didn't need to formally end things. She thought their best chance at continued friendship was to allow their time together to fade away, and to spare Kate the humiliation of being dumped.

Cloistered in Kate's apartment, she and Nicole were lighter together than they'd been when they were dating, unbound by expectation. It couldn't become anything serious, though. Nicole was with Jenna, who would help her become the adult she was destined to be. Whenever Nicole left Kate's apartment, she told herself it was for the last time.

Nicole stood up from Jenna's table and retrieved her purse from a hook by the front door. She slipped Jenna's offering onto her key ring, then spun it around on her finger in celebration.

Sitting back down for dinner, Nicole accepted a chicken thigh and some salad, and put Caesar dressing on both to mask the dryness of the poultry. As she chewed, she told herself she would be better. She would treat Jenna with the respect she deserved. She would not see Kate anymore.

Three weeks later, she climbed the stairs to Kate's apartment carrying a full-size cheesecake in a brown paper bag.

FROM INSIDE THE car, it didn't sound like metal slamming against metal, folding in on itself, becoming jagged and deformed. The sound Ethan heard was a thud, he said, like a bag of flour had fallen on the floor. Nothing too serious. He thought it would all be fine.

It wasn't. The sound Ethan heard was the airbag exploding into his face.

He was on his way home from a friend's house in New Jersey, where he and a few buddies had spent the day partying and playing video games. He knew he'd had a lot to drink, but he was a big guy with an enormous tolerance and he thought he could handle it.

"I was trying to be so careful when it happened," he pleaded to Gabe and Kate. He was sitting on a bed in the Columbia emergency room, his face tinged with green under the fluorescent lights. "I was trying to get into the left lane and I was watching my side mirror, trying not to rush. I must have watched the mirror for too long. I was looking in the wrong place." He put his face in his hands and tried to muffle his own scream.

Ethan had run a red light coming off the George Washington Bridge and hammered into a passing car, leaving its twenty-two-year-old driver with broken ribs, a punctured lung, and a pelvic fracture that ripped apart a network of blood vessels and very nearly killed her. Ethan totaled his old Ford Explorer, which had been with him since college, but he was okay. He had some nasty bruising around his eyes, but he'd been wearing his seat belt and was drunk enough that he flopped around on impact, which probably saved him from more severe injuries.

Gabe and Kate were sent back to the waiting room while Ethan got a head CT. They sat side by side in pink plastic chairs that were bolted to the floor. Gabe leaned forward and clenched his hands together so tightly that his fingertips turned white. This was not the first time Ethan's drinking had brought them to the hospital. He'd tripped down some subway stairs while he was drunk and broke a bone in his foot. Another time, he'd wandered into the ER covered in fresh bruises and passed out. He never remembered what happened to him that night, so it remained a terrifying mystery. But this had to be the last time, Gabe said, or he would leave.

Kate paced in front of the pink chairs and called Nicole. It went to voice mail, so she called again and again, the phone ringing like a car alarm in her ear, until Nicole finally answered on the fourth try.

"Jesus, what's going on?" Nicole whispered. "Are you okay?"

"Yeah." Kate walked toward the vending machine to put some distance between herself and Gabe. "Ethan was in a car accident."

"Shit, is he okay?"

"Yeah."

"Okay, good."

"But the person he hit might not be."

"Oh my God. I'm so sorry."

"He was drinking." Kate's voice sounded stiff, unfamiliar to herself. "Can you come here?"

"Can I what?"

"Can you come to the hospital?"

"The hospital? Like right now?"

"Yeah, now." Kate looked at a phalanx of candy bars sparkling under a white light. How could someone eat a Snickers while waiting to hear if their life was over?

"Kate," Nicole said slowly. "I can't come now."

"Oh."

"I'm so sorry. I'm at Jenna's. We're having dinner with her parents. I can't just leave."

It felt like a fist had landed in Kate's gut. Nicole and Jenna's relationship had the glow of authenticity. They were a couple that threw dinner parties, knew each other's friends, met each other's parents. Nicole and Kate were trapped in an endless loop of shadowy visits that would start and end in Kate's apartment. Kate was not a part of Nicole's real life.

"Gabe is there with you, right?" Nicole asked.

"Yeah."

"Good. And Ethan is okay, right?"

"Yeah."

"Okay. You're okay. And I will call you in the morning." Nicole's tone was firm, confident in her plan. "You guys take care of each other."

"Sure."

"I'll be thinking about you," Nicole said. "I really wish I could come."

"Okay," Kate said, and hung up.

Lying in bed with Nicole a few days later, a gentle rain falling on the fire escape outside her window, Kate found she didn't have much to say. It was not because she was nervous like she'd been when they first dated. She wasn't scrambling internally for an observation or a question that might spark conversation. She was angry. She wanted Nicole to draw her out, to plead and apologize, but she never did. It was clear to Kate that Nicole had made her choice.

That was the last time. Not long after Ethan's accident, Kate met a woman named Shirin at an *L Word* viewing party at a bar in the West Village. Kate remembered Shirin making two jokes that night, riotous, cutting remarks about the show and the scene at the bar, and otherwise, staying mostly silent. She looked like she was uncomfortable being as beautiful as she was. Kate got her number.

On the way home from her second date with Shirin, Kate pulled up a text message on her phone. She'd received it the day before.

Nicole: Hey there. You free tomorrow night?

Kate had looked at the message a dozen times without responding, and as she sat alone on an uptown C train, she decided she never would. She deleted the message. She deleted Nicole's number. Then she put her phone away.

11

GABE WAS IN his kitchen making a pot of coffee for people he despised.

In the next room, Ethan was talking strategy with Andrew and Robin from his campaign, joined by an assistant whose name Gabe didn't catch. It was unclear if the assistant was permitted to speak.

Chloe was with Gabe in the kitchen, perched on a tiny chair in front of a child-size table made of blond wood. She was swirling blobs of watercolor into a faint approximation of mountains. Or maybe they were animals.

Gabe sculpted a block of aged Gouda to hide the missing chunk he'd carved off for himself the day before. He set the cheese on a simple white plate with a bowl of kalamata olives and finished the arrangement with a wreath of water crackers. He put it all on a tray with five cans of Diet Coke, one for each of their guests and two for Ethan.

"I think the answer to the gay thing is that, yeah, I'm gay, and I also have brown hair," Ethan said, his voice wafting in from the living room. "One is as meaningless to who I am as the other."

"Exactly!" Andrew clapped his hands together. "We're not going to divide the country the way the left does, with gay people over here and straight people over there."

"Right!" Ethan said.

"But voters are going to have their opinions about gay people," Andrew continued. "So we also need to position you as a fighter. That the Democrat Party wants to destroy America and you are the pit bull who's going to stop them."

Gabe had NPR on the radio, his habit whenever he was in the

kitchen. For everyone's benefit, he reached for the little gray dial and cranked it up. It occurred to him that if he spat in the olives, just a bit, and stirred them around, no one would know.

Ethan really did feel that way about his sexuality, that it was a nonissue, incidental to who he was, probably because being gay had never been a struggle for him. His mother had always been supportive; one of her brothers was gay, so she had long been aware that gay men could lead happy, fulfilling lives. She attended New York City's gay pride march every year, regardless of whether her children agreed to join her. Coming out wasn't an issue for Ethan at school, either. He went to the same New York City private school from fifth grade all the way through high school, and by the time he came out at the beginning of his senior year, he had been the tall and handsome popular boy for the better part of a decade. New information about his sexuality did not diminish his social standing.

Gabe wondered how Ethan's perspective would be different if he'd been tripped in the hallway and called a faggot the way Gabe had been in high school.

"How much do we talk about the fact that the Democrats are bending over backward for the crazies in their party?" Ethan asked. "That's part of how they lost me. Or do we not talk too much about when they had me?"

"We don't want to get too specific on your old positions. Those don't matter anymore," Robin said. "We should pick a marquee issue, like freedom of speech, and use it to show voters how much damage the Democrats are doing to the country. You can't disagree with the liberal orthodoxy without getting canceled now, right? And you realized that despite what you'd always been told, the conservatives were the ones standing up for what's right. We're the ones protecting the freedom to debate issues that matter in this country. We're protecting the free exchange of ideas and an open society."

Gabe gripped the edge of his granite countertop and dropped into a fantasy about bursting into their conversation shouting rebuttals.

"And your background is what makes you an interesting story,"

Robin said. "So if you're out there talking about how you used to be a Democrat, if that's part of the message and the story you're telling, you'll get more coverage. That's how you're going to get on TV."

"Is Daddy going to be on TV?" Chloe asked.

"I guess he might be."

"Is he going to be famous?"

"I don't think so, honey." He gave her a kiss on the top of the head. "I'll be right back."

Gabe lifted the tray of food and pulled his shoulders back to brace himself. He pushed through the swinging door into the dining room and forced a rigid smile.

Ethan, his sleeves rolled up to his elbows, shot to his feet to take the platter, which he deposited at the center of their walnut dining table. "Thanks, babe," he said. "This looks perfect." Robin and Andrew sat opposite each other; the wordless assistant was to Andrew's left taking notes on a laptop. Robin pointed a quick smile in Gabe's direction while Andrew used that moment to tap something out on his phone. He muttered a "thanks" without looking up. Wordless Assistant kept his eyes on the computer screen.

Gabe wondered how long these people would remain in his house. It was only 7:00 p.m. At what point could he say it was a school night and they had to leave? He and Chloe had finished their dinner of buttered pasta and baby carrots, eaten at the tiny kitchen table. Ethan and his team planned to order takeout when they got hungry, but Gabe hadn't heard anyone mention food yet. Maybe he shouldn't have brought out snacks.

Then Gabe looked over at his husband, who was munching on a hunk of Gouda, beaming.

Ethan was radiating energy. He looked like he could gather every adult in the room into his arms and hoist them up six flights of stairs.

"This is delicious," Ethan said, waving a piece of cheese toward Gabe. "You've all got to try this. Thank you, hon. Do you want to stay and help us brainstorm?"

"No, thanks," Gabe said. It would be rude to add that he'd rather crawl across the West Side Highway blindfolded. "I'm going to stay with Chloe."

"Okay. Thanks, angel." Ethan put his hand on the back of Gabe's neck. "I couldn't do this without you."

Gabe was surprised by the intimacy Ethan showed in front of Andrew, Robin, and Wordless Assistant. He reached up and touched Ethan's cheek, the familiar roughness after just half a day of not shaving, and Gabe felt his mask melt away. He smiled at his husband, for real this time. "You're welcome," he said. Ethan grinned and popped open a Diet Coke.

Gabe walked back into the kitchen and dropped into a tiny wooden chair, where he took off his glasses and rubbed at his eyes with his fingertips. He could feel the first pinpricks of a headache in his left temple. Ethan had been ground down over the years, dimmed by a string of jobs he found tedious and empty. But tonight, he was bounding around their dining room like he couldn't wait to see what the next moment would bring. The conversation had lit him up.

"Do you want to paint with me, Abba?" Chloe asked, offering a thin purple brush.

"Yes, please. I think I'll paint our family on a deserted island, just the three of us."

12

KATE CHECKED HER reflection in the window of a store that sold tchotchkes and T-shirts to tourists. She and Nicole had arranged to meet at a bar on Forty-Fourth Street, next to a Broadway theater with a twinkling marquee that advertised the name of a movie star. She was curious to see Nicole after so many years, to find out what she looked like and what she did for a living, but mostly, Kate planned to spend the evening taking an elegant victory lap. She had never succeeded in holding Nicole's interest when they were younger, but now, she was a *Herald Ledger* reporter, an unmitigated story of professional accomplishment. Kate would stay for one drink, long enough to satisfy her curiosity and broadcast her achievements, and then she would leave.

She pulled open the heavy wooden door and scanned the room. It was full but not crowded, a parade of men in dress shirts who'd come from work and tourists wearing running shoes with jeans, colorful shopping bags resting at their feet. Kate felt a flutter of nerves in her belly and considered turning around and bolting back out onto Forty-Fourth Street. She forced herself to unbutton her jacket instead and made her way through the long, narrow room.

At the far end of the bar, which was polished to a high gloss, there was Nicole. She stood up from her seat and smiled.

"Well, hi," Nicole said, a dimple piercing her left cheek. Kate had forgotten about that dimple. She used to love that dimple.

"Hi," Kate replied. She hovered in front of Nicole for a moment, not sure how to navigate the space between them. Nicole dove in for a quick hug, then returned to her stool to watch Kate get settled.

Kate hadn't so much as seen a recent picture of Nicole in ten years, and it felt like she was looking at a woman who had fallen through time. Her face was the same, the same thick upper lip, the same almond eyes, and she still had those great curls stretching midway down her back. But her skin was different, lightly folding in on itself when she smiled. Kate was aware of the streaks of silver in her own hair; Nicole had either no grays or an expensive dye job. She was wearing a flowy white shirt without sleeves, though the chilly fall air called for a sweater. This made sense when Kate looked at her arms. Nicole's slender muscles sloped in below her shoulders and out at her biceps. She looked older. She looked good.

Kate took off her jacket. It was a beautiful gray peacoat, which she'd bought on sale even though it was a bit too tight, and she was conscious of how awkward she must have looked shaking her arms free of the sleeves. She put her coat on a hook under the bar and tugged her button-up shirt so it would hang open at the top, leaving her collarbone visible. She could feel Nicole's eyes on her as she ordered a Sancerre and a glass of water.

"So, how long have you been back in New York?" Kate asked, as though she didn't know where Nicole lived and how much she paid for her house.

"It's been about a year and a half. But I'm in New Jersey, actually. We," she corrected herself. "We are in Wickham."

The bartender put Kate's wine down in front of her, and she turned to Nicole, raising her glass by the stem. "It's good to see you."

"It's good to see you, too." Their eye contact was unbroken as they sipped their drinks.

They chatted about the basics—Nicole's move from Louisville and her house in New Jersey, Kate's apartment on the Upper West Side— and made rapid progress on their drinks, until Nicole supplied Kate with an opening.

"Tell me about your glamorous job!" Nicole said.

"It's really not glamorous." Truly, it was not. Kate slept in cheap hotels when she traveled and wrote a lot of stories in the front seat of compact rental cars. But she hoped it sounded like she was just being modest. "What do you want to know?"

"The last time I saw you, you were covering real estate, I think, for a paper in Hoboken. How'd you get to the *Herald Ledger*?"

Kate walked Nicole through the trajectory of her career. When she was in her twenties, the *Ledger* hired her to cover the New York State Legislature from Albany, which was a treat because there was always at least one lawmaker being indicted. She found it a terrible place to live, though. It was difficult to make friends, and it felt impossible to meet anyone her age who was gay, so she threw herself into the work, pounding away at her desk deep into the night and on weekends. She brought those work habits with her to all her subsequent beats.

After stints covering law enforcement and pharmaceutical companies, she became an international correspondent based in Mexico City. She traveled all over Central America writing about politics and culture, migration and social issues, powerful leaders and forgotten laborers. It was exhausting, but thrilling, too, and she accumulated prestigious awards for breaking news and investigative reporting.

Kate paused.

"Usually, when I tell this story, I piously focus on the work," she said. "Never the prizes."

"Of course. You're very pious." Nicole laid a hand on her chest. "I see it. You are above the prizes."

"That is what we call bullshit," Kate said. "I love those sexy trophies!"

Nicole let out her big laugh and clapped her hands. When Nicole laughed, people nearby would often startle, jumping in their chairs at the volume. Sometimes they turned around to make sure everyone was okay. Getting that woman to laugh was like throwing an entire party with one joke.

After four years in Mexico, Kate was tapped on the shoulder to come back to New York and cover politics. In truth, the duties didn't sound particularly appealing, and the stories she'd be writing would be much narrower, but it was a more prominent position. The *Ledger* had originally been a political paper before expanding into other areas like business and international news, and the upper leadership, which was stacked with political junkies, still valued campaign and Washington coverage most of all. The job would be good for her career. So she took it. She shared none of this ambivalence with Nicole, however, focusing only on her upward momentum.

Her professional dominance established, Kate took a sip of her Sancerre and smiled. She had done what she came to do and could leave the bar at any time.

"Wow," Nicole said. "I'm so impressed!"

"Don't be," Kate said, without meaning it at all. "Now, tell me about you. What do you do? Last time I saw you, you were getting your master's in art history."

"God, that was a million years ago," Nicole replied. "I take care of my kids now. That's what I do."

Really? Kate thought. "That's great!" she said.

Kate was surprised by this, and she hoped it wasn't obvious in the high register of her voice. Nicole had such big plans in her twenties. She was going to have her own art gallery one day, or be a curator or a professor. Kate remembered being dimly aware that Nicole wanted kids, but it was not a regular topic of conversation. Kate had another sip of her wine and wondered if she should have taken her career gloating down a notch.

"Yeah, it's okay," Nicole said. "The kids are wonderful. Henry is eight and Sarah's five, and I'm lucky I get to spend so much time with them. You know what they say, at the end of your life, you'll look back and regret the time you didn't spend with your family, not the meetings you skipped."

"Absolutely," Kate said. "When did you decide you wanted to stay home?"

Nicole paused. She watched Kate for a moment longer than was comfortable. "I don't know if I've decided that yet," she finally said.

Kate cocked her head to one side. "What do you mean?"

"There was no decision, exactly. Life just sort of took over." Nicole sipped her drink, some sort of bourbon or whiskey on the rocks, and Kate waited quietly for her to continue. "I got laid off when I was pregnant with Henry, which was fine in some ways because I hated that job, but the timing was bad."

"What was the job?"

"I was doing marketing for a ridiculous start-up that was trying to be a curated search engine," she said. "It had pre-vetted results, but it was fee based, so you had to pay for a small number of answers, or you could get them all on Google for free."

"Oh." Kate grimaced.

"Yeah. The master's program was a very expensive mistake, and I needed a job," Nicole said. "I didn't particularly like marketing, but I was good at it and they paid me well. Then Austin, my husband, was offered a big job in Louisville and I didn't have a big job in New York that was worth staying for, so we moved. I worked remotely for the search engine for a while, then it finally folded when I was seven months pregnant. I didn't think anyone was going to hire me with a body that screamed 'maternity leave!' So my plan was to wait, have the baby, and start looking after he was born."

"Makes sense," Kate said.

"Yeah, well, Henry was a terrible sleeper as a baby, up for hours every night. I was so exhausted that first year, I couldn't imagine putting on real pants, let alone looking for a job and convincing someone to give it to me."

Kate pictured Nicole in sweatpants and a T-shirt covered in spit-up. She'd still be hot.

"I didn't know what I wanted to do next anyway," Nicole continued. "So I figured I'd stay home until Henry could go to nursery school. But then we started thinking about having another kid, and I didn't want to take a job and then immediately go on leave. By the time Sarah was in school a few hours a day, Henry was five and our life was built around my flexibility. I was going to need to make a real amount of money if it was going to be worth paying for childcare. Then Austin got a job in New Jersey, so we were moving again, and I had to get us settled.

"And really," she said, "every day is just busy. Especially when the kids were little, there was always a mess to clean up, always a need to be addressed. I couldn't sit at my computer and read trashy websites for an hour if I was feeling hungover."

Nicole was speaking loudly now, her curls bouncing around her face. "Being a full-time mom is a hard goddamn job! I mean, where else are you expected to catch your coworkers' vomit in your bare hands?"

"Ew," Kate said.

"Sorry. It just makes me crazy how judgmental people can be about stay-at-home moms. Especially people in New York."

"Are they?" Kate asked, trying to sound innocent. She, too, was judgmental about stay-at-home moms, and she was beginning to feel faintly ashamed of this. It was a default position she'd never examined because she didn't know many women who did it. In New York City, who could afford to?

"Oh my God!" Nicole said. "It's like you completely disappear if you don't have a job here. Unless you're a man! If you're a woman and you stay home, you've given up your entire identity, but stay-at-home dads are a sexy catch. Which they are! I agree! But it is also fine if a woman wants to stay at home."

Nicole looked into her glass, which was almost empty, and seemed to draw herself back together. "Wow, I am on a tear here with some-body I really don't know. I guess you seem familiar still. You can prob-ably tell I don't get out very much."

"No, tell me all of this," Kate said. "I want to hear it. Really." Kate spent so much of her professional life being lied to and spun; Nicole's honesty felt like a cool hand resting against her feverish face.

"Do you like it, then?" Kate asked. "Staying at home?"

"Not particularly," Nicole said. "It's not a great fit for me. I like hanging out with my own kids, and I'd miss them like crazy if I went back to work, but I don't especially enjoy other people's children—and they take up a big portion of the day when you stay home!" She flashed a guilty smile, which gave Kate permission to laugh. "Honestly, now that my kids are in school all the time, I haven't quite figured out what to do with myself. I drop them off, I go for a run, I clean the house, I buy groceries, do some errands—and suddenly I have two hours until I have to pick them up again, which isn't really enough time to do anything productive. So, I don't know." Nicole tipped her head back and finished her drink. "I'm still figuring it out, I guess. Sorry, I am really unloading on you."

"No, please. I want to hear it," Kate said. And it was true. "Tell me more. Let me buy you another drink."

A S THEIR THIRD round arrived, Kate excused herself to go to the bathroom. Alone in a crowd of strangers, Nicole had a moment to sit with the fact that her drinking buddy was someone with whom she used to have lots of illicit sex. She took out her phone to text Austin, who had made the kids chicken tenders, toast, and apple slices for dinner and encouraged Nicole to stay in the city as late as she wanted.

Nicole: Still out. Should be heading for a bus around 9:30. Did S eat enough dinner?

Austin: Yep, she ate. We're all good here. No rush.

Nicole closed her messaging app and opened the camera, turning the lens on herself so she could use it as a mirror.

"I've got to make sure I'm drinking water," Kate said as she flopped onto her barstool and crossed her long legs. Nicole quickly put down her phone. She hoped Kate hadn't noticed her preening.

"Cheers," Nicole said as they clinked their matching tumblers. Kate had switched to bourbon on their second round.

"Okay, I have a question for you." Kate leaned heavily against the bar. "I may never see you again, so I'm just going for it."

"I'm intrigued." Nicole smiled flirtatiously. "Shoot."

"What the hell happened with us?" Kate's tone was light, as if she were asking about a silly plot twist in an overwrought movie. "It was all a hundred years ago and it does not matter anymore, but I have you in front of me and I'm curious. It just felt like you never gave us a real chance. Why was that?"

"Oh. Uh, okay," Nicole stuttered. "Yeah, we can go there."

"Sorry." Kate shrugged. "I ask uncomfortable questions for a living. If you want, I can also ask you how much money you make."

"That one's easy: Nothing. Zero dollars."

"Zero is an easy number to remember."

The light above the bar threw shadows around Kate's face, cascading from her sharp cheekbones and jawline. She really had great bone structure, Nicole thought.

"But how about my other question?" Kate said.

"Okay. Yeah, you deserve that." Nicole took a breath. "You're right. I mean, you know you're right. I didn't give us a real shot."

"Uh-huh."

"I was an idiot. It's because I was young and I was an idiot."

"Hm. You know, I'm a reporter," Kate pressed playfully. "And that's not a real answer."

Nicole laughed. Her nerves made her laugh even louder than usual.

Kate leaned toward her. "Can you be more specific?"

Nicole needed a moment to organize her response. She took a big sip of her drink—too big—then had to wipe a boozy dribble from the side of her mouth.

"I think," she began, "I wanted so badly to 'make it,' whatever that means—you know, professionally. So I was looking for someone who was already there, or already on their way, I guess. I had all these plans about what my life would look like. Honestly, I think I was looking to date a résumé more than a person."

She watched as Kate nodded, staring into her bourbon, which was molten bronze in the bar's dim light. Kate looked like someone receiving serious news—not sad news, necessarily, nothing shocking, but it was information she needed to parse.

"I'm sorry," Nicole said.

"You don't need to apologize," Kate answered. "It was a hundred years ago and everything turned out fine. Everything's great, right?"

Sure, Nicole thought. Everything's great.

"Well, I'm sorry anyway," Nicole said. "And I hope you do see me again. I don't know about you, but I'd like that."

13

KATE STOOD OVER her editor's desk. He was a tall man with shaggy receding hair, who wore a uniform of khakis and a white or blue button-down shirt every day like a prep-school boy.

"Hey, Mark."

"Are you quitting?" he asked, his eyes on his computer screen. Kate had requested a meeting.

"Not today," she replied.

"Great." He pulled himself out of his chair, laboring to reach his full height. Kate was tall, taller than most men, and Mark was one of the few people at work who made her feel petite. "Let's go find a room."

They settled into a nearby conference room, a sterile box with no windows, its only visibility to the outside world a tiny glass rectangle in the door that allowed colleagues to awkwardly peer inside. Mark waved his long arms above his head to activate the motion sensor lights, then folded himself into a navy-blue rolling chair. Behind him was a large framed photograph from the *Ledger*'s archives of something exploding, a cloud of dirt rocketing into the sky. Kate sat down.

"I need to tell you about a potential conflict," she said.

"Uh-oh."

"No, we'll manage. My brother is running for Congress, for Joe Bucco's seat in New Jersey."

"Shit." Mark grabbed the arms of his chair like it might slide out from under him. "Shit!"

"It's not that bad!" she said. Mark was not known for his equanimity.

"Yeah, yeah, okay, it's fine. It's inconvenient for me, but it's fine. You just have to stay the hell away from that race."

"I know that," she said. "That's why I'm telling you."

"Has he declared yet?"

"No. Should be soon, though."

"Does anyone know about this? Are we covering this race?"

"Not yet, but I imagine we will once he's in—having nothing to do with me, obviously. He's gay and he's running as a Republican."

"A gay Republican." Mark leaned back, nodding almost imperceptibly. "He got a family?"

"A husband and a five-year-old girl."

"Interesting," he said. "Has he raised any real money? Wait! Never mind. We shouldn't even be talking about this. Forget I asked. You will stay ten thousand miles away from this race at all times. You don't come to any meetings about it. You don't ask how we're covering it. If you overhear anything about what we're writing, you forget it."

"I know."

"The appearance of impropriety can be just as damaging as actually fucking up."

"I get it! That's why we're having this conversation." Kate didn't usually mind that Mark was gruff. It was efficient, which she appreciated, and he was never personally insulting. But she did not enjoy when he explained things to her she already knew. Journalism was less of a boys' club than it had been when she started out, but there were still plenty of men wandering around the newsroom who were eager to inform her that water was wet.

"Good," Mark said. "What's his name?"

"Ethan Keller."

"You hate each other or anything?"

"No, we get along. I see him pretty regularly. I introduced him to his husband, actually, my one and only success at matchmaking."

"Congratulations. So, we're done here?"

"We're done."

"Okay." He stood, leaving his shoulders stooped, as though he'd clipped his forehead on too many doorways to trust his full height. "Stay the hell away from this."

"I know that," she said. "Good talk!"

She was still sitting in her navy-blue chair when he opened the door and walked out.

14

THERE WAS NO going back. In the thin early light of a Monday morning, Ethan declared himself a candidate for Congress. His first campaign ad was released on YouTube and started running simultaneously on TV and Facebook. Ethan, Gabe, Andrew, and Robin all crowded together in front of Andrew's laptop, which was perched on their dining room table, to watch as the video went live.

My family has been in this country for almost two hundred years.

Ethan was walking down a suburban street Gabe had never seen before. He was wearing jeans and a white button-down, the sleeves rolled above his elbows, which he never did because he thought it felt bunchy.

Generation after generation, we've found opportunity here, and freedom. Now, I don't know about you, but these days, I'm worried about our great United States of America.

Where the hell did they film this, Gabe wondered.

Washington wants to tell us how to live our lives. The Democrat Party is bending over backward for the woke mob on the ultra-left. And they're running our economy into the ground! I know I don't have to tell you about the price of gas. We all feel it in this Democrat economy, every day.

Ethan stopped, stared into the camera, and started pointing aggressively.

I want to fight like hell to stop them. I want to fight the Democrats' open borders that are sending illegal drugs pouring into our country. I want to fight the censorship that's trying to silence us. I want to fight so you can make decisions about what's best for your own family. I want to fight for you! I am fighting for America! I'm Ethan Keller, and I'm running for Congress.

Gabe picked up his husband's hand and squeezed.

"I'm proud of you," he said, and searched for the part of himself that meant it.

ANDREW SAID THE announcement could not have gone better. Ethan was written up in the biggest newspaper in North Jersey the day his ads started running, which Robin had negotiated in advance. That story included Ethan's family, but it focused on his positions on local issues like property taxes and whether the government should pay to rebuild homes that had been repeatedly cracked in half by hurricanes. A meaty paragraph up high talked about his unlikely political evolution and the independence that required.

The next morning, the news was picked up by a New York City tabloid with a conservative bent and a gift for writing trashy headlines: "GAY-O-P Candidate in NJ," the bloodred lettering declared. Andrew was relieved they hadn't chosen to make it rainbow.

That afternoon, there was an item about Ethan on Rightward, a conservative website with a respectable national following. The writer ventured that if Ethan could get elected, it might be good for the party down the line. He could appeal to independent voters who would be open to a different kind of messenger, someone with strong conservative principles and a background they understood. Young people aren't as bothered by lifestyle choices, the writer added. But could a former Democrat be trusted?

And then it crossed over. The next outlet to cover Ethan was a liberal website that didn't quite know what to do with him. The story was a crisp six hundred words that was chewing off its own arm, trying to celebrate his queerness while firebombing his message and policies.

The stories were all different in their focus and style. But at the top of every piece, there was a picture of Ethan's family. There was Chloe in her pale blue dress and red high-tops. And there was Gabe, smiling in his windowpane button-down shirt because he loved his husband.

Texts from Ethan poured in to Gabe's phone, sending each article and updates from Andrew.

At 1:17 p.m.: Andrew says Rightward has the sixth biggest readership of any conservative website in the country!!

At 3:42 p.m.: My phone is blowing up!

At 3:45 p.m.: Lots of interest. Booking lots of meetings, lots of events.

At 4:39 p.m.: Love this picture of us all over the internet! Look at my sexy husband ;)

Gabe's phone was blowing up, too, but the tenor of the messages he received was different.

At 2:34 p.m.: Congratulations! I think?

At 3:01 p.m.: Ethan's a Republican??????

At 3:51 p.m.: Um … are you okay?

At 3:58 p.m.: Does this mean you're a Republican, too?

Gabe wanted to crawl into bed and stay there until November, or at least until the primary in June. Failing that, he hoped to make it through the workweek without barfing on his shirt.

NICOLE STOOD IN front of her six-burner stove scrolling mindlessly through Facebook while she waited for a pot of water to boil. Someone on the neighborhood giveaway group was offering a large multilevel cat house and scratching post covered in beige carpeting, retail value seventy-six dollars. "In search of disposable puke bags," another neighbor posted. "Anyone have a stash left over from pregnancy?" Also on offer was what appeared to be actual trash: a set of metal hair clips that were mottled in a reddish-brown rust. "They can be cleaned with rubbing alcohol," the post explained. Somebody had already replied "Interested!" Then there was a very cute picture of a golden retriever puppy, looking like a stuffed animal come to life, which had been adopted by a woman Nicole had known in graduate school. She gave that a "like."

Then—wait, she thought. Was that Ethan Keller?

Ethan's campaign ad was served into her feed right after the puppy. The last time she had seen Ethan he was twenty-something years old and completely shitfaced at a bar in the West Village. He spilled some of his vodka soda onto her open-toed shoes that night, a pair of strappy black sandals. It felt cold and slippery, but at least none of the ingredients were going to stain. Now, he was apparently running for Congress.

God, he looked so much like Kate. They had that same square jaw and wide-set hazel eyes. His hair was a sandy brown like his sister's, though Kate's now had more gray. Was Ethan two years older? Three? He was in good shape, none of that dad gut acquired by a lot of men in their forties.

Jesus, how did this guy become a Republican? Was he still gay? Nicole must be in his district. Were they neighbors? Man, he really looked like his sister.

"I'm Ethan Keller, and I'm running for Congress."

She thought for a second about texting Austin, who was on his way home, to tell him that years ago she'd gotten drunk with a congressional candidate who was going to be spamming them with ads and flyers until Election Day. But talking to Austin about politics was perhaps her least favorite activity, and she didn't particularly want to talk to him about Kate, either.

She put her phone down on the white marble countertop and dumped a box of spaghetti into the salted, boiling water.

15

IT HAD BEEN more than two years since Nicole had been to a proper party, the kind populated by adults drinking cocktails. These days, parties she attended were held in honor of small children, and she would inevitably leave these celebrations with at least one of her kids wailing as they plunged from a sugar high, clutching a party favor bag filled with plastic crap that would immediately break.

So here she was, on her way to a retirement party in suburban Westchester where she would be surrounded by pharma executives, and she felt like a college freshman gearing up for a Saturday night. She couldn't wait to make small talk with strangers and silently appraise the host's decor. She had changed her outfit three times, finally settling on a black cocktail dress that was probably too fancy and almost certainly too short.

Austin sang quietly along to Bruce Springsteen as he drove them to Westchester in his Audi SUV, keeping the beat on the steering wheel and humming over the words he didn't know. Nicole hated that. If he didn't remember the lyrics, she wished he would keep it down so she could listen to someone who did.

Seated beside her husband, Nicole found herself thinking about Kate. It had been good to see her, better than she expected. It was invigorating to have an honest conversation about real things. They'd been texting since their drinks, sharing tidbits from the internet and observations about their lives, ripples of excitement in the flat lake of Nicole's day. She was not at her clearest by the end of their evening together, but she knew she had taken Kate's hand when they said goodbye and squeezed. She folded her arms over her chest as the GPS announced their arrival.

Austin parked in front of an imposing redbrick house, the kind of place that looked like a nice colonial had eaten two or three pieces of *Alice in Wonderland*'s giant-making cake. They climbed out of the car and Nicole tugged down her dress.

"Ooh, honey, you look good," Austin said, running his hand over her backside.

"Thanks." She straightened her outfit where he'd made it bunch. "You look good, too." He did. He wore a white button-down shirt, a suede sport coat, and a pair of khakis. In the twilight, his blue eyes were almost luminescent. She noted this dispassionately, as if registering the particular brown of his shoes.

"I feel a little nervous," she said, gently scoffing at herself.

"You're going to be the most charming woman in the room, like you always are," he said, taking his phone out of his pocket and glancing at the screen. "And the sexiest," he added. He hadn't looked up.

Austin had always been the calmer of their pair. When they'd first gotten together, she'd loved that about him, how unflappable he was. Self-doubt was a concept he was familiar with but didn't really understand, like the physics of airplanes or the mechanics of an electric car. It was something other people dealt with. Austin could certainly get excited, but rarely got upset, and she found that soothing. She admired it. It wasn't that she considered his judgment superior to hers, that he was correct to assume things would always be okay, much less that he had the power to make it so. She never saw him as her protector. But she appreciated that he had a different perspective. It helped ground her to know that if she was worried about something, the worst-case scenario she saw barreling toward her was not what he considered to be the likely outcome.

In recent years, however, his equanimity just made her feel neurotic. That was the role she now occupied in their relationship, but it was, fundamentally, not how she saw herself. The shine had come off his self-possession, and she felt her eyes narrow when he told her absently, while looking at his phone, that she'd be the most charming woman at a retirement party.

He put his phone in the pocket of his sport coat and looked up at her. He took her hand in his and brought it to his lips, pressing a kiss into the knuckle of her right thumb. "Love you," he said.

She scolded herself silently. It was ungenerous of her to be annoyed by his compliment.

"Love you, too," she answered.

Still holding her hand, he knocked on the front door, where they were greeted by a waiter in a bow tie and a jacket that looked like it was made from the same stiff white material as a restaurant tablecloth.

"Good evening," he said, his eyes far away. "Please come in."

Nicole and Austin made a few passes around the party together. They said hello to Austin's boss, Adam, and to Adam's boss, Edward, the host, who was standing near the bar. "I like to hold position here because I know everybody will come by eventually," he bellowed.

Austin planted himself in front of the boss's boss, introduced Nicole, and quickly turned the conversation to baseball. Nicole was a lifelong Cincinnati Reds fan and could easily participate in banter about the current season, which charmed older men in a way she found irritating because their delight seemed to be rooted in surprise. She had once accused Austin of using this as a party trick. He said she was overreacting, that it was just a way to get everyone comfortable and on the same page. It was a safer topic than politics and more interesting than talking about work.

He had a point. When the conversation moved on to a new blood pressure medication that was beginning clinical trials, Nicole freshened her bourbon and excused herself.

The first order of business in any rich person's home was to check out the décor and the art. Edward and his wife (Veronica, was it?) had solid contemporary paintings in their living and dining rooms, big pieces with rich color palettes that looked like they'd been chosen to complement the furniture. A giant sculpture of a hand in the entryway must have been expensive, given its foreground position by the door, but it looked like a Rodin knockoff. In a hallway near the bathroom, there was a row of eight-by-ten school pictures, a phalanx of what must have been Edward's grandchildren, grinning forcefully through missing teeth, their hair askew, their clothing rumpled. It was the best wall in the house.

She finished her second bourbon and realized she hadn't spoken to anyone since she peeled away from Austin and Edward. Austin was no longer at the bar when she went back for a third, which was fine by her. She did not need a chaperone.

As she waited for her refill, she watched two women enter the party and be immediately intercepted by Edward's wife near the Rodin knockoff. One of them was cute, tall with big curls falling just below her shoulder. The other woman, who was shorter and had severe silver bangs, introduced Big-curls to the hostess, a hand resting comfortably on the small of her companion's back.

They had to be a couple. The lower back was not the place for a friend's hand, was it? They were moving toward the dining room now, guided by Edward's wife, and the hand was still in place. They were together.

Who were they? Were they married? The shorter one must work with Austin. What did she do? Did Austin know her?

Nicole floated toward them. Big-curls picked up two plates and passed one to her date. They began to graze a table of hors d'oeuvres, lifting slices of prosciutto and tiny quiches onto their plates. Nicole took a big sip of her bourbon and let it warm the edges of her tongue. She deposited her drink on the tray of a passing waiter, straightened her dress, and headed for the snacks.

"Are those quiches any good?" she asked the two women.

"We haven't tried them yet," the pharma-lesbian said, giving Nicole a quick smile.

Nicole stuck her hand out over the dip.

"I'm Nicole."

"I'm Kim," pharma-lesbian said. "And this is Liv."

"Nice to meet you," Liv said with a firm handshake.

The three of them stepped away from the hors d'oeuvres and found a place to hover nearby. Kim was a director in the research and development arm of Paxol Pharmaceuticals. Liv had a job Nicole didn't quite understand that had something to do with providing high-powered computers to financial firms. Nicole said she had recently moved back to the East Coast and was trying to figure out next steps. Neither of them asked how she had wandered into a Paxol retirement party, and she didn't offer. They told her they lived in Longbourne, New Jersey, that they missed the city, but it wasn't far away. They said they had an eleven-year-old daughter and that they'd been misled about when "teenage" sulking began. The three of them were groaning together, they were laughing together. Nicole was feeling good.

A glass of champagne had somehow materialized in her hand. She was halfway through it when she noticed a young woman with short hair and tight black pants walk through the front door.

"She's cute," Nicole said to her new friends.

They exchanged a look.

"Excuse me?" Kim said.

"I said she's cute," Nicole repeated, raising an eyebrow to give the announcement she'd just made about herself a little extra punch.

"Uh, she works for me," Kim said.

"That's Allison, right?" Liv added. She pressed her lips together.

"Yep, that's Allison. If you'll excuse us, we should really go say hello to Edward. It was nice meeting you."

Kim's hand returned to the small of Liv's back as they walked away.

"Nice to meet you." Nicole stood still for a moment, watching them move through the party. They did not look back.

Nicole could see the mortification in her future, a morass of self-loathing she would surely reach by morning. But for now, it was mercifully dulled by the fact that she was, most definitely, drunk. She left her champagne on a mahogany credenza, snickering to herself that she didn't use a coaster, and went looking for her husband.

16

KATE WAS IN pretty good shape. She lived near Riverside Park and went for a run two or three mornings a week. She preferred to say "run" rather than "jog" because it implied strenuous exertion, though really, she covered three or four miles at a leisurely pace. And that worked for her. She could still fit in her pants, and the combination of exercise and outside time helped sand down the sharpest edges of her anxiety.

Nicole, on the other hand, was in great shape, apparently. The disparity between their relative levels of fitness was on full display when they went to a cycling class together on the Upper West Side, in a windowless studio decorated with splashes of fuchsia, turquoise, and lime green along the walls. An attractive instructor shouted at them cheerfully from a podium at the front of the room. She had a long black ponytail that swished dramatically from side to side and wore a spandex outfit of neon yellow and orange that displayed her six-pack.

"Can we all just have a moment to acknowledge how much shit we wade through every day?" the instructor shouted, beads of sweat dripping from her chin. "How terrible the headlines are? How much bad news there is all the time? But you're here! Despite the news, you found the courage to be here today! To take care of yourself! And that's beautiful!"

Kate would never choose to do a thing like this on her own. She viewed exercise as a private endeavor, a time to be alone with her thoughts without distraction. She didn't even listen to music on her runs. She found she wandered into good ideas this way, and she could keep an ear out for oncoming traffic or bikes. Once in a while, she didn't even bring her phone.

Nicole said they didn't have this particular chain of cycling studios in New Jersey, but it was worth crossing the bridge for because the controls on its stationary bikes were intuitive and it had the most charismatic instructors—she didn't say they were the hottest instructors, but Kate assumed that's what she meant. There was also cucumber water and soft, fluffy towels in the locker rooms. Nicole texted to say she was thinking of going to an early-evening class, maybe on Sunday, and asked if Kate was interested.

They went, and Nicole killed her. They were not technically competing, but they were riding steel stationary bikes side by side and Kate could see their speeds and resistance levels flashing in shouty red numbers. Kate was not comfortable losing under any circumstance, so she pushed as hard as she could manage. She found herself gasping and making loud grunting sounds, along with many of their classmates, but it did no good. Nicole never lost control as the muscles in her thighs and calves shifted and flexed, her sweaty body sparkling under the room's pinkish lights. Kate felt like she might go flying over the handlebars at any moment, crashing into the hot instructor in her traffic-cone spandex.

"Okay, that was hard," Kate said as she wobbled out of the studio. "I think I might die."

"They really push you, right?" Nicole dried her face and the back of her neck with a towel then dabbed at her upper chest, above her sports bra. Kate noticed that she had just the barest touch of loose skin around her belly button and a clear line of muscle down her stomach.

"They do," Kate said. "But now it's my turn to pick the activity. Let's get some ice cream and then go have a drink." Nicole laughed, and the bottle blonde walking out of the room in front of them jumped a bit, startled by the volume.

"It's cold out."

"Who cares?"

I **HAVE A QUESTION,"** Nicole said as she wiped chocolate ice cream off her lips with a paper napkin.

"No, you can't have any." Kate pulled her cone away with a flourish.

"I don't want that. Who orders cantaloupe sorbet?"

"It's refreshing!"

"How could such an intelligent woman be so misguided?" Nicole teased. Even this tiny flirtation gave her a thrill. "Anyway, no, I have a different question. Is your brother running for Congress?"

"He sure is," Kate replied. She turned onto a side street and Nicole followed, looking for a stoop they could sit on while they ate. "He just announced."

"I think I might live in his district."

"That would make sense," Kate said. "I'm not sure exactly where the lines are, but you're a little south of where he lives and that's where he's running."

"I was wondering if he was my neighbor," Nicole said, simultaneously disappointed and relieved this wasn't so. "Why isn't he running where he lives?"

"Because he's a Republican. Democrats always win in his district. How's this one?" She motioned to a limestone stoop without any visible puddles or stains. Nicole answered by plopping down on it. The stone felt cold against her leggings. It was unseasonably warm for the beginning of winter, but Nicole still wished she was wearing real pants.

"I've seen some of his ads," she said. "He's running to fight the woke mob, I believe."

"That's him." Kate bit into her cone.

"How did he become a Republican, exactly?"

"He's always been kind of conservative. Given where we grew up, it's shocking what a centrist he was when he was young. And then he worked for that terrible attorney general, Willard Keyes."

"Which Keyes was that again?"

"The one with all the bribes."

"Right," Nicole said. "I remember him."

"I think Ethan was really disillusioned by that guy. Not only the criminal behavior, but also just the way he did business. He really threatened and terrified people into going along with him, though Ethan doesn't focus so much on that part. The way he tells it, he got an up-close look at Willard's policies, which were very mainstream Democratic ideas, and he saw that they didn't work as advertised and put too much power into big government bureaucracies. But who knows. I think he was always going in that direction, and then he got really into conservative podcasts. He started listening to two or three of them a day, on his commute and at the gym, and suddenly he was getting a huge amount of information, all of it from a very specific point of view."

A drop of pale orange liquid fell from Kate's cone onto her jeans, and Nicole had to stop herself from reaching over and blotting it with her napkin.

"His views have really solidified in the last five or ten years," Kate said. "He's not one of those people who has been a Republican forever and watched the party change around him."

"Austin's like that," Nicole said.

"He's like what?" Kate asked. Nicole heard a shift in Kate's tone, like she was trying to keep it casual but not quite pulling it off. Austin's name was heavy in the air between them.

"He grew up a Republican and has always been one," she said. "Small government. Fiscally conservative. That kind of thing."

Nicole finished her ice cream and popped the tip of the cone into her mouth. When she and Austin were dating, she was crestfallen when she learned about his politics one night over dinner. They were at an expensive Italian restaurant with white tablecloths and a separate leather-bound binder for the wine list. He was a rich kid from Lexington who had gone on to make his own money, and he wanted low taxes and an aggressive foreign policy; he liked to say that people were better off when they worked for what they had, which she found incredibly annoying. She had grown up solidly middle class and didn't mind chipping in so everyone in the richest nation on the planet could have health insurance.

The difference in how they conceptualized these issues was disappointing, but every potential partner had to have something wrong with them, and so this, she decided, was Austin's thing. It wasn't going to stop her from being with him. She was from Cincinnati. She knew and loved plenty of Republicans. It felt like an unfortunate difference of opinion, but a divide that existed within many couples.

His preferred candidates now frequently lost in the primaries to more aggressively conservative challengers, but he never considered changing his registration. He was a Republican, just like he was from the South and had blue eyes. He saw it as an irrevocable part of himself. She found it increasingly distasteful, but their routines revolved around pickup and drop-off, childcare and soccer practice, family dinners and Austin's commute, not debates about the role of government or tax policy. Politics had become just another area where they'd grown apart.

Nicole felt immediately guilty for bringing him up, and aware of how close she and Kate were sitting to one another. She glanced at her watch. She had told Austin she was going to the city for a cycling class and hadn't mentioned doing anything afterward. She also hadn't said whom she would be meeting. She didn't need his permission to see a friend, but she should keep an eye on the time.

"We just don't ever talk about it," Nicole said, hoping to wrap up that portion of the conversation. "That's how we deal with it. But it's a pretty easy topic to avoid, really, because there's so much day-to-day garbage to organize."

"Sure, that's how Ethan and Gabe usually handle it."

"Wait, Gabe is not a Republican, then?" Nicole asked.

"Oh my God, no, he is not. He is as progressive as they come, and I think a part of him dies every time someone asks that question."

"I guess I just assumed, otherwise how could he stand it? I can't imagine anything worse than my husband running for office—or my wife." It seemed important to throw in a theoretical wife she did not have. "Even if I agreed with them."

"Me, neither." Kate grimaced as though the words tasted of old yogurt. "But it's like you said, their life is the day-to-day stuff. They've got jobs and a kid and a mortgage, and they're just moving from one thing to the next like everybody else. And honestly, they're great together. I mean, they're married, so they fight and they drive each other nuts sometimes, but it's like they compete to see who can spoil the other one more. My ex-wife and I were never like that. Which is probably not a thing I should admit!"

Kate had a few strands of silver hair hanging over her right cheek. Nicole wondered if her hair felt different now, the parts that had gone gray. She wanted to reach over and tuck the hair behind Kate's ear. She twisted her dirty napkin instead.

"They started dating when they were so young, and in most ways, they've really grown together," Kate said. "So what's Gabe supposed to do? Does he blow up a pretty excellent daily life for something that feels abstract? I don't think most people would."

"I get that," Nicole replied.

"So." Kate turned her body toward Nicole. "Are you going to vote for him?"

"Will you be mad when I say no? Because hell no." Kate laughed. "But I bet Austin will."

17

ON THE THIRD Thursday of every month, a rotating group of teachers and other staff from Gabe's school went out for happy hour. Their usual spot was a bar a few blocks from work that called itself a pub and pushed harder than was necessary on some ill-defined affiliation with Irishness, labeling cans of beer as "tins" on the menu and slapping shamrock decals on a multitude of surfaces. The bar always had plenty of room on Thursday afternoons and pitchers of pilsner for thirteen dollars.

About a dozen of Gabe's coworkers generally came for happy hour, but on that day, rain was pouring down sideways so their crowd was thin, just a handful of teachers, a secretary from the main office, and a paraprofessional who helped kids with special needs in the classroom. After an hour, their party had dwindled and only Gabe, another tenth-grade history teacher named Armando, and the paraprofessional, Erica, remained. Gabe went to the bar and bought them another pitcher so they'd stay.

"Thanks for the drink, man," Armando said as Gabe poured a fresh beer onto the side of his glass. "How's your husband doing? He still in that job he hates?"

"Well, actually," Gabe said, "he's on leave from his job."

"Shit, is everything okay?" Armando asked. Gabe had meant to deliver this information lightly, but perhaps he'd failed.

"Yeah, everything's fine. It's good, actually." Gabe took a big sip of his beer. "He's—he's actually running for office."

"Oh my God, really?" Erica shouted. "That's so cool! Is he going to be president? Are you going to be the first gentleman? I think you'd be really good at that. You'd be such an elegant host, and you look so nice in pictures!"

"God, I hope not," Gabe said.

"That's great, man!" Armando added. "What's he running for? Dog catcher?"

"Ha ha, no. He's running for Congress."

"Holy shit!" Armando said, embracing his turn to scream. "That's huge. We are going to be close to the seat of power, right here. Are you going to move to Washington? Don't you dare leave me in those planning meetings without you."

"Are you campaigning with him? Like doing events and stuff?" Erica asked. She leaned forward on the worn wooden table, then made a face when something sticky pulled on the skin of her arm.

"Not yet," Gabe said. "He just announced."

"So where is he today?" Armando asked, nodding, a big smile on his face.

Gabe couldn't lie about it. Running for office was among the most public things a person could do. There was no keeping his secret any longer. He tugged at the collar of his shirt.

"I think he's at the Fairgreen Republican Club," Gabe said, trying to keep his voice level.

His colleagues paused.

"Sorry, where?" Erica asked.

"It's kind of near Princeton." Gabe was stalling, trying to buy himself a few extra seconds. "It's about a forty-minute drive from the bridge."

"No, no, I don't need directions," Erica said. "I mean, I don't know where that is, but I also don't care. Did you say Republican club?"

"I did," Gabe answered slowly. "Ethan is a Republican."

Armando peeled himself away from the table and leaned back in his chair, crossing his arms over his chest. Erica looked at Gabe, a profound puzzlement knitting her eyebrows together.

"Are *you* a member of any local Republican clubs?" she asked.

"No! God, no. Look, he wasn't always a Republican. His views have changed over the years. But I wasn't going to divorce him when he switched parties."

"You weren't?" Erica asked.

"No," Gabe said forcefully. "This is not my favorite thing. But he is my husband and he has always wanted to run for office. He'll regret it if he doesn't give it a shot, so I'm trying to be supportive."

"Well, that's admirable, I guess," Erica said. "So what does *he* support?"

"What do you want to know?"

"How about gun control?"

"He supports some limits," Gabe said.

She raised an eyebrow. "Like what?"

"High-capacity magazines."

"What does he think about abortion? Is he anti-choice?"

Gabe took a breath. "Personally, he is, yes. But he thinks those laws should be decided by the states."

"Well, that's terrible," she said. "What about kids like Rahim and Damian?" Rahim and Damian were two of their students who were open about the fact that they were undocumented, brought to the country by their parents when they were very young. "Those are good kids."

"I know they are," Gabe said.

"Well?"

"Ethan doesn't want them to leave the country, necessarily, but he doesn't think they should be able to jump the line for citizenship." Gabe considered knocking the entire pitcher of beer into his own lap to create a diversion.

"What about Republicans like Brett Cooper and what's-her-face," Erica said, "you know, the openly racist one who wants creationism taught in every public school. What does she call the Democrats? Is it the party of pedophilia?"

"No!" Now it was Gabe's turn to raise his voice. "Ethan's going to have to be careful about how he talks about that wing of the party, but he thinks they're awful."

"How about gay marriage?"

"Very funny. Armando, you're very quiet over there."

Armando's arms, still crossed over his chest, rose and fell under a deep sigh. "I don't know what to say, man."

"He's my husband."

"I get it," he answered. "I'm just glad I'm not you."

Armando said this with sympathy, and Gabe appreciated that his situation was being seen for the shitstorm it was. But the conversation left Gabe feeling exposed, as if he'd torn open his shirt in the middle of the bar. The pitcher he bought was still half full, but Gabe decided it was time to go home.

18

NICOLE DROPPED A bag of frozen mango in the center of the dining room table so the kids would consume some vitamins if they declined their vegetables. Bits of fuzzy-looking frost were forming on the outside of the bag, across a photograph of a beach and what appeared to be a coconut tree. She had made overcooked pork chops, baked sweet potato "fries," and a salad for dinner, and with every bite of spongy meat, she felt vaguely humiliated that this was what she had to show for her day. The kids drowned their food in so much ketchup they'd never be able to taste the difference, but she wondered if the chops might strain Sarah's jaw. Nicole cut her daughter's meat into especially tiny pieces.

"I'm going to play eighteen this weekend with some clients," Austin said. "Eight a.m. tee time on Saturday work for you?"

Austin had started playing golf when they lived in Louisville, then brought the hobby back with him to New Jersey, where it was approximately a hundred times more expensive to play. He had been on a Division I tennis team in college and had the sort of natural athleticism that meant he could wander into any organized sport without embarrassing himself, and with the help of some lessons, his golf game improved quickly. He loved that it was a social event but a solitary competition, where he was ultimately trying to best himself. Playing eighteen holes meant he had a good four hours outdoors, a sustained respite from the stresses of everyday life. He found it restorative. Energizing.

Nicole considered it a repellent waste of money, in addition to being somehow both difficult and boring. The last time she joined him on a golf course, she had broken protocol and embarrassed the hell out of him by failing to move quickly enough through the game, declining to pick up her ball and surrender on the fifth hole, even after a young guy wearing the club's insignia on his polo shirt zipped over in a golf cart to hurry her along. They had paid two years' worth of college tuition to be members here, so no, she would not be rushed. Austin hadn't encouraged her to tag along since.

But they had no plans on Saturday, so fine. She would take the chit and cash it in for her own modest break from family life. Maybe she and Kate could do something.

"Sure, go ahead." Nicole took another bite of her terrible pork chop.

"When I played with Rob last weekend, I just couldn't hit them off the back," he said. Austin didn't normally talk with his mouth full, but the meat took so long to chew he appeared to be making an exception. "I should've quit after nine—"

"I watched a video at school today about the moon!" Sarah announced. She was wearing a puffy pink dress that shimmered when she moved. Her extravagant sense of style mystified Nicole, who had been a tomboy as a child.

"Honey, you've got to wait until Daddy's finished. He's in the middle of a story." Nicole was also more interested in the moon, or really anything other than golf, but she was trying to raise polite children. "Remember what you were going to say, and as soon as Daddy's done, we want to hear it."

"Thank you, honey," Austin said to Sarah. "Rob had a good round, though. I even had to pick up my ball a few times."

Sarah tried whispering to her mother across the table: "On the moon you can float!"

"Honey," Nicole whispered back, "you're still interrupting."

"Can I come with you on Saturday?" Henry asked his father.

"Don't talk with your mouth full, please," Austin said. "This time it's a work thing, so it's just for grown-ups. But let's go next weekend. How about that?"

"I want to come!" Sarah chirped.

"That's great, sweetie. Let's all go to the driving range." Austin motioned toward Henry with his fork. "College recruiters love a golf player."

"He's eight," Nicole said.

"And I'm five!" Sarah was not one to be forgotten.

"And you're five," Nicole added. "Exactly right. What were you going to say about the moon, honey?"

"I forget." Sarah was busy drowning a piece of sweet potato in ketchup.

Fabulous, Nicole thought. She missed a rare story about Sarah's day so she could hear about Rob's golf game. She wished Austin would finish his meal in the kitchen.

"It's never too soon to start thinking about that sort of thing." Austin finally swallowed his food. "I'm not going to push anybody, but if they have the interest and the natural ability, then why not? I'll tell you, a white boy from a comfortable background is going to need any advantage he can get."

Oh, Christ, Nicole thought.

"Let's not make anyone here feel embattled, okay?" she said.

"What do you mean, Daddy?" Henry asked.

"Everyone at this table has just about every advantage you could hope for," Nicole replied. "We should be grateful for what we have."

"That's all true," Austin said. "But come on, let's be real—"

"No," she said. "Let's talk about something else."

Austin pouted at his rubbery meat, and for a few strained moments, they ate in silence, pointedly refusing to make eye contact. Nicole looked up from her plate to see Henry's eyes darting nervously between his parents. The details of what had transpired weren't clear to him, but he knew something was off.

Nicole's phone vibrated in the pocket of her leggings and she pulled it out to glance at the message.

Kate: Hi there. How was your day?

Nicole felt her evening swell with potential. She told herself she would get the kids to bed on time, even a little early, so she could curl up in her bedroom reading chair and quietly text with Kate.

"Mom, don't look at your phone during dinner," Henry said.

"Sorry, honey. It was just a news alert." The unnecessary lie flew unexpectedly out of her mouth. "But you're right," she said. "No phones during dinner."

Nicole helped herself to some salad and noticed that everyone was eating not just their sweet potatoes but their pork chops, as well. She hadn't done such a bad job after all. She smiled at Austin through her lifted mood and asked about his day.

19

I **HAVE SOME NEWS,"** Gabe said into his husband's chest. Ethan had just arrived at home for their once-weekly dinner and they were wrapped in each other's arms by the kitchen sink, where a tower of dirty dishes emitted a musty smell.

"Are you running for Senate?"

"Not yet. We're getting a snake."

"A what?" Ethan yelped.

"A snake."

"Why are we doing this?"

"The mornings have been rough," Gabe said, pulling away and walking toward the fridge to unload ingredients for dinner. At Ethan's insistence, they'd hired a woman named Judy to take care of Chloe in the morning and drop her at school. Judy was a recently retired middle school teacher who was earning extra money by arriving at their house every weekday at 7:00 a.m.

"I thought Chloe liked Judy?"

"She does, but not enough to make up for the travesty of you and me leaving the house first. There was so much screaming and crying and clinging this week. I had to peel her off my body every day and try to slide the door closed without pinching her fingers. It was awful." He rested his forehead on Ethan's shoulder. "So this morning, I may have told her that if she showed me that she could stay calm when I left, we'd get her a snake."

"You couldn't have suggested a lizard?" Ethan made a face like something mysterious had just dripped on him from above.

"Lizards eat bugs. I don't want to deal with keeping bugs around the house."

"Okay, fair."

"Snakes eat mice," Gabe continued. "You just keep a bag of dead baby ones in the freezer."

"Oh." Ethan nodded. "And this is better?"

Gabe took off his glasses to clean them with his undershirt. He knew at the outset of the campaign that Ethan would be gone a lot, but the intellectual awareness was not equal to the experience. Ethan often got home after Gabe was asleep and then would be out the door again while Gabe was still drinking his first cup of milky coffee. Duties they used to split were now Gabe's responsibility, like getting Chloe up in the morning and ready for bed at night. And there were tasks Ethan normally took care of that Gabe kept forgetting to deal with, like the dishes. In their regular lives, Ethan would go into Gabe's backpack every evening and retrieve the stainless steel Tupperware he used as a lunch box. Ethan would always rinse it for him and put it in the dishwasher. Gabe had remembered to do this exactly twice since Ethan declared his candidacy. On all the other days, he'd woken to find the smelly container still in his bag.

Ethan had promised to be home for dinner at least once a week, and while Gabe was aware this required planning and sacrifice, one family meal every seven days didn't feel like much. They saw each other so infrequently that if Gabe woke in the middle of the night to use the bathroom and found Ethan lying beside him, he felt a tickle of excitement. Ethan was an incredibly sound sleeper—the man could sleep on a bag of rocks—so Gabe would spend a few minutes rubbing two fingers gently along his husband's stubble, into the cleft of his chin, before drifting back to sleep.

"I don't need any criticism for bribing our child with a reptile, please," Gabe said.

"I didn't."

"We're past internal motivation here."

"I get it."

"This week was so terrible." Gabe kept going. "I just needed some help."

"Hey." Ethan put his hands on the sides of Gabe's face. "This is a lot. I know it is. Do what you've got to do." Gabe nodded into Ethan's hands, which felt cool against his cheeks.

"Buy as many reptiles as you need." Ethan smiled. "Maybe they can run for office next."

20

THEY WERE WALKING down Broadway when Nicole grabbed Kate by the hand and tugged her toward a nearby shop. Her touch left Kate's hand feeling suddenly hot. Nicole might as well have licked it.

"Wait, can we stop in this bookstore?" Nicole asked. There were towers of books in the window carefully stacked under a warm yellow light.

"Sure," Kate said, still thinking about their hands. "I love a bookstore."

"Me, too. I never seem to get to them, though." Nicole pulled back a heavy blue door and stepped aside to let Kate walk through first. They crossed the threshold into a narrow room that took every advantage of vertical space, with white shelves extending from the ceiling down to the birchwood floors. Nicole unbuttoned her wool coat as she walked toward a small table piled with new nonfiction. She picked up a history of the Manhattan Project, which had a mushroom cloud on the cover, partially obscured by a gold sticker declaring the book's victory in a major literary prize.

"That looks uplifting," Kate said.

"It's on my list." Nicole tucked the hardcover under her arm. "This is number four."

"You have an actual list, like with numbers?"

"I do. I'm very devoted to my list. At the start of every year, I have twelve books I know I'm going to read, usually a mix of novels, history, and memoirs. I pick a lot of award winners from the year before, and then I always throw in one classic that's new to me. Like this year I read *Middlemarch*."

Nicole was talking fast, excited to be sharing this part of herself. It was cute. Kate felt the left side of her mouth curve into a half smile.

"It's so nice in here." Nicole looked like she had just stepped onto the beach on the first warm day of summer, her eyes closed and her arms stretched open, as though the sun were pressing down on her from a high shelf in the biography section. She opened her eyes and caught Kate staring. "What?" Nicole asked.

"Nothing." Kate shook her head but let the smile linger on her face. "I've never read *Middlemarch*. So you read a book a month?"

"No, I read a book from my list every month, but I read a lot more than that. My goal was to read seventy-five books this year."

"Wow. Well, the year's almost over. How many have you read so far?"

"Seventy-seven." Nicole picked up another hardcover and opened to the inside flap. "I like to think my list keeps me reasonably current and using my brain. It's like a curriculum I design for myself. And then I can read whatever trash I want on top of that."

Nicole nibbled on her thick upper lip while she read a blurb about European fascism in the twentieth century. Kate had been watching Nicole since they walked into the store and had yet to pick up a book herself.

"Excuse me." A woman with long gray hair was trying to squeeze past Nicole.

"Sorry." Nicole looked Kate in the eye and took a step toward her.

Sandwiched between two display tables, long rectangles of wood painted white, their bodies were just inches apart. Nicole reached over and touched the burgundy scarf that hung around Kate's neck. "This is nice." She smiled. The scarf wasn't particularly nice, or at least not anymore. Kate bought it on the street in Marrakech about a decade earlier, and it was nearly threadbare after years in heavy rotation. Kate looked down to watch Nicole rub the thin fabric between her fingers. If Kate lowered her face just a few inches, she could have reached Nicole's thumb with her lips.

"Thanks," Kate said. Nicole smiled again, flashing her solitary dimple, then stepped away. She walked into a tightly packed aisle filled with paperback fiction and Kate followed.

Nicole's curls were loose around her face, and she wore a black sweater with a deep V-neck under her coat. A gold necklace made of large interlocking loops hung almost down to her navel. Kate could see the notch at the base of her throat, a shadow cast across it like a half moon. She used to love the precise definition of Nicole's collarbone. Its lines and ridges were sharper now, and Kate wanted to know how it would feel under her fingertips.

"Can I ask you a personal question?" Kate said.

"Of course." Nicole turned to face her. "Ask me anything."

Kate took a step closer so they could have a private conversation in that hushed public space. The shelves on either side of them reached to the ceiling, creating the illusion that they were alone.

"Were you surprised that you ended up with a man?" Kate asked.

"Not surprised, exactly. Maybe a little disappointed." Nicole was flirting, but Kate wanted a real answer.

"Why were you disappointed?" she asked. "Did you not want to marry a man?"

"I could have married a woman or a man."

"Then why were you disappointed?" Kate pressed. "It's got to make your life easier. It probably makes me a bad gay for saying that, but that's the world we live in."

"You're right, it does make things easier," Nicole said, scanning the shelves. "But I lose something, too."

"What do you mean?"

"I don't know." Nicole pulled out a thick novel and stacked it on top of the hardcover from her reading list. "Because I'm married to a guy, it feels like I don't really get to be queer anymore, you know? It feels like that part of me has just disappeared. The whole world sees me as straight."

She looked up and stared Kate right in the eye.

"Even though I still think you're cute."

Kate held on to her coat so she wouldn't reach out and grab Nicole with both hands. This was a deliberate escalation, not a thing you'd say to a person you used to sleep with unless you meant it.

"Excuse me, ladies." A man in a puffy black jacket was trying to pass them in the narrow aisle.

"Come on," Nicole said as she started toward the register. "I really hate to say this, but I have to go back to New Jersey. First, though, I'm buying this for you." She waved a copy of *Middlemarch* over her shoulder as she took Kate's hand and pulled.

21

J ESUS!" GABE YELPED when Ethan opened the door to their bedroom. "You scared me. I wasn't expecting you home so early."

It was 9:30 p.m. and Gabe had just put on his pajamas.

"Sorry, I wasn't trying to sneak up on you. Though that could be fun." Ethan raised an eyebrow in exaggerated flirtation and put his hand on Gabe's backside. Gabe gave him a kiss hello, then pushed him away. He wanted to floss and go to sleep.

"How was the candidate's day today?"

"It was good." Ethan dropped onto the edge of the bed and started taking off his shoes. "I was at the train station in Wickham for a couple of hours this morning trying to meet some commuters. Nobody spat on me, and a few people even talked to me!"

"It's only because you're cute," Gabe said with floss between two incisors.

"Then I made about four hundred phone calls to potential donors and supporters." Ethan walked into the bathroom and tossed his crumpled dress shirt into the laundry basket. "And in the afternoon, I had a round table at a garden club."

"Did you ask them how much space we should give our rhododendron so it stops poisoning the bushes?"

"You know, I should have asked them that. They probably would have found it charming."

"Who needs a campaign manager when you have me?"

"Someone did ask me if I own a gun."

"How nice." Gabe dropped his floss in the garbage. "Did you tell them you'd rather stay married?"

"It probably wasn't great that I had to say no, to be honest. But it did lead to a good conversation about gun safety in the home."

"Not this again, please."

"You know we would be responsible gun owners."

"I will never be a gun owner."

"Thousands of people, probably hundreds of thousands of people, use guns for self-defense every year."

"And how many people accidentally shoot themselves or a family member instead? How many kids find those guns?"

"We would keep it in a safe."

"No," Gabe said.

"It's naïve to think we can protect our family with a sticker on the window that says our home has an alarm system."

"No."

"There are so many illegal guns out there."

"No! How many times do we have to have this conversation?" Gabe said, throwing up his arms in exasperation. "God, you drive me crazy."

"Crime isn't just something that happens to other people." Ethan was calm and measured, which was incredibly annoying. He unfastened his wristwatch and put it on his bedside table, going about his bedtime routine as Gabe became furious.

"The idea that you and your gun are going to stop a home invasion is a fantasy," Gabe said, pulling decorative pillows off the bed. "It would never happen."

"If someone was in the house and we only had sixty seconds to respond to the situation, the police wouldn't be able to help us."

"Stop it!" Gabe slammed a pillow against the duvet. "I can't stop other people from having guns in their homes—I think it's really stupid, but I can't do anything about it. But I will never have a gun in my house. Not around me. Not around my kid. Nowhere! And I can't—"

"Okay, okay," Ethan said gently. He crossed the room and took Gabe's face in his hands. "I'm sorry," he said. "I shouldn't have brought this up before bed. Not my greatest move."

"No." Gabe wanted to extract a promise from Ethan, that he would never buy a gun and that they would never have this conversation again. He knew it wasn't possible, but he did love it when Ethan held his face like this, one thumb gently stroking his cheek. The outer edges of his anger were beginning to melt into Ethan's palms.

"I love you," Ethan said firmly. "And I'm sorry."

Ethan kissed him, warm and full on the mouth.

Gabe was not turned on by fighting with his husband. He hated it. He hated the distance it created between them, and at first, when Ethan kissed him, Gabe kept his arms unyielding by his sides. But he kissed Ethan back, and as their mouths opened wider and their lips moved together, Gabe's body responded. They breathed together, pressed their hips together, and the tension between them started to melt.

Gabe pulled off Ethan's undershirt and ran his hands down his chest.

22

NICOLE WAS VACUUMING her bedroom in leggings and a sports bra, deciding whether to blow up her life.

She had gone for a six-mile run that morning after dropping her kids at school. Jogging through her neighborhood, her lungs burning from the cold, she passed one house and then the next and the next that were all just slightly different versions of one interchangeable life. When she and Austin bought their home in Wickham, it was a drab yellow stucco, the color of Big Bird with a hangover. But it was on a corner lot with a big yard and a good local school. It was close to the city, but Austin's commute farther into New Jersey would be manageable. So they bought it. They had since painted the house white, and Nicole had done a nice job on the inside, where her design emphasized clean lines, natural materials, and a soothing color palette with lots of beiges and blues.

None of this improved the clumsy ostentation of the exterior. It had an overly large semicircular driveway, as if a horse-drawn carriage might arrive at any moment, and there were two giant columns out front that were too wide for their height, ornate Corinthian flourishes at the top. Every time she walked through the front door, she had to look at those trashy columns. She usually went in through the kitchen.

She expected that over time she'd grow to love the house, or at least accept it as the envelope of her life and her family. Instead, the things she disliked only grated on her, leaving her raw to its ugliness.

If a different house had been available when they were looking to move, another place that was roughly the right size in roughly the right area, they would have bought that one instead. It was all a function of inertia and timing. Just like her life. She knew she was crucial to its functioning, but she felt incidental to its design. It didn't reflect her talents, her taste, or her desires. She didn't even like her damn house.

She wondered, sometimes, how much her marriage had also been a function of timing. She and Austin had met and fallen in love at just the right moment, when they were both ready to enter a new phase of life, both starting to think about having kids. It filled her with a fluttery panic to imagine that the foundational decision of her adulthood had been so random, like she'd gotten on the Austin train because he happened to pull into the station when she was ready to go.

He was forty-three and divorced when they met, his hair almost fully silver. She chatted him up at a holiday party thrown by a mutual friend, a woman who outranked Nicole at her first gallery job and had a dispiritingly small apartment for someone in their thirties. The steam heat was blasting in the cramped living room and Austin had claimed a spot by an open window, where he was telling a story at the center of a group of people. She waited for him to get to the punch line before she approached.

"Move over" was the first thing she said to him. "Share that breeze."

Austin was by far the best-looking person in that room, with his sturdy jaw and eyes so blue they almost looked fake. He had dated wildly when he was young, been married for a few years in his twenties, and then dated wildly again; by the time Nicole met him, he was still the mayor of every party he attended, but he was less interested in having a crazy night out, more open to settling down, for real this time. He had a career, a navy-blue BMW convertible, and a two-bedroom apartment in a doorman building in Brooklyn Heights. Nicole had never heard of a guest room in New York City. She'd never seen success like Austin's up close.

Nicole unplugged the vacuum cleaner and moved on to the bathroom, where she planned to scrub the grout with an old toothbrush. She was not a naturally tidy person, but she wanted to do something nice for Austin, who hated the way mildew collected unchecked in their shower. They had a housekeeper who came twice a month, but Nicole couldn't bring herself to ask the woman to do a more thorough job on the bathroom, of all places. She pulled on a pair of yellow rubber gloves and shook Bon Ami cleaning powder on the tile that lined her shower.

When they were first dating, Austin had bought her gifts, like a suede sack-style purse and an expensive winter coat that was intended for skiing, a sport she had never tried. What really impressed her, though, were his baked goods. His first wife had gone to culinary school to become a pastry chef, and he'd picked up an interest. Baking appealed to his sense of order and his aesthetic eye, and Nicole would arrive at his house for dinner and be presented with a molten chocolate cake or crème brûlée. Once when they were dating, he made her a lemon meringue pie for no particular occasion; it was just a Sunday and he wanted a project. She read a novel in the living room while he strained lemon juice and whipped egg whites. He set a paper napkin on fire with his pastry torch in the process, but he handled the incident without spectacle, calmly tossing it in the sink and dousing it with water, then turning back to his meringue. The pie was delicious, if not sufficiently chocolaty.

She had been crazy about him then. She used to love to rub her hand against the back of his neck, across the velvety hairs he kept neatly trimmed. The way his quads looked in a pair of tennis shorts. His troublemaker's smile. Their age difference hadn't mattered, but it was starting to now. He was calcifying, becoming rigid and routinized, while she was still figuring out what she wanted. They were bored with each other, yes, but it was more than that. Somewhere along the way, the tide had gone out on their marriage and never come back.

Nicole was scouring a stubborn spot of mildew on the grout with so much force, her bicep was starting to ache. She leaned her body into it and added more Bon Ami.

If she had stayed in New York instead of following him to Kentucky, she might not be washing the walls of her shower in the middle of a Tuesday. Without the narcotic ease of his money, she would have had to hustle and make her own way. By now, she could be an executive at an auction house or an overpriced interior designer.

A bit of soap sprayed off the brush onto her cheek, removing her from her fantasy. But that was fine. She didn't really enjoy such hypo-theticals anyway, thinking about alternate lives she could have lived. Because if she hadn't stayed with Austin, she wouldn't have her kids.

Sarah was her exuberant ball of energy, shy of no one, invited to every birthday party. Things came easily to her, and she seemed like the kind of kid who would breeze through life. Henry was their compli-cated child. He had big feelings that were hard for him to manage, and when he was nervous, he got a bit of an edge to him. He was only eight inches shorter than Nicole now, but he still curled up in her lap when he was upset, trying to fold himself into a space where he no longer fit comfortably. It wasn't that he was her favorite—Nicole would walk in front of a bus for either of her children, and Henry could be a real pain in the ass in a way his sister wasn't, at least not yet. But there was a fe-rocity about her attachment to him that she had nowhere else in her life.

It was unfashionable to feel the way Nicole did about her kids. On the playground, huddled with the other addled grown-ups, it was ac-ceptable only to gently trash your children, to talk about their harmless absurdity and the multitude of disruptions they brought to adult lives. They woke you up too early, rejected all the food you made that wasn't pasta, considered a plastic bag filled with dirty sticks to be a prized col-lection that belonged in their sock drawer forever. No one wanted to hear that Nicole had stumbled into somebody else's life by accident, that she had spent years drifting through a fog of indecision and regret, and that Henry and Sarah were her only salvation.

So much of Nicole's life felt accidental, but Kate represented a choice, one that would be made not for her husband or for her children, but for herself. It was a choice that meant her path was not yet settled, that she could still have something of her own. Being around Kate elevated parts of Nicole that were relegated to the periphery of her life, like her intellect, her interests, her body—which was not just the body of some-one's mother. It made her feel like a version of herself she recognized.

Standing partially clothed in her shower, scrubbing at the tile like there was gold underneath, Nicole decided that she needed to sleep with Kate.

In some twisted way, she thought, this could bring her back to herself and allow her to stay in the life she and Austin had built together. Or maybe she had just chosen him and their shared life enough. This time, she would choose herself.

She heard a scraping sound and realized she'd flattened the bristles of the toothbrush and was now attacking the wall with a piece of rigid plastic. She threw the mangled brush in the garbage then peeled off her rubber gloves and damp running socks, which she left in a corner by the door.

She grabbed her phone from the bedside table and started typing.

Nicole: Hey! I'm going to be in the city again on Friday. Can I buy you dinner?

The reply came in seconds.

Kate: You're becoming a regular. Sure!

K ATE SHAVED HER legs, just in case.
She was meeting Nicole at an Italian restaurant on Amsterdam Avenue called Lulu's, a New York institution that had been around since at least the 1980s. It had exposed-brick walls, a famous Bolognese sauce, and a menu that probably hadn't changed since Kate was in high school.

It was also five blocks from her apartment. The restaurant had been Nicole's suggestion, and the proximity did not feel accidental. Nicole knew where Kate lived, and she'd chosen this dimly lit restaurant nearby, which had itty-bitty tables that forced diners to crowd together, breathing into one another's pasta.

Nicole was married, Kate reminded herself. Married. With two kids and two cars and a life in the suburbs. But she almost never talked about her husband. Kate did not love the idea of sleeping with a married woman. She'd been married, and she understood how painful screwing up in that context could be.

When Kate applied for a reporting position in Mexico City, she and

Shirin had been married for four years. Shirin did not speak Spanish, and her mediocre French wasn't going to do much for her in Mexico, but she didn't particularly like her job teaching at an expensive Manhattan private school and she had never loved New York. (Why did everyone just accept that the streets smelled like garbage in August?) She was from Los Angeles and liked the idea of living somewhere warm again. A fresh start appealed to her. So they went.

But to Shirin, it never felt like an adventure they were on together. She taught English to adults a few days a week, but she was introverted by nature and had trouble building a network of friends in that unfamiliar city. Kate was on the road two or three weeks out of the month, and over time, the quiet strains in their relationship began to splinter. They were stubborn in similar ways, so their disagreements simmered, and with Kate traveling all the time, rifts would stretch on for days, weeks even, through an entire reporting trip. When Kate would finally come home, they'd grown used to that sour feeling, even if the original disagreement had been over something minor, like a small critique of a meal Shirin had spent forty minutes preparing. Shirin didn't love talking on the phone, which made the distance harder. After a while, it felt like they were living separate lives, sometimes in close proximity.

Deep into their third year in Mexico, they went to Tulum for a long-planned vacation, some badly needed time alone to remember what they liked about one another. They took a late flight down from Mexico City and it was dark when they arrived at their hotel, but they could taste salt on their tongues and hear waves sliding into the sand. In the morning, they sat on their balcony with cups of strong coffee and watched the water, which was the same pale blue as the sky, stretch toward them. Shirin liked the beach, but what she really wanted to do was go snorkeling in the underwater caves that were threaded beneath the ground in that part of the Yucatán. She and Kate were just selecting a location, a network of caves where turtles would sometimes join the tourists for a swim, when Kate's phone started buzzing in Shirin's hand. The picture of gentle turquoise water on her screen was swallowed by the words "INTERNATIONAL DESK."

Kate's editor was calling. A US border patrol agent had shot a nine-year-old boy at a border crossing and there were protests on both sides of the fence that were threatening to descend into riots. The closest reporter was a correspondent based in El Paso, Texas, whose Pulitzer Prize slotted him a few steps above Kate in the hierarchy.

The Pulitzer winner was also on vacation, and he declined to come back early. Kate wasn't given a choice. She left Shirin that morning and didn't come home for three weeks.

Things disintegrated quickly after that. In their apartment, which was filled with large, fluffy houseplants, the air became almost viscous with tension. Any anodyne conversation could explode into battle.

"Are we out of eggs?" Kate asked one morning. Her face was in the fridge and cool air tickled her cheeks.

"I don't know," Shirin said sharply as she rinsed a mug in the sink. "I don't keep track of your eggs." Shirin hated eggs.

"I know, but have you bought any recently? Looks like we're out." Kate shuffled containers of leftovers from side to side, as if a single egg might be hiding behind three-day-old rice.

"If they're not in the fridge, we don't have any."

"That's too bad." Kate let the fridge door close. "I guess I'll figure out something else to eat."

"I don't mind doing all the grocery shopping," Shirin said, in a tone that made clear she very much did mind, "but you need to tell me when you're running out of something. I'm not going to keep a list of what you have for breakfast."

"I appreciate that you do the shopping," Kate replied, enumerating in her mind all the household duties she handled herself. She made sure they paid their taxes and their rent on time, in addition to doing her job, which felt sometimes like a firehose spraying directly down her throat. "We both contribute in our own ways."

"Do we?" Shirin asked, her words like daggers sailing across the room. "I understand that your work is *very important*, but I also have a job, and *you* are also capable of going to the fucking grocery store." She went to the front door and shoved her feet into canvas slip-ons. "I'm going for a walk."

They didn't discuss their disagreement when Shirin came back. Instead, they avoided each other around the apartment, slamming doors and cabinets to register their continued displeasure. Kate left that afternoon for a reporting trip, and when she got in the cab and asked the driver to take her to the airport, she felt a tightness in her chest unwind. Those trips had always been an adventure for Kate; they had become a relief.

A few months later, when Kate moved to New York to cover politics, Shirin did not come with her. She went back to LA instead.

The divorce was quick. They didn't have kids, they didn't own a home together, they didn't even have any pets. One day, they were married, and the next, they were nothing to each other. There was no reason to call, no excuse. It felt like a death, like someone had stepped off a cliff and out of her life forever.

Nicole was married, and she very much had kids. But Kate knew nothing about her marriage. Austin might have been cheating on her for years. Maybe Nicole was miserable and it would be better for everyone, her kids included, if the marriage ended. Maybe she didn't have the fortitude to do it any other way.

Or, Kate could be spectacularly misreading the whole scenario. After an uneventful dinner at the dimly lit Italian restaurant, she might go home, watch *Dickinson*, and go to bed.

It had been years since Nicole tore through Kate's life, burying her in longing and humiliation. They had been frenzied and reckless for each other, then Nicole would toss her aside. It was a loop that made Kate feel pathetic.

Their dynamic was completely different now, balanced and easy, and Kate wasn't angry anymore, not exactly. But as she checked her eyeliner in the bathroom mirror, she recognized that she did not feel particularly inclined to protect Nicole, either. Kate was lonely, and Nicole was a grown woman who could make her own decisions. If she wanted to fuck up her marriage, Kate wasn't going to stop her.

Kate put her hand on the light switch by the front door and turned around to scan the apartment in case she had company later. She had tidied the open kitchen, which was carved from a corner of the original living room, and wiped down the Formica countertops. She'd cleared a pile of newspapers off her red sofa and arranged two notebooks, a charger, and her laptop into a neat pile on her dining room table.

It all looked fine. She flipped off the light.

23

THEY SPLIT A bottle of Barbera over dinner without so much as grazing fingertips. Then they shared a dish of hazelnut gelato. Kate watched Nicole lick her spoon clean and dip it back into their melting dessert, swirling the pool of liquid sugar at the bottom of the ceramic bowl.

Nicole leaned forward onto the table, shadows from a votive candle between them gliding across her face, and she asked Kate if she knew a good place for one more drink.

They crossed the street to a much larger restaurant, which had a long bar up front where patrons waited for their tables with fun cocktails and warm nuts spiced with cayenne. Kate ordered herself a mezcal margarita on the rocks. Nicole asked for a bourbon.

The restaurant was full and the blue and white tiles lining the walls amplified the volume of its patrons, every voice counting for double. Kate and Nicole had to get close to hear each other. When Nicole laughed, she held on to Kate's upper arm or laid her hand on Kate's thigh just above the knee. She took a sip of Kate's margarita without asking, turning the glass so she drank from the spot where Kate's lips had already cleared away the salt. For a few seconds, the only thing Kate could see was Nicole's mouth.

"Wait, I'm sorry," Kate said, laughing. "I got distracted and I totally missed what you just said."

Nicole hollered with laughter and grabbed Kate's bare arm.

"Okay," she said, tossing back the last of her bourbon and dropping the glass on the bar. "I see I'm not holding your attention. Let me try something else."

She narrowed her eyes and pulled Kate toward her, putting her face against Kate's cheek.

"There's something I've always wondered," she said, pushing Kate's hair out of the way. Her breath was hot against Kate's ear. "When we first got together, you talked kind of dirty to me. And then it stopped." She drew her face back just a few inches, far enough that she could look Kate in the eyes. "Whatever happened to that?"

Kate's lips fell open, and she could feel cool air on the tip of her tongue. "Come home with me."

NICOLE HELD THE restaurant door open just wide enough that Kate would have to brush past her body as she walked by.

"Which way?" Nicole asked.

Kate pointed and they started down the street.

They walked in silence. Nicole was afraid that conversation would snap their momentum. They moved quickly, not touching, not speaking, as if on parallel tightropes.

Nicole followed Kate up the steps of the brownstone where she lived, and as Kate fumbled for her keys, Nicole gently placed her body against Kate's back, pressing into her almost imperceptibly. She breathed in the smell of Kate's hair, a dusting of lavender and peppermint, and opened her mouth. She let her breath dance on the back of Kate's neck.

Kate jammed the key into the lock and shoved the door open, standing aside for Nicole to pass.

"That one," Kate said, pointing down the narrow hallway toward her front door. As Kate unlocked the dead bolt to her apartment, Nicole stood behind her again, now pressing firmly against her. She put her hands on Kate's hips and felt Kate suck in her breath—then she paused, her key in the door. Nicole moved her hands to the front of Kate's body, flattened her palms against Kate's hip bones, angled them down.

Kate exhaled through her open mouth like she was trying to fog glass. She pushed the door open, then spun around and grabbed Nicole's face in her hands. Kate kissed her, and Nicole felt something inside of her erupt.

It had been fourteen years since Nicole had kissed anyone other than Austin, and she felt her entire body rise up to meet Kate's mouth. Inside the apartment now, they were frantic and clumsy with each other. Nicole pushed Kate up against the door and yanked off her jacket, giving it two strong tugs when it caught at Kate's wrist. She pulled off Kate's shirt. Nicole kissed her hard and the back of Kate's head hit the door with a thump. Nicole's hands were on top of Kate's bra, then underneath it. Kate's fingers were in Nicole's hair.

Kate pushed off the front door and led them, still tangled together, to the back of the apartment. In the bedroom, Nicole peeled off her own shirt and pushed Kate onto the wrought-iron bed. Nicole closed her eyes and gasped as she lowered herself gently on top. God, she had missed this, the softness of her bare chest touching another woman.

Nicole pulled Kate to the edge of the bed and tugged off her jeans. Down on her knees, Nicole stopped to look. She grazed her fingertips along Kate's body. Her skin had more give now, but that made it softer, velvety and plush. Kate had a birthmark near her right hip bone, in a place nobody would see it unless she was undressed. Nicole remembered the first time she saw it, how it felt like Kate had told her a secret. She traced it with her finger. Kate shuddered and arched her back.

"Nicole," Kate gasped. "I want you to fuck me."

KATE OPENED HER eyes and propped herself up on her elbow. The dark room gave a little swivel. Nicole was kneeling at the edge of the bed again, but she was back in her clothes, black boots zipped on her feet and a suede purse hanging from her shoulder. She had her hand on Kate's arm and gently squeezed. "Hey," she said. Seeing Nicole fully dressed, Kate felt uneasy in her nakedness and reflexively tugged the sheet up a few inches to cover her breasts.

"Hi," Kate said groggily. "What time is it?"

"Almost midnight," Nicole said, running her hand up and down Kate's arm. "I've got to go."

"Okay."

"I had a really great time," Nicole said, her words dripping out slowly. "Can I see you again?"

"I'll think about it," Kate replied, offering a half smile she hadn't planned.

Nicole leaned in, letting her lips hover just over Kate's mouth.

"A really great time," she said. She pressed her lips to Kate's and kept them there until Kate kissed her back.

"I'll walk you out," Kate said.

"No, go back to sleep."

"I've got to lock the door." Kate pushed back the covers and looked around for the shirt she wore to dinner, or for any shirt, really, but she didn't see one. Fuck it. She stood up, naked in front of a well-armored Nicole, who seemed even to have touched up her makeup. Kate wasn't twenty-five anymore, and in the intervening years her body had started to shift and soften. But that didn't matter. She wanted Nicole to watch her. She wanted Nicole to see that she was comfortable in her own skin.

Kate smiled and started walking toward the front door. Nicole followed. She watched.

As Kate reached for the brass doorknob, Nicole grabbed her wrist and spun her around. Kate felt a shock of cold run up her back as Nicole pressed her into the door and kissed her.

"If I don't go now," she whispered against Kate's mouth, "I'm never going to leave."

Kate turned the doorknob behind her. "Good night."

24

AS INSTRUCTED, KATE showed up for dinner at Gabe and Ethan's house with two boxes of pasta, lettuce, and a jar of sunflower seed butter for Chloe's lunch. Peanut butter was no longer permitted in many schools because of allergies, and Chloe's generation was under the misapprehension that sunflower seed butter was an acceptable substitute. Kate had tried it. It was bitter, reminiscent of emulsified cardboard. This did not appear to bother Chloe.

Kate hadn't decided if she was going to tell Ethan and Gabe about Nicole. She was not the kind of person who needed to discuss every detail of her life, but a part of her still couldn't believe it had happened. Talking about it would make it feel real.

The person she really wanted to tell was her mother, who would listen without judgment, always on Kate's side. She'd been dead for six years, and there was still a dull daily ache of missing her humming in the background, like static on a poorly tuned radio. Until she started to wilt from pain and exhaustion at the end, her mom had rolled through life like a tank in sensible heels. She had advanced in the legal world at a time when she was almost always the only woman in the room. Once, when Kate was in college, her mother somehow argued with her cell phone carrier until they waived three hundred dollars' worth of over-age charges Kate was contractually obligated to pay. Kate never got the full story on how she did that. Kate's father would complain that such furious tenacity made her mother difficult to live with, but it showed Kate how a woman got shit done in the world.

With her mother gone, Ethan and Gabe were her people now. She wasn't looking forward to the inevitable judgment from Gabe, who would not find it cute that she'd slept with a married woman. Kate didn't find it cute, either. She found it embarrassing. But she could handle Gabe's judgment.

Ethan opened the door in a white undershirt and sweatpants, and Chloe blew past him before he had a chance to say hello.

"Aunt Kate! Come see my Legos!" Chloe grabbed her hand in a tiny vise grip and yanked her toward the dining room table, where a *T. rex* composed of precise green and brown blocks stood waiting, baring its teeth.

"Rooooar!" Chloe lunged toward Kate with the dinosaur in her hand, practically hurling it across the room.

"That looks great!" Kate said. "And terrifying! I'll have to bring you another one."

"Please don't," Gabe said, appearing behind her and taking the bag of groceries from her hand. "Thanks for these." He gave her a peck on the cheek.

"Abba!" Chloe was outraged. "Why?"

"We have so many, and the pieces are just everywhere," he said. He turned to Kate. "There is no pain like the corner of a Lego stabbing into your bare foot at one a.m."

"A pterodactyl could be cool," Ethan chimed in, putting his hands on Gabe's shoulders. Gabe arched an eyebrow at him, not pleased at the suggestion. "If we found a way to keep them organized and tidy," Ethan added cheerfully, "then a few more wouldn't be a problem."

"A girl can dream," Gabe said, sliding his husband some side eye.

Gabe brought the groceries into the kitchen and Kate followed. Under normal circumstances, Gabe was an exceptional cook who always seemed to have something marinating in the fridge alongside a mason jar of homemade pickles. But doing the cooking and the cleaning and the childcare in Ethan's absence was wearing him down. He'd texted Kate earlier in the week devastated because his sourdough starter had died. Now, he informed her, he only prepared food that came out of a box. He was making pasta with red sauce for dinner that night, along with a simple salad that included the lettuce Kate brought over and a single chopped apple. When he opened the salad spinner, he found a toy horse with a purple mane trapped inside. Kate was always impressed when Chloe ate salad—an inconsistent accomplishment, but an accomplishment nonetheless, even if her lettuce was luxuriating in a pool of dressing.

"Aunt Kate! You have to come with me!" She grabbed Kate by the arm and yanked with the weight of her whole body. "Now!"

"Honey, how do we say that in a more polite way?" Gabe prompted.

"Now, please!" She pulled her aunt up the stairs and into her bedroom, where she instructed Kate to sit on the floor.

"This is Fang!" Chloe announced.

She held a thin snake in her hands. It was white with reddish-orange stripes and pink eyes the color of radioactive bubble gum. He—Kate was assured that he was a he—looked like an undulating candy cane with scales.

"Wow," Kate said, sitting cross-legged on the floor of Chloe's bedroom. "He's kind of pretty, in a snaky sort of way."

"He's an albino milk snake," Chloe said proudly, hoisting Fang toward Kate's face. Kate instinctually leaned back, bracing herself against the carpet.

"Is that his cage?" Kate asked, pointing to a glass tank filled with wood shavings toasting away under a heat lamp. "I wonder what he looks like in his cage."

"Do you want to hold him?" Chloe asked.

"No, thanks. I like snakes," Kate lied, "but I prefer to look at them in their tanks."

"Okay," Chloe said, looking a bit deflated. "I'll put him back."

She placed Fang gently onto the bed of shavings and slid a screen cover over the top of the tank, securing it in place with two metal pins. Fang's apartment was situated on the opposite end of the room from Chloe's bed, which seemed to Kate not nearly far enough. Ethan and Gabe had decorated Chloe's bedroom in a loose animal theme. The drapes were white with drawings of dogs on them. There were elephants and giraffes on the bedding and a beanbag chair in the shape of a dolphin. None of it quite went together, but Chloe was happy. She had recently started augmenting the décor by sticking her artwork to the wall with reusable adhesive putty and brightly colored masking tape. There was a paper plate decorated with gold and purple glitter. A snowflake made out of silver pipe cleaners. A drawing of the sky—or was that a whale?

"Fang seems very nice," Kate said.

"Yeah. I got him because Daddy can't take me to school anymore."

"I'm sorry, honey. It won't be forever," Kate said. "But I'm sure it's hard right now."

Chloe stared into Fang's tank, watching him glide into the darkness under a rock. She looked so much like Ethan. Like pictures of Kate when she was a girl.

Kate pulled her niece onto her lap and snuggled her nose into Chloe's chestnut hair. Kate had always liked kids, but being a mother had never been her priority. Her job came first, and she traveled too much to be a parent on her own. It wasn't like she was going to get pregnant by accident, but when she was younger, she assumed that the perfect confluence of circumstances would one day present itself, and she and her theoretical partner would recognize that moment as the time to go out and buy some sperm. Now, at forty, she had settled into the idea that she probably wouldn't have children of her own. It didn't feel like the wrong choice, but sometimes, it was lonely. Being part of Chloe's life took some of the sting out. She had grown to need that kid.

Kate was still conflicted about Ethan's campaign—really, she only wanted him to win in that she wanted him to have nice things. But if he did actually make it to Congress, he would be out of town a lot, traveling or in Washington, and Kate would be happy to step in for him at home. That could be a bright spot.

"Is it hard having Daddy gone so much?" Kate asked.

"Yeah."

"You know he misses you, right?"

"Yeah."

"And he loves you a lot. So, so much."

"I know."

"I love you, too."

"I know. I love Fang."

"Well, he's very lovable." Kate climbed to her feet and extended a hand to this miniaturized version of herself. "Come on," she said. "Let's go hang out with your daddy. Bye, Fang."

HOW AM I doing?" Gabe echoed dramatically. "I've become Nancy fucking Reagan! That's how I'm doing."

Ethan laughed and laid his hand on Gabe's back.

"She was one tough bitch," Kate responded, leaning against the kitchen counter. "Just like you." She smiled, and Gabe gave her the finger. "So how's the campaign going, Nancy?"

"Everyone thinks I am personally standing at the border ripping migrant children from the arms of their parents. My coworkers, my family, my friends—they all assume I'm a Republican!"

"Republicans also assume he's a Republican," Ethan chimed in. "And he looks very handsome while deceiving them."

Gabe leaned into Ethan's side. "You're lucky you're cute or I'd have to murder you in your sleep."

"Aw!" Ethan said. He smacked Gabe on the backside, then turned toward the sink to continue the dishes. Gabe put some leftover pasta into a small metal container for Chloe's lunch the next day.

"Mr. Ronald Reagan." Kate turned to her brother. "What do you have coming up this week?"

"Too much," Ethan said into the sink. "I'm going to stop by a couple block parties this weekend. I'm going to a libertarian book club event at a library at some point."

"What kind of library?" Kate asked. "Please tell me it's a libertarian event at a public library."

"It is, actually." Ethan laughed. "Maybe it's the only space they could get?"

"That is too perfect!"

"And I'm going to church, I don't know, three or four times on Sunday."

"Please don't tell my mother," Gabe said, mostly joking.

"I'm also going to a synagogue this weekend."

"That's an interesting choice," Gabe replied. "Are you going to talk to them about George Soros and your party's favorite anti-Semitic dog whistles?"

"Come on, there are bad apples everywhere," Ethan said. "And conservatives are the staunchest supporters Israel has these days."

"No, let's not—"

"Boys," Kate said. "Let's move on, please. Ethan, what else do you have coming up?"

"I'm having breakfast with the leaders of Mothers Love Freedom on Monday. It started on Long Island as a Facebook group and now it's basically—"

"A cult!" Gabe interjected. "They say they're all about parental rights, but what they mean is they want to help ban books about gay people from school libraries."

"I wouldn't frame it quite like that."

"What's your pitch to them?" Kate asked.

"Well, I think parental choice is a good thing," Ethan said. "Why shouldn't parents have more of a say in their children's education? And if that means they want to decide when their kids encounter certain topics, and they want to be the ones to guide those conversations, and they want to do it at home, they should be able to make that decision."

"I'm sorry, did I just walk into a campaign event?" Kate teased. "Because if so, I'd like to leave."

"They're also big on school choice." Ethan ignored her. "Gabe and I disagree on this, but I want to increase funding for charter schools, and Mothers Love Freedom supports that, as well. We have a lot to discuss."

"Just because they're privately run does not make charter schools better," Gabe said. He could feel a knot forming somewhere in his gut.

"Sure, but the really successful ones have pretty incredible results," Ethan replied. "How can you tell a parent they can't send their kid to a place like that? And look, I understand you think they're bad for the school systems—"

"They're terrible!" Gabe whisper-shouted. "They suck the most motivated families out of the public schools, then they kick the toughest kids out of the charters—and where do you think those kids go?"

"But how can you look a kid or a parent in the eye and say, you can't go to this school where the test results are phenomenal—"

"Phenomenal?" Gabe shouted, a bit less of a whisper this time.

"Or even just really good." Ethan's tone was steady, his expression calm. "How can you tell them they can't go there, that they have to go to their crappy local public school instead? Of course some public schools are great, but some of them are horrible."

"I can't believe you really think this shit," Gabe hissed. The knot in his stomach was growing, spreading into his chest, reaching up into his throat. "It's not like there's an infinite pot of money for education. The money that goes to charter schools is money that does not go to public schools."

"I just don't think it's right to tell that kid or those parents, you don't get to have this opportunity because—"

"Not every kid can go to a charter school!" Gabe hit the moment, always predictable, when he lost control and started yelling. Ethan was unruffled, his expression pensive, as if to signal he was listening, though nothing was getting through. "The 'successful ones' have good test scores because they kick out the difficult kids! What's the solution for them?"

He wanted to grab Ethan by the shoulders and shake him.

"Why should bright, ambitious poor kids get an inferior education because other kids are disruptive?"

"I cannot believe—" Gabe heard himself. He was really shouting now. Ethan had learned never to suggest that Gabe calm down during these conversations. It only made things worse. But Kate reached over and put her hand on Gabe's arm.

"Hon, you're going to wake up Chloe," Kate said.

"She sleeps like a rock," Gabe snapped, snatching Chloe's lunch container off the counter and bringing it to the fridge. "But let's change the subject."

"Okay," Ethan said, perfectly content to drop the conversation, just as he'd been untroubled by having it. He picked up a colander and rinsed it under hot water. "What's going on with you, Kate? How's work?"

"It's fine. You have complicated my life, asshole." She jabbed a finger toward Ethan.

"Get in line!" Gabe cried.

"I love my husband!" Ethan called over his shoulder from the sink.

"No, I'm kidding," Kate said. She wasn't kidding, but she didn't want to contribute to the tension in the kitchen. "I can't write about you, but there's plenty going on this cycle. I'm mostly trying to focus on a few Senate races and doing some big-picture stories on how social issues are animating voters. You know, whatever is making people crazy and whatever the crazies are excited about. And there's the usual deluge of news that needs tending."

"I hear there is a great story to be done on some Republican fairy running in New Jersey." Ethan grinned at her. "That should be on the front page."

"Of course it should be," she said. "But I will not be the one to write it."

"Are you liking your job any better?" Gabe asked.

"Not really." She took the colander from Ethan and started drying it with a dish towel. "I was hoping I might like it more with an election getting closer, but in some ways it's worse. There's more pressure now to do whatever horse race story of the day everyone else is chasing. I feel like one tiny part of a really big machine. So that's fun.

"On the plus side," she said, "I am, objectively, killing it. I'm on the front page a couple times a week."

Whenever she made that pivot, Gabe felt sad for her. Front-page bylines were a measurable signifier of success at the *Ledger*, and something nobody outside the world of media noticed at all. She cared about them far too much. He handed her a grapefruit-flavored seltzer from the fridge.

"But I do have some gossip." She raised an eyebrow, cracking open the seltzer.

"Do tell," Ethan said.

"Well"—she took a sip of her drink—"I may or may not have slept with Nicole."

"You what?" Gabe squawked. "But she's terrible!"

"Is she still terrible?" Ethan asked. "I mean, genuine question. We were like twenty years old when you two had your mess. I was a raging alcoholic then who did terrible things and hurt people. But now I'm an upstanding citizen." He unraveled his most exaggerated stump-speech smile. "A loving father. A model husband." He wrapped an arm around Gabe's waist. Gabe sighed and dropped his head against Ethan's shoulder.

"You're a pain in the ass," Gabe said. "But seriously." He returned his attention to Kate. "She was terrible to you. And now she is married!"

"I know," Kate said. "That part isn't good. But what do I know about their marriage?"

"Maybe he cheats on her," Ethan said. "Maybe it's her turn?"

"Yeah, maybe they take turns. Like in chess," Kate added sarcastically.

"Never play chess," Gabe said to Ethan.

"I don't think I'm going to marry her or anything."

"Since she is married already," Gabe said.

"Since she is married already, yes," Kate repeated. "But I don't know. We have a lot of fun together. There are no games. And I think this is the first time I've actually been excited about a woman since Shirin."

"Gabe does have a point, though," Ethan said. "You were totally in love with her, and I'm sorry, but if she said jump, you would've said, 'Great! Off which building?'"

"It was not my finest moment," Kate said. "It was an extended moment, and not my finest. But I was like twenty-three years old."

"Right. Obviously things are different now," Ethan said.

"*I* am completely different now. And so is the power dynamic. When we dated, or whatever it was we did, she seemed like she was on her way to being hot shit, and I was panicked about becoming some extravagant failure. I was terrified of her. Now, she seems kind of lost, and I'm the one with a great career and a shelf full of awards."

"It's a very pretty shelf," Gabe said.

"Yes, it is," Kate agreed. "And you know what else? She's pursuing me. She is always the one who makes the plans, always the one who reaches out. The last time we got together, she picked this romantic restaurant with itty-bitty tables like five blocks from my apartment."

"There's a woman with an agenda," Ethan said, giving Gabe's bicep a squeeze.

"But it worked," Gabe offered.

"Correct," Kate said. "And you know what? She's very smart, she's very hot, and I like spending time with her. The last few years have been relentless, and I just want to enjoy myself for however long this lasts. I've been in such a funk since I got back from Mexico, and I need to snap out of it."

"That makes sense," Ethan said. "Have fun with her. Just be careful."

"I still hate that bitch," Gabe said.

"Noted," Kate replied.

"But obviously," Gabe added, still nestled in Ethan's arm, "you have to tell us everything."

25

A **MAN IN SHARP** white gloves pulled open a spotless glass door, welcoming them to the opulent Upper West Side apartment building where Ethan's fundraiser was being held. As they strode across the lobby, their dress shoes clackity-clacking against the checkerboard of marble, Gabe considered what would happen if he reached over and held Ethan's hand.

They hadn't always been big on public displays of affection. Eighteen years ago, when they first got together, it felt dangerous for two men to walk down the street holding hands at night, even in New York City. People stared. They had friends who had been walking hand in hand when they were punched in the face.

When Chloe was born, they became, very publicly, a family. They weren't going to hide it, and often, Gabe in particular wanted to broadcast it. It made him angry, especially when Chloe was a baby, that people might assume he and his husband were just friends. His family had to prove what they were, while straight people got to stumble into an assumed cohesion. So if Ethan was pushing the stroller, Gabe started taking his hand or threading an arm around his waist, making sure passersby saw the three of them as a unit.

Kate said something about Ethan once that kept tunneling around in Gabe's brain: If voters wanted to forget Ethan was gay, they probably could because he read as so straight. This made Gabe want to lick Ethan's face on national television or plaster his campaign website with photos of them making out. This was his family. How could anyone forget?

But the men working in this fancy lobby did not give a shit if the tall dude walking past was gay. Gabe's anger had nothing to do with them, so he kept his hands in his pockets.

They rode the elevator with a porter whose job was to stand in the elegant wooden box and push buttons. They got out on the ninth floor and were greeted by an avuncular private equity executive named John Beckwith.

"The guest of honor!" Beckwith boomed. He pumped Ethan's hand like he hoped oil might shoot out of his mouth. "And this is Gabe, is it?"

"It is." Gabe leaned toward him and found his hand being yanked up and down and squeezed. Beckwith shook hands not like he was threatening you, exactly, but like he wanted you to know that he could.

"Come on in," he said, putting his hands in his pockets and taking a wide stance. "We'll take your coats." He took a few steps back, making no move toward their outerwear. A young man in a cheap tuxedo materialized behind him already reaching out his arms for their jackets. Beckwith and Ethan used to work together, and Ethan's campaign manager, Andrew, suggested getting back in touch. Beckwith had family money in addition to his master-of-the-universe salary, and he liked to think of himself as a kingmaker. He wanted to shape the future of the Republican Party from behind a curtain of money.

Andrew and Robin were already there, radiating stress. They greeted Gabe politely, then took position on either side of Ethan. They steered him and Beckwith into the next room, whispering notes about the expected attendees. Ethan turned and mouthed over his shoulder as they shuffled him away, "You okay?" Gabe smiled and shooed him off with his right hand, then went to look for the bar.

"What can I get you, sir?" the bartender asked. Gabe wondered whether he was being called sir because he was in the home of a very rich person, or because he looked old.

He considered ordering the girliest cocktail he could think of, to be the husband delicately holding a pink drink by the stem. Maybe something with a cherry in it that was named after a flower. It could be his little act of rebellion this evening. But the only drink he could come up with was a cosmopolitan, which sounded revolting; he was more of a beer and scotch drinker. He ordered an IPA. The bartender poured it into a highball made of paper-thin glass; it felt cold in his hand and like it would shatter if he squeezed.

Ethan and Gabe had arrived a few minutes early so the candidate would be there when guests began to trickle in for the cocktail party. This was not a fundraiser that charged by the plate. Ethan wasn't there yet. The goal was to get as many potential donors in the room as possible.

Ethan was standing in a circle with Beckwith, a woman Gabe assumed was his wife, and Andrew, so Gabe slipped quietly into the next room. The apartment was decorated with expensive mid-century modern furniture, the real version of the stuff Gabe and Ethan bought at West Elm. There were slate-gray Eames chairs around the dining table, with molded plastic seats and wooden legs arranged in a crisscross pattern. Gabe lifted one an inch off the ground as he passed by, curious how it felt. It was heavy. A few years ago, he and Ethan bought a knockoff version of these chairs in white on the internet. They required weekly maintenance because the screws that held the legs together would pop out. Periodically, a piece of metal would shoot across the room when you sat down.

It was clearly an expensive apartment, with a double front door and pink marble on the floor of the entryway. But the view was what really made the place smell like money. The outer walls were floor-to-ceiling glass, and beyond them the Hudson River and New Jersey were painted against the night sky. It always struck Gabe as funny that rich New Yorkers considered North Jersey a prize to look at, but not a desirable place to live.

Gabe wished the mansion-apartment were smaller. He couldn't imagine that his gay Republican was going to get much of a turnout, and a meager crowd would be less jarring in a normal-size living room.

He found a corner where he could hover by a window to sip his beer and look at his phone. He opened the *Ledger* app and scrolled down.

There was an article about how to cater a dinner party for fourteen people using only sheet pans. There was a movie review about a remake of the 1950s musical *Seven Brides for Seven Brothers* that reimagined all the characters as gay. And there was a story about the future of the Republican Party, how Brett Cooper's cultish magnetism was drawing in a younger crowd. Gabe read a few paragraphs and then scrolled back to the top. Kate wrote that. Even after so many years of her writing for the *Ledger*, it still made him smile to catch her byline in the wild.

"Gabe, it's nice to see you," Andrew said, clapping a hand on his shoulder. "It's showtime. Put the phone away, please."

"Sorry," Gabe said, sliding his phone into the front pocket of his dark blue suit pants. "What can I do to be useful?"

"Love that attitude!" Andrew said, slapping him on the back. "I'm going to introduce you to some folks, but mostly what I need you to do is keep your eye on our guy tonight, so if he calls you over, you can jump into whatever conversation he's having. And don't be on your phone, please. I don't care if you'd rather be anywhere else in the world but here." He winked. "Let's not make it obvious."

Gabe raised an eyebrow. This was not a relationship he understood. Andrew worked for Ethan, technically, but Ethan needed him more than the other way around. Andrew probably considered Gabe a challenge the campaign needed to overcome. Which, in fairness, was likely true since he was an outspoken Democrat and a nattily dressed externalization of Ethan's sexuality. Gabe and Andrew were not buddies, and he appreciated that Andrew didn't pretend otherwise.

More to the point, Andrew was right. Gabe did not want to be there, and that was not a fact he should broadcast.

"Okay, let's schmooze," he said.

Andrew nodded. "Good."

FOR THE NEXT hour, Gabe was treated to a stream of conversations that made him want to run screaming through the floor-to-ceiling windows.

Ethan seemed like he had the balls to take on the woke mob that was destroying the lives and careers of good American men who did a little flirting at the office.

Ethan was just the guy to tackle the international left-wing conspiracy (international left-wing conspiracy!) run by a bunch of European organizations that wanted to drag down living standards in the United States so they could reset capitalism and the international order.

Affirmative action, critical race theory, and diversity initiatives were destroying the country, and especially the lives of Black people. Wasn't affirmative action one of Ethan's big issues?

"Yeah, I think that's on his website," Gabe said, trying to hide his misery with a neutral, factual statement.

"Well, I want to know what he really thinks," said an older white man wearing a sweater the color of egg yolks under his blazer. "I'm a practical person. Not every red-meat issue is going to be one he really cares about. I get that. But affirmative action is racist!"

Gabe felt a tennis ball take shape in his throat.

"What could be more racist than hiring someone based on their race?" the man roared. "It should be the same as it is for schools. Because what happens when they get to Harvard or wherever—I'm a Harvard graduate, myself—what happens if they get there, and they can't keep up? It's not right. And it's bad for the country! I'd like to support a man who knows that."

Gabe's eyes felt dry, which alerted him to the fact that he had stopped blinking. He forced himself to take a breath and looked desolately at his empty beer.

"He is not in favor of affirmative action," Gabe said to the bottom of his glass. "He feels pretty strongly about it. I think you'd appreciate his position."

Gabe was dimly aware that the man in the egg-yolk sweater was shouting his approval at this new information, but he had trouble listening. His body had gone cold.

He was here for Ethan, and he knew that arguing with potential donors about affirmative action would not help his husband. He was not going to convince this man anyway, even if he had a hundred awful years in which to try. Tonight was about Ethan. But Gabe had let that racist garbage stand. He felt like a hypocrite and a coward and like he needed more to drink.

He excused himself and was heading back toward the bar when Robin grabbed him by the elbow and yanked him in Ethan's direction. The candidate was standing by a window, nodding as Andrew whispered in his ear.

"He's going to make his speech," Robin said. "Let's have you stand nearby as the supportive spouse." She deposited Gabe three steps behind Ethan and a bit to his left.

Beckwith hit his bourbon glass with a tiny spoon to draw the crowd's attention. There were more guests than Gabe had noticed. A lot more than he'd expected.

"Good evening!" Beckwith began, taking that wide stance and leaning back, his hips popped forward and his chest puffed out. He looked for a moment like he might tip backward. "I want to thank you all for coming, and I'll keep my part short because I know you aren't here to listen to me. I want to introduce you all to my friend Ethan Keller. An absolute pit bull who also happens to be the future of the conservative movement!" The crowd applauded politely. "This guy is going places, and I want to be along for the ride. I hope y'all will come along with us. So here he is: Ethan Keller!"

The room applauded again as Beckwith and Ethan pumped each other's arm and exchanged handsome, toothy grins.

"Thank you all for coming," Ethan said. "I'm honored that you're all here tonight. Truly honored. You are titans of business. You are members of families that have helped guide this great nation for generations. You are leaders. And you are all working to defend our great nation from a full-frontal assault on our values, on our way of life, and on the free market system itself. And on freedom of speech! Anyone remember freedom of speech? We used to have that in this country. Now we have freedom of speech until you disagree with me—and then you're canceled!"

A low rumble of laughter rolled through the room.

"First, I want to tell you a little about what I plan to do when I'm in office, and then I'd like to tell you what I bring to the table." He had one hand in his pocket now and his other hand in what Gabe was coming to realize was its speechmaking position, rigid and straight like he might reach out and slap somebody for emphasis.

"Here are a couple bullet points: I want to secure ballot integrity. We are one of the only countries in the developed world where you can vote without showing ID. It's insanity! It's like we've put up a big sign that says please commit voter fraud here, we promise not to ask any questions."

More laughter, a bit louder this time. Gabe shifted uncomfortably on his feet.

"I want to increase police presence and police pay. I want to increase nuclear power to lower energy costs. And I want to make sure that any institution in New Jersey that uses affirmative action in hiring or admissions loses any funding or license it receives from the state."

"Yes!" Gabe's new friend shouted, bursting into applause, which the rest of the room quickly followed. Gabe forced a stiff smile and hoped nobody would notice he wasn't clapping.

"And speech!" Ethan continued, jabbing into the air with his slapping hand. "I am going to protect our speech and our political views from the relentless attacks we face from the left. If race and gender are going to be protected in the workplace, then political views should be, too. No one should be intimidated, fired, or shamed for their values."

The applause was louder this time. Gabe kept one hand in his pocket while the other gripped his empty glass.

"And the companies behind so much of the censorship we're seeing, the rules need to change for them. Tech giants like Facebook and Amazon are some of the most powerful entities in the world, more powerful than a lot of countries. They're not more powerful than the great United States of America, though, that's for sure. But right now, the First Amendment only protects your speech from the government. The government can't shut you down, but a private company can do whatever it wants. So Facebook can shut down groups organizing perfectly legitimate conservative protests, and Amazon can ban a book half the country wants to read."

Murmurs of approval fluttered through the crowd.

"Free speech protections should apply to these giant, liberal companies as well. They should not be able to silence conservative Americans just because they don't agree with us!"

More applause. Andrew had his arms crossed tightly over his chest, one finger tapping rapidly against his bicep. But he was smiling.

"Now." Ethan shifted, bringing his tone down a bit, like he was talking to several dozen of his closest friends. "I want to tell you more about me. We're all sophisticated people here, and we know there are things about me that make me an unusual candidate. But I'd like to take them head-on, because I know that, ultimately, they will be advantageous, not only to me but to the conservative movement.

"First, I think we all know that twenty years ago, when I was twenty-three years old, I was a Democrat. I even worked for one. This isn't a secret. I'm not going to hide it. And a lot of people don't trust it, which I understand. Now, I'm not the only conservative with this kind of history. Ronald Reagan was a Democrat and a big supporter of FDR before he became a Republican. And let's leave aside that there are probably a lot of things we all did when we were twenty-three that we would not choose to repeat today." He laughed, giving the room permission to laugh, too.

"But it's more than that," he continued. "This doesn't just mean that I've seen the light and come to my senses—which I have, by the way." Another chuckle from the crowd. "My political journey says important things about me, and about our shared conservative principles.

"I wasn't raised conservative. I came to these views on my own, and it required questioning many of the bedrock beliefs I had been taught all my life. But when I started listening, really listening, I realized that conservatives were the ones protecting what Americans value. Conservatives were the ones who knew that I should be making decisions for myself and my family. Conservatives were the ones promoting American interests at home and abroad. Conservatives were the ones protecting families, promoting families. Conservatives were right, and I had just been taught never to hear them.

"Now, I'll be honest, this was a difficult position to take in the world I was coming from. It required some very real personal and professional sacrifices, and it would have been much easier for me not to go down this road. But I am not afraid to take strong conservative positions. I can take the heat. And I will do that in office, too.

"Our ideas are better, we all know that," he continued. "The challenge these days is to get people to listen. And I believe I can do that. There are independents and even Democrats who will see me and say, 'I know that guy.' They won't have the same gut reaction to me that they have to some Republican candidates. I am a conservative they will listen to. They'll hear how I changed my mind, and maybe they'll be open to changing theirs, too."

Gabe surveyed the room and saw Ethan's targets, drinks in hand, nodding. In this era where not just politicians but neighbors and friends—even spouses—had their hyper-partisan knives out, he wondered why Republican voters would bother with someone who used to play for the enemy. But Ethan was making a good case. Of course he was. Gabe looked around and felt a swell of pride lift his chest. Ethan had this room. They were rapt. They were laughing. A lot of them, Gabe realized, would be convinced.

"And let's address the other biographical detail that makes me unusual." Ethan looked at ease with all those eyes on him, rating and assessing. He smiled. "I've got a husband. He's right over here." Ethan looked to his right, then found Gabe on his left. Gabe stepped forward with a tight smile and waved to the crowd. "There he is. We've been married for nine years, and we have a little girl named Chloe.

"This is unusual for a conservative candidate. I know that," he said. "But we all know that anyone can be a conservative. Black, white, gay, straight, Christian, Jewish, immigrant—anyone. And I have much more in common with a conservative pastor in the South than I do with a liberal gay man in New York City.

"We are not going to divide the country into groups the way the

Democrat Party does, with white people over here and Black people over there," he said. "We're not going to do that. But I know that I would be an asset to the party. Let's talk it through. Having a conservative member of Congress who happens to be gay isn't going to do anything to hurt a conservative running for governor in Wyoming. They had nothing to do with me getting elected. And the fact that I'm gay isn't going to be disqualifying in New Jersey. But in parts of Virginia or Georgia, states that are turning purple and that we need to hoist back over to red, I know I could help. Gay marriage is not the issue it used to be, not for young people in this country, and even for medium-young people like myself." The room chuckled. Gabe was impressed that Ethan had gotten them to laugh during the gay part of his speech. "Now, there are people who feel strongly about this, particularly people of faith. I understand that. But they are conservative to the core, and they're going to vote conservative no matter what.

"But the Democrat Party has moved so far to the left, so far into the fringes, that they've abandoned a lot of moderate and conservative Democrats who feel totally alienated. So we have an opportunity to say to them: Hey, look at our party. We are here to welcome you, whoever you are. We don't care how other people label you. Anyone can be a conservative. This is an opportunity to really change people's minds. This is the future of the conservative movement. And we want to say—to as many Americans as possible—that we are the party of common sense, and we represent you. We—we—are America."

He got a round of firm applause. Gabe was stunned. Ethan had told a room full of Republicans they should give him money because he was running as a former Democrat and a fag, and he got real, enthusiastic applause.

"Now, I look forward to talking to each of you this evening, one-on-one. I'll try to make it around the room, but please come grab me if we haven't connected yet. Thank you all for coming, and I look forward to working together."

The room erupted in a storm of approval, and Gabe felt a proud smile creep across his face. Beckwith jumped forward to pump Ethan's hand and slap him on the back. Gabe scanned the crowd, which was awash in the kind of applause that sounds like heavy rain. They were nodding. They were smiling. They were impressed.

Holy shit, Gabe thought, his pounding heart kicking him in the chest. He might actually win.

26

Mike (former Brett Cooper aide): The man likes a cold room. Especially when he gives speeches. Cooper doesn't want to look sweaty on TV, so he has every room set at 58 degrees.

Kate: Perfect. 58 degrees exactly?

Mike (former Brett Cooper aide): Yep. Whenever possible.

KATE HAD JUST confirmed her long-held suspicion that when covering Cooper's events, it was wise to bring a chunky knit sweater or some gloves. After freezing her ass off at several consecutive speeches, she checked casually with a few other reporters, who were also tired of taking notes with stiff, frigid fingers. Then she called members of the Georgia state legislature and was rewarded with pithy quotes about chattering teeth and cold noses. One state senator said she carried a pashmina in her purse whenever she was in the capital in case she had to be at an event with the governor. An assemblyman kept gloves in his briefcase.

"Morning," an editor greeted Kate as he pulled off his jacket.

"Morning," Kate replied from her desk.

This article was not going to win her a Pulitzer, but an editor had asked her to find a quick story to write, something that would attract attention. She dashed off an email to Cooper's communications director.

Greg,

I understand that when doing public appearances,
Gov. Cooper likes to keep the temperature at 58 degrees
whenever possible, especially when giving televised speeches.
We're going to write a short, scene-y piece about this. Any
comment you want to share? I'm on deadline so please send
ASAP.

Thanks,

Kate

She knew she'd get some grief for this story on social media, and at
least a few reader emails with the outraged subject line: "This is news???"
She agreed that American democracy was in a precarious moment, but
there was still room to needle a politician's vanity.

Kate stood up to get herself some free office coffee, sniffing the mug
she kept on her desk. It was purple with "Nobody cares. Work Harder"
written in flowery script. It could use a rinse.

Her phone buzzed. A response from Cooper's press secretary:

That's a lie. Totally untrue. Of course he doesn't care about the
temperature.

Kate sighed and dropped back into her chair. Navigating other people's falsehoods was a regular feature of her life and a fixture of her job.
A reporter's foundational purpose was to ferret out what was true, what
was spin, and what was outright bullshit. The best reporters got a charge
out of that daily street fight, even silly battles like this one. But this low-
stakes, naked deception made Kate want to drop her phone in the toilet.

Cooper's denial didn't matter, though. She knew it was true and had
it confirmed. She'd start writing after her morning meeting.

Kate picked up her laptop and headed into a large conference room where the Politics department assembled for its regular Monday debrief. Framed newspapers flanked the windowless room like fading soldiers standing in a tidy row: The front page that ran after Osama Bin Laden was killed. The front page from the blackout of 1977. The front page from when the Berlin Wall came down.

A group of journalists—mostly white, mostly rumpled, mostly male—took their seats around a long conference table. A speakerphone perched in the middle piped in reporters who were based in Washington or were out on the road in other parts of the country. When journalists who covered the most sensitive stories sat in that conference room to discuss their reporting, they would unplug the speaker and leave it outside, just in case someone was tunneling in to listen.

The Politics department went around the room to share updates on stories they planned to tackle in the coming week, which included a piece about redistricting in and around Atlanta and an article about how politicians who wanted to send everyone with a crack problem to jail in the 1980s were now tripping over themselves to say they would help victims of the opioid epidemic. Mark, who was everybody's boss, sat at the head of the table and called on them one by one.

Kate viewed this exercise as a blend of aspiration and performance, because in the reality of their day-to-day, there was almost no time for the larger enterprise stories she wanted to do, the pieces she felt might actually move the national conversation forward. The news cycle had become so unrelenting, the candidates so extreme, and the political hostage taking so unpredictable, it was all they could do to keep from drowning in news. Kate's cold-room story about Cooper was pretty close to what passed for enterprise these days; it would only take a few hours and was the kind of headline that attracted clicks. The tech billionaire who owned the *Ledger* was very interested in clicks.

"Okay, who's next?" Mark grumbled, scribbling illegible notes on a yellow legal pad. "Kate. Shit, Kate's here."

"Nice to see you, too," she said.

"No, hi, great to see you," he said dryly. "Tell us what you're work-ing on and then get out of here."

"Excuse me?" She felt her neck grow hot.

"We need to talk about Keller for Congress." A glint of irritation sliced through his words. "So you need to leave the room."

27

NICOLE HEARD A mug of coffee land on her bedside table with a thump.

"Get up, babe," Austin said as he walked out of the room. His next stop would be to get the kids out of bed, giving Henry a playful shake and Sarah a rough kiss on the cheek. Once they were upright and Nicole had her caffeine in hand, Austin considered his morning contributions to be concluded. Nicole pulled herself out of bed to face the day and went to the bathroom to brush her teeth.

Her mouth was a froth of minty suds when Austin came in behind her and grabbed a fistful of her ass. They'd had sex the night before, which wasn't a terribly regular occurrence. It happened about once a month—like a full moon, except it didn't last that long. Inevitably, they were both tired and ready to go to sleep after a routine and not totally unsatisfying quickie.

But last night was awful. She was on top, as usual, and she couldn't get into it. Until she started thinking about Kate. Then she felt herself moving more quickly. She kept her eyes closed. She kept her hands on her own body so she wouldn't feel Austin's slackened skin or the roughness of his chest hair.

Then she looked down after God knows how long to see Austin grinning at her, exhilarated to see how much she was enjoying it. She felt so guilty she thought she might throw up on him. Nicole shut her eyes again and tried to finish him off as quickly as possible, faked her way through an ending, and immediately declared herself exhausted. In the past two weeks, she'd slept with her husband once and Kate twice.

"What do you think of this sweater?" Austin spread out his arms and shifted his body from side to side, displaying different angles while she ran her toothbrush under the faucet. She examined his reflection. The sweater fit well in the shoulders and it looked like a quality cashmere, but the cut was almost an A-line, which left an excess of material pooling around his middle, emphasizing the small paunch he'd recently developed. It wasn't good.

"No," she said. "You look like Santa Claus."

"What? I like this sweater."

She shrugged. "You asked my opinion."

"How do I look like Santa Claus? This sweater is green."

"Okay, then you look like a Christmas tree."

Austin furrowed his brow. "I think it's nice. It's got this zipper here." He pulled the zipper up and down at his collar to demonstrate.

"Nifty," she said. "It's not flattering. Where did that sweater come from?"

"I ordered it."

"Send it back."

"You're ruthless," he said.

"You don't want me to say it looks good when it doesn't."

"Yeah, yeah." He pulled the sweater over his head as he walked out of the room.

"You're welcome!"

Downstairs, she laid out bowls of cereal for the kids and had just turned her attention to making lunches when Henry appeared beside her.

"Mom, guess how many Pillar Cards I have!" Henry said, hoisting a stack of worn and moderately sticky playing cards toward his mother's face.

"That's great, sweetie. I mean, how many?" Each Pillar Card had a vicious cartoon character printed on it, along with a rating system that cataloged how strong it was (from 1 to 100) and how resilient (1 to 10). It had been explained to her, many times, that this was how you knew which Pillar character would be victorious in a head-to-head battle, and which one would be dead.

"I have a hundred and seventy-three!" he said.

"Wow, a hundred and seventy-three!" She mustered as much enthusiasm as possible after just one cup of coffee.

"I almost have two hundred."

"That's right. How many more do you need to get to two hundred and fifty?" she asked.

"Uh." He paused for a second, then a smile broke across his face. "Eighty-seven!"

"That's the right idea, but actually you need seventy-seven," she said gently.

"No, I don't." He looked betrayed. "It's eighty-seven."

"No, honey," she said, pulling out two slices of bread for his peanut butter sandwich. "It's seventy-seven. Here, let me show you." She shuffled through papers on the countertop near the fridge, a repository for garbage that hadn't yet made its way to the trash.

"You're wrong," he said.

"Sweetheart, I've been doing math for a long time. I'm a lot older than you."

"I know just as much math as you!" he declared, his face bunching up in anger. God, she wished he would just eat breakfast right when he woke up.

"Use a quiet voice with me, please," she said, working hard to use her own quiet voice. She found a flyer from school about silly hat day (more familiar to her as stressful last-minute-craft day) and started jotting down a few numbers on the back that she thought might be helpful.

"I'm not looking!" He ran into the living room and threw himself on the couch, the Pillar Cards spilling dramatically from his right hand into a heap on the floor. "It's eighty-seven!" he screamed. "I know it!"

She watched him through the doorway, the silly-hat flyer still in her hand. For the most part, he had grown out of these tantrums, but he could be a challenging kid, and she was now treated to the occasional outburst expelled from a larger body with more powerful lungs.

Sarah, meanwhile, was never one to waste an opportunity. She scurried over to the Pillar Cards, scooped up a pile of them in her hands, and ran away toward the stairs, a pink tutu bouncing around her middle. Henry lifted his torso off the sofa and howled.

"Those are miiiiiiiiiiine!"

He launched himself at his sister and flattened her against the carpet.

"Get off!" she cried.

"They're MINE!"

"No, they're not!"

"Henry!" Nicole screamed. "Get off your sister! Sarah, don't take things from your brother! Everybody," she yelled, "stop yelling!"

Austin trotted down the stairs and straight to the front door. "Bye, family!" he called out in his Southern lilt, just loud enough to be heard over the screeching children, and he was gone.

NICOLE WAS SITTING in her SUV, parked in the driveway of her trashy-looking house. She turned off the engine and wrapped herself in the sound of rain falling outside, pattering on the sunroof of her car in plump, heavy drops. She felt guilty for yelling at the kids and irritated with herself for teaching them bad habits. She'd grown up in a household of yellers, and in the manner of so many adults who do not themselves have children, she had sworn that she'd never be like her own parents in that way. Now that she fought her own battles not to strangle her kids, she realized her mom and dad did their best, and that they too probably felt like failures once the volume had come down.

After breaking up the fight that morning, there hadn't been time to force Henry and Sarah to put away the toys they'd ritualistically dumped on the floor, so her choices were to clean up after them and raise spoiled demons or spend her day stepping on Legos. Usually, when faced with these options, she chose to live in a dump. She had just dropped them off at school and she wasn't yet ready to face it.

She closed her eyes and thought about Kate. How she had pushed her palms up and down Kate's thighs as she fumbled to get her key in the lock. How she threw Kate against the inside of the door and stripped off her clothes. Sitting in her booster-seated SUV, Nicole pictured herself kneeling over Kate. She heard Kate say, "Come here to me," as Nicole grabbed the headboard for support.

She and Kate hadn't been shy with each other when they were in their twenties, but there was something performative about the sex they had when they were young and still figuring out what they liked. They used to joke that they had sex as if somebody, somewhere must be watching. Now it felt focused. Nicole loved when they talked about what they were doing, when they asked for what they wanted.

It had been so long since she felt like she was at the beginning of something, she had forgotten about that delicious phase when it was a perfectly legitimate activity to sit quietly and let the other person waft around your brain. To think about what they tasted like. What they did with their hands when they kissed. What had she thought about when she and Austin first got together? Probably his quads, or the way he used to lift her up and carry her into the bedroom. He didn't do that anymore because it hurt his back.

Stop it, she told herself. She forced the memories from her mind as if shoving them away with both hands.

She went back to thinking about Kate.

When Nicole was going down on her, Kate braced herself against the door, gripping the knob with her left hand and twisting it while she moaned. Her other hand crumpled Nicole's hair.

Nicole grabbed her jacket from the passenger seat and draped it over her lap. She unbuttoned her jeans.

Her car was parked in the driveway, a few yards in from the street with her back to the sidewalk. A neighbor could walk up through her blind spot and knock on the window to say hello. But going inside the house she shared with Austin, to the bed she shared with Austin, felt like more of a betrayal.

Nicole put her right hand under her jacket.

Kate had pulled Nicole onto her lap.

Nicole closed her eyes.

Kate held Nicole in place with her left hand and pushed her right hand inside her.

Nicole felt a tightness in her lungs.

Kate was kissing Nicole's chest, running her tongue along her neck. Nicole grabbed Kate by the hair, and gave a gentle tug to pull her mouth away. "Look at me," Nicole said. Kate smiled, and pushed harder.

28

KATE SLIPPED OUT of her bedroom, apologizing profusely because her editor had left a message and she had to call him back. Nicole didn't mind. She was happy to inspect Kate's room without an audience.

The wrought-iron bed where she lay in a tangle of sheets was set against an exposed-brick wall. Two tall windows looked out over the backyards of adjacent brownstones, a patchwork of bluestone, potted plants, and illegal firepits. They'd left the shades open, Nicole realized. There was a tower of paperbacks by the bed, mostly novels, and a pile of hardcovers about current events and politics balanced against a large white dresser. On a wall opposite the bed, rectangular frames displayed old front pages from the *Herald Ledger*.

There were two framed photographs on the dresser, and Nicole got out of bed to examine them. As she crossed the room, she registered that she was standing naked in someone else's home in full view of their open windows. She put a hand over the loose skin across her belly and felt the muscles underneath.

One of the pictures was of an older woman who shared Kate's wide-set eyes and angular jaw. The other was of a little girl in a red winter jacket who was hanging upside down from a set of monkey bars, a still photograph that looked like it might fly across the room, propelled by all the motion trapped inside. That was Ethan's daughter; Nicole recognized her from the ads.

"Sorry about that." Kate appeared beside her holding out a glass of white wine.

"No problem," Nicole said. "Cheers." She took a sip, just enough to feel the tartness of the wine on her tongue. "That's your mom, right?" She pointed to the woman with the square jaw.

"That's her," Kate said. "You never met her, did you?"

"I didn't."

"That's too bad. You would've liked each other. Though I did tell her what was going on with us when you were dating Jenna. She was not your biggest fan at that moment."

"That's delicately put. She probably wanted to decorate Central Park with my head on a spike."

Kate laughed. "She probably did. But she died a few years ago, so you're safe."

"Oh. I'm sorry," Nicole said. She paused for a moment, then rested her hand on the small of Kate's back.

"Thanks. It still feels strange living in the city without her. She was such a New Yorker, she didn't even particularly like going away on vacation. 'I have the culture, I have the beach, I have the food—I have everything in the world here!'" Kate mimicked a deeper register and the round vowels of a girl from Queens. "'Why would I leave?'" She smiled and settled back into her own voice. "She died a few months before I went to Mexico City, and since I moved back here, it's felt . . . hollow."

She straightened out her posture and took a sip of wine. "And that over there"—she pointed at the upside-down child—"is the future president of the United States. That's Chloe, Ethan and Gabe's daughter."

"She looks like Ethan," Nicole said. "She looks like you. I see Ethan's face everywhere, by the way. I feel like he's stalking me."

"He is stalking you. You're a voter in his district."

"Did I read somewhere that one of his opponents thinks transgender therapies should be illegal?"

"He sure does. No gender-affirming treatments, including for adults," Kate said. "That's James Caruso. He's a member of a local town council, where the damage he can do is fairly limited, but now he's Ethan's main competitor. He's the kind of guy who's great in a primary because he's basically foaming at the mouth, but he's got a whole menagerie of creepy policy positions. The trans thing. He thinks women who get abortions should sit in prison for years. And he really seems to believe that contraception should be illegal, though he's been cagey about that one."

"Jesus."

Kate and her wine went back to the bed. She sat, leaning against a pillow, and covered herself up to the waist with a sheet, leaving her breasts exposed to the afternoon light. Nicole felt aware for a moment of what having two kids had done to her own breasts, which behaved as though they responded to a different gravitational pull than the rest of her body. She followed Kate to the bed and sat down beside her.

"And what are those?" Nicole pointed to the framed newspapers.

"Those are some big stories I've written," Kate answered. "I don't think it says anything good about me that they're visible from my bed."

"Oh, stop. What are they about?"

"That was my first fronted article at the *Ledger*—God, that would have been like fourteen years ago now. The middle one was an investigation about pharmaceutical companies falsifying research on painkillers. That won a couple of awards. And this was my first front-page byline as an international correspondent in Mexico. That was a good day."

"I bet." Nicole sipped her wine. It was three in the afternoon and she was already light and warm all over.

"That was always the dream, to be an international correspondent," Kate said. "But the dream kind of stopped after that. It seemed so impossible when I was starting out that I'd ever get there, I never really imagined what would come after."

"Seems to have worked out."

Kate shrugged. "Not really. I have a great beat. It's too bad I hate it."

"You hate it?" Nicole cocked her head to the side. "I thought you loved being a reporter."

"I used to." Kate took a swig from her glass. "You know what's really depressing? I have built my whole life around the *Ledger*, but I am totally replaceable. If I quit tomorrow and never wrote another word, not a single reader would care. No one would notice. My bosses would hire a new reporter within a week, someone just as smart as I am who works just as hard—or probably harder at this point. Honestly, the paper would be better off with a reporter who really wanted to be doing the job. There's this saying that there are people who love the uniform more than playing the game. I'm afraid I've become like that."

Nicole paused, unsure of what to say. "Do you ever think about doing something else?"

Kate tipped her head back to empty her wineglass. "I'm Kate Keller of the *Herald Ledger*. What else would I do?" She adjusted the sheet around her waist, then turned to Nicole and smiled. "What time do you have to go?"

"The kids have activities until five fifteen today, so I should leave by four." Nicole set her wine down on the bedside table, a geometric structure made of pointy bronze bars and a sheet of glass. She pictured Henry and Sarah standing in front of their school waiting for her, the last lonely kids to be picked up—the last lonely kids who would not let her forget about it for days. She couldn't lose track of time.

"Can I ask you a question?" Kate said.

"You can ask me anything." Nicole wanted to repay the openness she'd just received.

"What are your kids like?"

"My kids?" Nicole repeated.

It would have been additionally disloyal to have a chat about Austin in somebody else's bed, but her kids were a part of her. She wanted a life that was individuated from them—a life she did not currently have—and she appreciated a few hours a day without them underfoot, brawling with each other and demanding snacks. But they delighted her. They were weird little creatures who would curl up in the laundry basket to read a book, or who would tell her they loved her more than their favorite food: She was better than sandwiches. Some part of her had slipped into this life because she preferred hanging out with her kids to the other options that seemed available to her at the time. Austin knew that, and in her more generous moments, she could see how he confused this with volition.

"They're monsters," Nicole said. "But they're also the best. What do you want to know?"

RICH BEAMS OF afternoon light stretched across Kate's living room as Nicole walked out of the apartment. Kate heard her open the heavy wooden door to the street, then let it fall closed, the latch clicking into place with a rattle. Nicole's footsteps were quick down the building's front stairs, and Kate stood listening until they faded away. The silence left behind was an almost physical presence, like a wall Kate might slam up against.

Shit, Kate thought to herself. Nicole was going home to her husband, and Kate was standing naked in her living room feeling sad about it.

She needed to reset, to focus on something else. She would shower and go find some work to do.

★ ★ ★

Gabe: Fang has escaped!!!!

Brother Ethan: Wait what?? There is a snake loose in our house??

Kate: LOL

Gabe: Not funny!! What do I do???

Brother Ethan: Gabe!! Are you telling me there is a snake loose in our house??

Brother Ethan: Gabe!?!?!?!

Gabe: He could be anywhere!

Brother Ethan: NIGHTMARE

Kate: LOLOL

Brother Ethan: Well he's not on the Upper West Side! Kate, I'm moving in with you.

Kate was curled up on her couch with a glass of white wine. Instead of working on a story, she was watching a cooking show, in which blind-folded contestants were making desserts that all had to be set on fire. She chuckled to herself and wondered why anyone would buy a snake.

Kate: This is a one bedroom. You're not invited. When did you notice Fang was missing?

Gabe: Like 20 minutes ago. Chloe and I have been looking everywhere for him. Well, I have been looking everywhere and Chloe has been wailing. WAILING!

Brother Ethan: Poor baby! She must be so upset! I'll come home so we can find him.

Kate: Kids, you're not gonna find a tiny snake in your big suburban house. He's in the walls somewhere or he's outside already, but either way he's gone. Also, he looks like a candy cane and he's in New Jersey… his chances are not good!

Gabe: WAILING!!

Kate: He's probably been eaten by a housecat already. Very undignified end for a $500 reptile.

Gabe: $125

Brother Ethan: Ughhhh I guess we've got to get another snake.

Kate: Guys, how about a bunny?

Kate felt bad for Chloe, who loved that creepy snake, and she felt bad for Ethan and Gabe, who did not need to be dealing with one more thing. But their conversation about the fugitive reptile was also a comfort. Nicole had a family, but Kate had a family, too.

BY THE TIME Austin arrived home that evening, Nicole had mapped out an entire fictional day for herself.

After dropping the kids at school, she'd gone into Manhattan for back-to-back cycling and weight-training classes. They played eighties music for the cardio, Nicole decided, and contemporary hip-hop for lifting. She was starving after all that exercise so went to a Mexican restaurant for lunch. She even concocted a story about a woman at the table next to her spilling water into the lap of her dining companion; Nicole thought that detail would give her fabrication some texture. Then she came home to get her car and went right back out again to pick up the kids.

None of this was true. In reality, she'd gone for a run in the morning, then went to Kate's. On her way over, Nicole had bought an order of tacos to go and immediately dropped them in a trash can on the street corner. She wasn't hungry, but she wanted her credit card statement to match her story. There wasn't time to shower after her visit, so she built that into her narrative, as well. She'd need to rinse off before getting into bed, and in the meantime, her frizzed curls were hidden in a topknot.

"Hey, babe." Austin walked into the kitchen. Nicole was at the counter slicing sweet potatoes into wedges. They'd become the only vegetable Sarah would reliably eat.

"Hey. How was your day?"

He groaned and ran a hand through his silver hair. "It was long. Can you pass me a glass?" She reached into the cabinet and handed him his favorite tumbler, which had wavy lines sliced into the crystal.

"Thanks." He bent down and kissed her on the cheek.

Just a few hours before, that same cheek had been resting against

Kate's bare thigh. Nicole wanted to grab a kitchen towel and scour Austin's lips. But he stepped away, untroubled, to pour himself a bourbon, and she forced herself to make conversation. "Why was your day so long?"

"Someone blew a deadline and I had to clean up their mess. It's amazing how far incompetent people can get in life, you know? But I don't want to bore you with this. It's boring. How was your day?" He took a sip of his drink and pursed his lips against the sting.

"It was good," she said.

"Good. I'm going to go sit down." He took out his phone and started scrolling as he walked out of the room. "Let me know when you need me to set the table."

"Okay," she said.

He was already gone.

Nicole stood alone in the kitchen, the knife heavy in her hand. The stories she'd created about her day would go unused.

29

AN ARTICLE ABOUT Ethan was published before dawn on GSNN.com, the website for the biggest news channel in the country. Ethan shot out of bed to read the story on his phone at 5:45 a.m. while pacing in front of their triptych of bedroom windows. He was thrilled with the coverage and jumped on the phone with Andrew to cheer about it in the morning darkness. Gabe, on the other hand, was not ready to face it first thing. Just thinking about it made his temples throb.

When he was settled on a commuter bus headed into Manhattan, yellow light filtering in through a badly scratched window beside him, Gabe took several deep breaths and read the article. At the top, there was a familiar picture of Ethan, Gabe, and Chloe from Ethan's campaign website, looking preppy and suburban.

He expected to feel an overwhelming urge to toss his phone out the window, or that a stress headache would explode into his morning. But those things didn't happen. He was surprised to find that reading about his husband under the familiar banner of a huge news organization was, in a way, kind of fun.

Ethan Keller is not your textbook Republican candidate.
    Not only did he once work for Willard Keyes, the former Democratic attorney general of New York and a member of the Democratic Keyes dynasty, he is also a gay man running in an election cycle where his party is leaning hard into social issues in an effort to get their base to the polls.

"I'm a strong, committed conservative, but I'm not a conservative by default," Keller said in an interview. "I was raised to be a Democrat, and I came to these principles on my own."

The article went on to describe Ethan's professional background and his usual spiel about freedom of speech. The story implied that living outside the district could be a bigger problem for Ethan than being a gay former Democrat.

And there was a bit about Gabe:

Keller and his husband, Gabriel Alter, were married nine years ago. The couple was introduced by Keller's sister, Kate Keller, an award-winning reporter at The Herald Ledger who covers politics. The couple live in Longbourne, New Jersey, with their daughter, Chloe, 5.

Raised in the Long Island town of Bennett, NY, Mr. Alter, 40, is a history teacher at the elite Manhattan Arts High School on the Upper West Side.

They'd found a picture of Gabe in the classroom pointing at a smart board, a photo that looked vaguely familiar to him as something a colleague once posted on Facebook. His hair hadn't been that long since Chloe was born, so the picture must be at least five years old. Great! His curls looked good and thick. There was a spot in the back that was thinner now than he would have liked, though Ethan assured him it wasn't noticeable. Maybe he should start using Rogaine.

Simon, a friend they used to go dancing with but whom they'd barely seen since becoming parents, was the first to send a text: "Sexy picture. Can you sign my bra?"

Their friend Brian, who was Ethan's law school classmate, texted them both: "Ethan for President!"

A woman named Lauren, who was the mother of Chloe's best friend, wrote: "Chloe's on GSNN! How'd you get her to wear that dress?"

Kate, who was on her way home from a reporting trip, called from an airport in Phoenix to see how Gabe was doing. He'd been sufficiently energized by his day to actually make dinner, and was cooking breaded chicken cutlets, broccoli, and brown rice when the phone rang. "I'm good," Gabe said. "I think I mean it, too. They used a nice picture of me, thank God. And some people I haven't heard from in forever are getting in touch. It's not so bad, really."

"They've left that story on the GSNN home page all day, so it must be getting good traffic," Kate said. "If no one was reading it, they'd have moved it by now."

"It's weird thinking about all these strangers you've never met seeing your face and knowing who you are. Do you ever think about that?"

"Are you kidding?" she answered. "No one thinks about print journalists. We're not famous."

"Well, now that I'm famous, I promise to think about you, but only on occasion," he said. "What I really need to think about are all my new Instagram followers! I've gotten so many today, including some very attractive news anchors with nice hair."

"I do wish that the article hadn't mentioned me," Kate said.

"Why?"

"I'm supposed to be an objective observer in this election, but actually, I'm a candidate's baby sister. The fewer people who know about that, the better it is for me. I really don't need to be included in these stories."

"It's too late for us, my dear," Gabe said. "We don't get to hide from this anymore."

GABE TOOK HIS customary position in the library fishbowl, a small glass office that had been added to the space, tacked on to the wall farthest from the windows. Gabe was required to be there every day during third period so students in need of extra help could come for guidance or another pair of eyes on a history paper. In theory, any student could drop by, even if they weren't in his classes. He had the expertise of a subject-area teacher and he was there to answer any questions.

In practice, almost nobody ever came, certainly not for help with their homework. There were two or three emotionally needy students who would show up periodically, looking for reassurance more than anything, and there were kids who popped by to chat. His regulars were Damian and Jaden, two beanpole juniors. Damian had been in Gabe's AP World History class the year before, and both he and Jaden were gay. Gabe talked openly at school about his husband, wanting to model for his students a happily married gay man, and Damian and Jaden wanted to know more. What was his husband's name? What did he do for a living? Did they have kids? Gabe wasn't supposed to share a lot of personal details with students, but putting meat on the bones of his happy gay life seemed fine, and like something these kids needed. They would come by the fishbowl a couple of times a month—sometimes separately, sometimes together—and they would talk. Ethan called them Gabe's groupies.

On most days, however, no one came and Gabe could use the time for grading or lesson planning. But it had been two days since the GSNN article was published, and Gabe had important research to do. He opened his laptop and started googling his husband under the harsh fluorescent lights.

SURPRISE CONGRESSIONAL CANDIDATE MAY FIND SURPRISING SUCCESS

KELLER DRAWS A CROWD IN MERYTON

HERE'S HOW KELLER COULD WIN

He couldn't help feeling tickled by Ethan's new prominence, by watching the world discover him. He was proud his husband was doing well. He was almost happy about it. Surely, this was not what Gabe would have chosen for his family, but the situation wasn't entirely terrible.

"Hey, Mr. Alter." Damian flopped down in a blue plastic chair and let his backpack fall to the floor, landing against the linoleum with a thud. Jaden followed and closed the glass door behind him. "Hey, Mr. Alter."

"Hey, guys." Gabe closed his laptop. "How are you doing today?"

"All right," Damian answered. "You?"

"You know," Gabe said, "I'm not too bad."

YOU'RE BLOWING UP!" Kate said into her headphones. She didn't call Ethan from the newsroom anymore, but she was working from her living room that afternoon, slumped into her bright red couch. "All the DC politics websites have had items on you. A bunch of the big conservative sites are following you. The *New Jersey Eagle* has a piece today. It's the dream pickup."

"It's crazy," he said. "Andrew and Robin are geniuses."

"Maybe," Kate replied. "But you're also an interesting story. Everyone is so sick of the same old candidate."

"Conservative fag at your service," he said brightly.

"Now that you're getting real attention, you and your geniuses have got to deal with your DUI. If you don't tell the world, someone else is going to tell the world for you."

"I know, I know. Everything has just been so nuts, we haven't had a chance to really sit down and plan how we're going to tackle it."

"No," Kate said. "You've got to make this a priority. You almost killed that girl because you were shitfaced. You need to get out there and make yourself a story of redemption before you look like a shady politician who's trying to hide his past from voters. And look, you can spin this into a positive—I mean, it's not good you hurt the woman, but she's fine now, right?"

"She's fine," he said. "She's got some hip problems, last I heard, but she also got a bunch of insurance money she used to start her own business. She supplies personal assistants to executives now."

"Good. So she's fine. And you are a story of redemption. You're a candidate who is truly sympathetic to people suffering from addiction because you have been there."

"I don't know, that makes me nervous," he said. "'Vote for the conservative fag who is also an addict' feels like a step too far."

"I don't think so. There's a lot of sympathy for addiction right now because the opioid crisis has been killing a lot of white people."

"Come on, it's not that simple," Ethan started.

"Let's not have a debate, okay? Nervous or not, you've got to get this done. Like, you should hang up on me right now and go call Andrew. Find a friendly outlet and a reporter who does more human interest than hardball politics and go offer them an exclusive."

"You're right, you're right," he said.

"I know I'm right. Now go!"

30

AT THE END of dinner every night, Nicole and Austin would divide and conquer the evening. He would do the dishes while she got the kids cleaned up, changed, and ready for bed. Some evenings, she would handle both Henry and Sarah. On nights when she hadn't set off a bomb of food scraps and prep dishes in the kitchen—she was not a cook who cleaned as she went—Austin would come upstairs and peel off one of the children. Sarah was in bed by eight, Henry by eight forty-five.

The adults rarely came together anymore once the ritual was complete. Usually, Austin deposited himself on their living room sofa and she floated upstairs to read a book or watch something on their bedroom TV. But tonight, when Austin dropped onto the couch, she sat down beside him. She lifted up his left arm and placed it over her shoulder.

"Well, hi," he said, giving her a kiss on the side of the head. "This is nice."

She missed him. She missed the idea of him, at least. He had been the center of her life once, but now they walked around their shared existence in individual bubbles. They could spend an entire evening at home together and only look at each other when he asked her to pass the salad or she wanted him to fetch a child. Every exchange was a transaction arranged to accomplish a household task. She needed to make more of an effort.

Nuzzled into the crook of his arm, she slid a hand between the buttons of his shirt. She could feel his face swiveling around, investigating whether she was trying to start something, but she didn't look up.

"What are we watching?" she asked.

"I was thinking *Criminal Masterminds*. That work for you?"

"Sure."

He turned on the TV and clicked over to a streaming service that included seventeen years' worth of *Masterminds*, a crime procedural she found oddly calming even though every episode was about something terrible, like a murder or a kidnapping. It was the longest-running series in television history, and while she enjoyed the show, it always made her wonder what was wrong with humanity that so many people were soothed by watching one hideous act of violence after another.

Austin picked an episode and pressed play.

"Do you remember freedom of speech?"

It was Ethan. Ethan's face—Kate's face—was on her TV. She tried not to let her body tense. Shit.

"I do! But today, it's freedom of speech until you disagree with someone— and then you're canceled. Honest, hardworking Americans are being called bigots just for questioning the Democrat agenda. And I'm tired of it!"

He was standing outside on a suburban street, some modest homes blurry behind him. His smile was perfectly symmetrical in a way Kate's wasn't—the left side of her mouth came up a little higher than the right—but their eyes squinted and creased in just the same way.

She felt Austin moving. She looked up. His head was bobbing up and down in a slow nod.

"We need to restore common sense to our great country, but we're going to need to fight for it. They're trying to censor us, to scare us into being quiet—but I won't let them! I'm going to fight them! I'm Ethan Keller and I approve this message, and I'm here to fight for you, every day."

"Excuse me, honey." Austin reached over her toward the bourbon he'd left resting on the coffee table. The coaster he was using had a miniature Rembrandt on it, a painting of a brightly lit wave about to knock a boat into the ocean. She took Austin's movement as an excuse to sit up.

"I've got to say," Austin told her, taking a sip of his drink, "I think that guy makes a lot of sense."

She could feel the pull of every muscle in her face as she smiled at him. "He's not my type. Actually, I think I'm going to go read my book."

"Babe, I'm sorry. I know that's not your favorite conversation. Stay. I'll drop it."

"No, no, it's not that, I'm just not in the mood to watch anything." She gave him a quick peck on the lips. "Enjoy your murder show." Austin settled back into the couch as she stood up to leave the room.

Halfway up the stairs, she checked that Austin was not behind her and took out her phone. She texted Kate.

Nicole: Hi there. What are you doing right now?

31

GABE AND CHLOE were holding hands in the brightly lit produce aisle of the grocery store, loading baby carrots and clementines into their shopping basket while they negotiated what they'd have for dinner.

"I want burgers," she said.

"We had burgers last night, honey," Gabe reminded his carnivorous child. "Let's have chicken. What kind of chicken would you like?"

"Let's have steak," she replied firmly.

"Not tonight, sweetie."

"Then I want a hot dog."

"Chloe, tonight we're going to have chicken. We can either have—"

"Hey! You're that guy's husband!" A woman wearing black leggings and a pink sweatshirt was pointing at them over the Honeycrisp apples.

Gabe looked around instinctively, wondering if she was speaking to someone behind him. "Excuse me?"

"Keller!" She snapped the fingers of her right hand. "Took me a second but I got his name. You're Ethan Keller's husband."

"Oh." Gabe paused. This could go any number of ways, many of them terrible. He put a hand protectively on Chloe's shoulder. "That's right."

"He's got my vote. He seems like a real person, you know?"

"Oh." Gabe let out his breath. He didn't actually know what she meant, but okay. "Thank you. I'll tell him."

"You know, you're cute, too."

"Oh!" Gabe chuckled a bit through his surprise.

"You're both cute. We could do a lot worse!" She laughed. "Anyway, enjoy your shopping." She smiled at Chloe. "You take good care of your daddies, honey. Nice to meet you."

"You, too," he called after her.

There in the produce aisle, Gabe felt his first sparkle of celebrity. And he liked it.

★ ★ ★

Kate: Hey. I need to ask you a question.

Brother Ethan: Shoot

Kate: I need you to be completely honest with me. Okay?

Brother Ethan: Okay. What's up?

Kate: Really though. Brutally honest

Brother Ethan: Sure. What's going on?

Kate: Well…

Brother Ethan: …??

Kate: Do you think Fang is still living in the walls of your house??????

Brother Ethan: I hate you.

Kate: Sssssssssssssss

GABE WAS READING *New York* magazine in bed when Ethan opened the door with a gentle nudge. He wore jeans and a light blue button-down shirt, the sleeves creased and bunchy from being rolled up all day.

"Yay, you're still awake," Ethan said as he crawled across the bed. He put his face up to Gabe's neck and inhaled, then draped his body across his husband's.

"You are wearing your outside clothes on my bed," Gabe scolded gently, his right eyebrow raised into a peak.

"I know, but you feel good," Ethan said.

"Well, that's nice, but I don't need you anymore," Gabe replied. "Some lady hit on me in the grocery store today."

"Of course she did." Ethan's face rested on the thin white T-shirt that covered Gabe's chest.

"She recognized me. I'm Ethan Keller's husband now. But apparently I'm also cute."

"You're extremely cute." Ethan lifted his head and looked up at Gabe. "Someone recognized you?"

"Someone did." Gabe rubbed his thumb across the cleft in Ethan's chin, the gentle pinpricks of his sixteen-hour stubble.

"That's amazing. I guess we're starting to get some traction." Ethan's smile was wide. "But do I need to fight this bitch for trying to steal my husband?"

"Oh, definitely," Gabe said. Ethan stretched up and kissed him on the mouth.

32

NICOLE KNOCKED SOFTLY on Henry's door as she opened it. "Honey, it's time to read," she said.

No response.

He was sitting on his turquoise carpet assembling the Empire State Building out of Legos, putting it together on a low table he reserved for construction projects. His bedroom was still that of a little kid, decorated with cars, trucks, and rainbows—he had always loved rainbows, and she encouraged it so his room wouldn't look like a pantomime of 1950s boyhood. But he was getting older now. She wondered how long the rainbow curtains would last.

The bricks spread in front of him were a pale brassy color, with shiny bits of black plastic set aside for the windows. She knew that once it was built, it would become a monument he would refuse to disassemble, along with his Lego airplanes and Lego cars, his Lego Statue of Liberty, his Lego robot, and his other Lego robot, which coalesced to form a collection of crap that threatened to take over her house and would never biodegrade. She wished people would stop giving him these kits.

"Honey, I know you're having fun, but you've got to stop."

He picked up a block and snapped it into position. He had built the platform and the base of the building and was now working on its shaft. He could have a thousand pieces left. But it was getting late and he was supposed to read independently for twenty minutes every night, then catalog his progress in a notebook with a dappled black-and-white cover.

"It's really time to read."

No response.

"Henry."

Still nothing. God, she hated it when he ignored her.

"Henry!"

He pushed another brick into place.

"I'm going to count to three, and if you don't stop, I'm going to take it away. One."

Nothing.

"Two." He picked up a long skinny piece and examined it.

"Okay," she said. "Three." She reached around him to grab what he'd built and he threw his body in front of her.

"No!" he yelled. His shoulder, swinging in from the left, slammed into the tiny skyscraper, which fell to the floor and cracked into bits, pieces of it dropping silently onto the carpet.

"Honey, I'm sorry, I didn't mean to—"

"You're so mean to me!" Henry screamed at full volume. His body was rigid and his hands were balled into little fists.

"Henry, it was an accident. But you need to listen to me. You cannot just ignore me when I talk to you."

"I worked so hard on it and you broke it!"

"I'm sorry."

"Stop being mean to me!"

"Honey—"

"I don't have to listen to you!"

"Oh, yes, you do!" Nicole felt herself shout back, a sharpness in her throat from hitting such a volume. "You cannot just ignore me or I will throw all of this in the garbage!"

"NO!"

"If you do not stop screaming at me," she yelled, "this is going in the garbage right now!"

"Hey, hey, hey, hey, hey!" Austin's hand was suddenly on her hip. "I'm tapping you out. Go ahead downstairs. Henry," he said firmly. "You absolutely have to listen to your mother. And right now, it is time to read."

She left.

She went down to the kitchen and took a seat at the marble kitchen island. It was cool against her elbows as she let her face fall into her hands.

She should have handled that better, but she felt powerless when Henry ignored her. She hadn't expected fights like this until he was older, and it terrified her to think of how this would go when he was a teenager. She would yell and threaten, and her kids would hate her. Austin had always been more patient. Even when Henry was a baby, when he rolled into hour two of crying and she was ready to jump headfirst into a wall, Austin was unruffled. He would wait it out, just hold the kid for as long as it took. Austin's equanimity felt like an insult when she was the one arguing with him, but it helped when dealing with melting children.

She picked up her phone and started scrolling through Facebook, giving herself and Henry some time to cool off.

HENRY, HONEY." NICOLE poked her head into his bed-room. "Can I come say good night?"

Henry was lying in bed, a row of stuffed animals wedged between his body and the wall. The detritus of the Lego collision was still scattered across the floor, visible by the glow of his night-light. Nicole waited in the doorway, and wondered if she'd be going to bed without giving her kid a hug.

When he spread his arms open, Nicole felt washed with relief. She crawled on top of his comforter and tucked her body around him.

"I'm sorry I lost my patience," she said. "It's important that we listen to each other, but I shouldn't have yelled. I love you, honey."

"I love you, Mommy." He didn't always call her Mommy anymore, and the word landed in the center of her chest. A peace offering.

He clasped his arms together behind her back and hugged her as tightly as he could. "Now you're stuck here forever!" he announced.

"Good." She squeezed him back until he groaned and laughed, the air forced out of his lungs.

Feeling calmed and forgiven, she pulled the blankets up to Henry's chin and went downstairs. In the kitchen, she found Austin standing by the fridge in his undershirt and the charcoal slacks he'd worn to work, eating his single bite of chocolate ice cream while scrolling on his phone. Nicole pushed his arms out of the way and rested her forehead on his chest. When was the last time she'd done that?

"Thank you," she said quietly.

"Hey." He scooped another bite from the container. "We're a good team."

He handed her the spoon, and she was swept with an unreasonable sadness that he hadn't offered to slide the ice cream directly into her mouth.

"Don't be too hard on yourself," he said with businesslike efficiency. "We all lose it sometimes."

"I guess." Nicole lost it sometimes. Austin almost never did.

"I'm sure he's over it. He never stays mad at you. Do you want me to leave this out?" Austin gestured toward the pint.

"Sure."

"Okay." He nodded. "I'm going to go watch the golf." He swept out of the room, his attention back on his phone.

Nicole stood alone in their silent kitchen, the spoon still in her hand. Theirs was not a perfect partnership, but the idea of being a single parent filled her with an almost existential dread, like she was watching a plane fall out of the sky. She resented that the childcare and household chores fell primarily to her, even on weekends, but Austin was there as a backstop when she lost her temper or needed a break. He helped take the kids to their Sunday activities, and he helped keep Henry calm. He balanced her out. Nicole didn't know how to be a mother without her husband.

33

A UNT KATE?" CHLOE was standing in a patch of grass near a rumpled baseball diamond warming up for her Little League game. Kate played softball in high school, in deference to her stereotype, and had brought out her old glove to play catch and help Chloe warm up. Her glove had been black years ago but was now a dingy gray, the color of a concrete sidewalk after it rains. Chloe's glove was purple and came already broken in, which felt to Kate very much like cheating.

"Yes, Chloe?" Kate lunged sideways trying to catch Chloe's wild throw, but she was about six feet short. "Hang on one second." She trotted away to get the ball, which didn't get far in the shaggy grass. Gabe and Ethan, who were standing just a few paces away, made no move to help her.

"Okay, I'm back." She tossed the ball gently toward Chloe. It dropped directly into her glove (Kate congratulated herself on her aim) before popping out again.

"Aunt Kate," Chloe continued as she picked it up, "do you remember the time you hit me with a baseball?" Gabe and Ethan snorted with muffled laughter.

"By accident! When I hit you with a baseball by accident! Yes. Sometimes that happens when old people who are out of practice try to pitch."

"Honey, it's time for you to get on the field and stretch," Gabe said. "Your coach is calling you."

"Okay!" she yelled as she ran away.

"I can't believe you're here," Kate said to her brother.

"Yeah, well, I'd like her to remember that I exist occasionally," he replied, glancing at his phone. "Andrew was not pleased."

"You probably had to miss a perfectly good gun-polishing contest for this," Kate said.

"Something like that."

"That new ad from your favorite opponent is interesting," Kate said.

"What are we talking about?" Gabe asked. "I try not to follow politics."

"James Caruso has a new ad out in which every member of his family, including his two young kids, are holding semiautomatic rifles in their living room," Kate explained. "I think one of them is like nine."

"Jesus," Gabe said. "That's fucking terrifying."

"Not a decision I would have made," Ethan said.

"Well, I guess you could be worse, then!" Gabe offered brightly.

Ethan let out a deep bark of laugher. "That's the spirit!"

"Oh yeah, he's way worse than you," Kate said.

"But he's definitely my main opponent. At this point, he's the only real threat. The hard right loves him and we still haven't figured out what to do about him. Great job, honey!" he shouted at Chloe.

"She didn't do anything," Kate said.

"She's running around the bases."

"With her whole team. They're warming up."

"Whatever. I'm here to distribute as many compliments as possible." Ethan took a sip of Diet Coke from his American flag thermos. The patriotic accessorizing Andrew insisted upon felt like a parody. He'd run around plastering "We the People" stickers and eagle decals on every available surface, slapping them on Ethan's phone case, his laptop, and his car. It made Gabe want to tattoo a rainbow on his forehead.

"Excuse me," a man said as he approached Ethan. He was about their age, wearing a few days' worth of graying red stubble and a Mets hat.

"Hi there," Ethan said.

"Are you Evan Keller?"

"Yes, I am Ethan Keller." He stuck out his hand and greeted the Mets fan with an enthusiastic shake and the most subtle correction. Gabe and Kate floated backward to give them space. "What's your name?"

"I'm Nick Zikas. I just wanted to say that I like what you're doing and I hope you win."

"Thanks, man. I really appreciate that." Ethan slouched so he wouldn't tower quite so much over his potential voter. "Hey, here's my card. If there's ever anything I can do for you, or if there's an issue you think should be getting more attention, please get in touch. Anytime."

"Okay, I'll do that," the Mets fan said. "It's nice to meet you. Keep fighting the good fight."

"I think," Gabe whispered to Kate, a smile dancing across his face, "my husband's kind of famous."

NICOLE SAW THE horn first. It was long and solid, shaped like a waning crescent moon. A wrinkled gray face followed onto her TV screen, with eyes that were docile and black.

The camera panned back to show a rhinoceros in a sad zoo enclosure, one stubby tree off in a corner. The animal was approaching a big puddle of mud.

"Do you want this guy representing you in Congress?" a deep voice from the television asked Nicole.

The rhino wedged its face into the mud and nuzzled around, emerging with its horn caked in thick sludge.

"No? Then you don't want this guy, either!"

An unflattering photo of Ethan popped up on the screen. Frozen in the middle of exaggerated laughter, his arms outstretched, he looked like a man trying to sell a bag of sunshine. The rhino was still nosing around in the dirt behind him.

"Ethan Keller is a RINO!" the voice intoned. Ethan's face disappeared from the screen, replaced by an explanation of the acronym, which appeared one row at a time:

Republican
In
Name
Only
RINO!

The commercial cut to a man in his mid-fifties with gray hair in a high-and-tight military cut. The muddy rhino was gone, replaced by a bright red background that made it hard to look at the screen.

"If you want a real conservative who will represent real conservative values, there's only one choice. I'm James Caruso. I'm a true conservative, I've always been a conservative, and I approve this message."

34

A **T THE LAST** fundraiser Gabe attended, he felt like an uninvited stranger who had wandered in off the street wearing his wedding suit, stumbling into some rich person's apartment by mistake.

This time, the gravity in the room centered dramatically around Ethan. Faces drifted toward him. Small crowds gathered around. There were plenty of people who wanted to talk to Gabe, too.

The event was held in an excessively tall residential building on West Fifty-Seventh Street, a skinny column of glass and steel that looked like a shiny middle finger extending to the top of the skyline. Gabe and Ethan stepped off an elevator directly into an apartment that was so sparsely furnished it felt like a museum, which, in essence, it was. The hosts lived in Miami, and they used this exorbitant apartment as a sometime hotel and a reliable place to park several million dollars. It wasn't a home so much as a monument to their money.

Michael and Savannah McCoy were major Republican donors, national players with influence and access, Andrew said. Their support and their network could help elevate Ethan's campaign into a different sphere.

Immediately upon entering, Ethan and Gabe were swept in different directions. Andrew put his hand on Ethan's shoulder and steered him toward the living room while Robin guided Gabe into the dining room, which held a long wooden table that could seat twenty people. Central Park lay resplendent down below, wrapped in a warm pink sunset. The height made Gabe a little queasy.

"Mr. Ethan Keller, right?" a woman said, offering a firm shake with a manicured hand, her nails a buffed ruby. She was tall, with stiff blond hair cut abruptly at her chin. "Well, the other Mr. Ethan Keller," she said, laughing without a trace of awkwardness.

"Sure," he said. "Gabe Alter."

"Gabe," she repeated. "It's so great to meet you. I'm Savannah Mc-Coy. My husband, Michael, and I—you haven't met him yet, but you will—we are very excited about Ethan." She spoke quickly. "We need a shot of life in the conservative movement and we think he's just the ticket. Here, take this." She snatched a glass of champagne from a passing tray, causing the waiter's collection of drinks to wobble. She handed the glittering beverage to Gabe. "Would you like a tour?"

"I'd love that," Gabe said. Ethan often teased that Gabe became a real New Yorker when he started snooping on other people's real estate. Colleagues, friends, the families of Chloe's classmates, he looked up all their apartments on real estate websites before heading over for a dinner party or a playdate. He liked to see a floor plan, but the real prize was to find out what they paid. This, Ethan said, represented a New Yorker's vampiric thirst for property intel. It was on the same continuum as wondering when your next-door neighbor, whose apartment would yield a pleasing combination with your own, might finally die. Gabe had been gratified to learn this activity was just as enjoyable in the suburbs.

Gabe had, of course, looked up Michael and Savannah McCoy's apartment. They had paid $16.5 million for their vacant piggy bank.

Savannah sailed with Gabe from room to room. The views were spectacular in all directions, and they paused to take in each vantage point: uptown to Central Park, visible rivers to the east and west, and a polished Manhattan cityscape to the south. The decor was modern, mainly low-slung furniture without arms. Almost every piece of upholstery was white or pale gray. The apartment contained none of the clutter that indicated actual lives being lived—no stacks of books or aspirational magazines, no spare reading glasses or tangled cell phone chargers. The entertaining spaces were large and open, made to feel more so because of the floor-to-ceiling windows. But somehow, there were only three bedrooms. They had spent $5.5 million for each one of them.

All along the tour, Savannah showered Gabe with questions about himself. What part of Long Island was he from? How did he find his way to teaching? What were the families like at his elite public school? What was Chloe like? Savannah said her kids were seventeen and twenty-two, and that Gabe should hug his baby long and often while she was still happy to squeeze him back. Her older son had come to New York to go to undergrad at NYU, Savannah said, which was why they'd bought an apartment here.

They arrived in the smallest bedroom, which contained a queen-size bed, a clear Lucite desk, and no hint that a young person had ever set foot in there. Gabe gravitated to the west-facing window, where he could see clear to New Jersey. He gazed in the general direction of Longbourne and wondered if Chloe was listening at all to her babysitter that evening. Then he heard the door behind Savannah click shut.

"I have another question for you," she said. "A bit more delicate."

"Okay." He turned to face her. "Shoot."

"Do you want your husband to win this race?"

"Excuse me?" He couldn't possibly have heard her right.

"Do you want your husband to win?" she repeated more slowly, stressing each syllable like she was beating a quiet drum.

"Of course," he said, clearly flummoxed. He felt trapped, and his eyes darted instinctively around the room.

"You know, before my husband and I invest in someone, we do our homework," she told him. "You're a registered Democrat. You vote in every election, every primary. You've donated to Planned Parenthood, the ACLU, and Lambda Legal. And you must do a better job of cleaning out your social media history, my friend. You do not have a sterling opinion of our Republican Party."

Gabe was stunned. She stood between him and the door, her arms crossed in front of her. She was probably five foot nine, only about an inch shorter than Gabe. He was broader, but he wondered if she could snap him in half through sheer force of will. If she managed, she was definitely rich enough to get away with it.

"My husband did not want to invest in Ethan because of you," she continued. "Politics is a nasty business, and it's hard on a family. The scrutiny, the distance, the time a candidate has to spend away. It's really best if everyone believes in the mission.

"But I won this particular argument," she said. "I want you to understand why I felt it was worth the risk. And your husband is a risk, which I'm sure you know as well as anyone, with his sexual preference and his past—which I do know more about than the average bear, if you catch my meaning."

"Sure, he's a risk, but he's a very talented man and—"

"I'm not finished," she said.

He paused for a moment, then nodded.

"Your husband is worth the risk because I need the conservative movement to embrace people like him. I have invested a lot of time and a lot of money into this GOP over the years. The party is not perfect, but there are people in it who want to run this country like the exceptional nation that it is. And the Democrats will run this place into the ground if we give them the chance!

"So I need there to be a place in the Republican Party for your husband, because I need there to be a place in it for my son," she said. "Because my seventeen-year-old is gay. He hasn't told me yet, but I'm not an idiot. I accept it, and I will do everything in my power to make this difficult road easier for him." Her voice lowered. "And I will burn this party down to make sure there is room for him in it. Do you understand me?"

Gabe nodded. His hostess took a breath, and thrust a smile onto her face.

"I agree with you that your husband has talent," she said, back in a more even tone. "And that's why, despite all the risks, I think he is the horse to bet on to help bring the Republican Party and the conservative movement into the future. I think he's right that he can cast a wider net, bring in more independents. And I don't want the image of this party to be dominated by shirtless lunatics storming the Capitol Building.

"So." She narrowed her eyes. "Do you want your husband to win?"

He paused, making sure it was his turn to speak.

"I do," he said. "I wasn't entirely sure in the beginning, but I do now. The Republican Party is not my favorite, that's true." He was speaking slowly, trying to be careful. "But my husband is a good man, and I'd rather have him steering that ship than somebody else."

She watched him for a moment, appraising his response. Neither of them spoke.

"Good," she said. She turned away from him and opened the door.

"Shall we go back to the party?" Her face was arranged into a careful smile. "I'm sure the guests are starting to arrive, and we need to show you off."

"Okay," he said, hoping he could leave the room without turning his back to her.

"And one more thing," she said, her hand resting on the doorknob. "If he doesn't win, you've got to move to a more conservative area. He's got enough working against him. He doesn't need to be running out of district."

She led them straight to the living room bar and ordered herself a white wine. Gabe traded his empty champagne flute for a light beer, nothing too boozy, so he could stay on his toes.

The apartment was starting to fill up. Ethan was on the opposite end of the room, speaking loudly in a circle of people, gesticulating with sharp, jerky movements, like he was trying to keep the adrenaline from shooting out his fingertips. All eyes were on him.

Despite the endorsement he'd just given his husband, Gabe felt like an interloper, like he was watching the scene from far away. Savannah McCoy's interrogation had left him off balance. Standing in the cold, lavish apartment, Gabe wondered if Ethan belonged with these people now, instead of with him.

35

NICOLE'S EYELIDS FELT like they were made of heavy blankets. She was lying in Kate's bed, wrapped only in a sheet and the warm afternoon light. They'd met for lunch at a Greek restaurant before going back to Kate's apartment. When they finished their food, Nicole suggested they visit the single-occupancy bathroom together, a tiny room with tiled walls and a sink the size of a shoebox. She flipped the lock and pushed Kate up against the door, then wedged her foot against it to keep it from rattling. It felt exciting and risky on the way in, but stupid and reckless on the way out, as they exited the closet-size bathroom together. A man with a neatly trimmed salt-and-pepper beard was waiting outside for his turn in the unisex stall, and he gave Nicole a knowing, lecherous look.

"Don't let me fall asleep," Nicole groaned, her face resting on Kate's chest. "Sarah woke me up at five this morning and I am toast."

"I'll get you some coffee." Kate gently lifted Nicole off her body.

"Ugh, I guess so. Thanks." The coffee Kate kept in her apartment was strong and acidic, like sipping facial astringent out of a warm mug. Kate took her coffee black, so she never had milk in the house. Nicole had to add two heaping teaspoons of sugar to make the dark roast palatable, if way too sweet. But today, she needed the caffeine.

Kate returned to the room and put a WNYC mug in Nicole's hands. Nicole looked down and saw that the coffee was a light caramel brown.

"I bought you milk," Kate said. "Two percent, right?"

It was the perfect gesture, considerate and attentive, a signal that whatever they were doing together would continue—but in a low-pressure, available-in-the-dairy-aisle kind of way.

Nicole took a sip. With milk, Kate's coffee tasted like dark chocolate and black cherries. It was delicious.

THE KIDS WERE calm. The kids were quiet. The kids were watching television.

Henry and Sarah had been fighting like rabid animals recently, but they were so cute when they watched TV. They were nestled on opposite ends of the sofa, Sarah's curls frizzy and askew from an afternoon spent running around outdoors, Henry's long legs spilling over the couch in gray sweatpants. His feet were almost as big as Nicole's now, and the round cheeks she used to love had all but melted away. But why was he wearing only one sock?

Nicole leaned against the living room doorway and retreated into her mind. She thought about when she could next see Kate. She could say she was taking a dance class in the city on Wednesday. Maybe Kate could take the afternoon off.

"It's my turn with the remote!" Sarah complained.

"No, it's not!"

Nope, not dealing with this, Nicole thought. They could work it out themselves. She spun around and removed herself from the situation, heading into the kitchen to start dinner. She felt like the United Nations when her children fought, nominally in charge of conflict resolution but without any real tools to create lasting peace.

The kitchen was bright in the afternoon sun and Austin was getting ice from the dispenser in the refrigerator door, tapping his foot to the beat of a song that played in his head. He performed this mundane task in the home they shared, while she thought about when she could next fuck somebody else.

She crossed the threshold into the kitchen. She was going to come up behind him and put her arms around his stomach. She wanted to comfort him, comfort him over something that was completely her fault, something of which, she felt certain, he was entirely ignorant. The stress of lying to him all the time was starting to grate on her. She'd been grinding her teeth in her sleep and she woke up most mornings with a throbbing pain in her jaw that radiated to the right side of her skull. She bought a plastic mouth guard online, which Austin smirked at and called sexy. The mouth guard had helped her jaw pain, kind of, but not the headaches.

She took two steps toward her husband—then stopped when her bare foot landed in something sticky. Gross. Was that a piece of banana? At least someone was eating fruit.

She hopped over to the paper towel roll, which lived on a wooden pin next to the sink. She wiped at her foot until she was satisfied she wouldn't track sugar around the house, then returned to the gluey section of floor to clean it. By the time she finished and dropped the paper towel into the trash, Austin had left the room.

HOW WAS THE play?" Austin asked as he poured himself a cup of coffee.

She had not been to a play the previous night. She had been with Kate, who had summoned her with just a few hours' notice.

> Kate: I keep picturing you pinned to my headboard. I'm gonna need to see the real thing before I can focus on anything else. Come over.

Nicole told her husband she'd won a raffle on Facebook and that the prize was a last-minute ticket to a Broadway show, where they must have been trying to fill empty seats. Sure, he told her. He'd take care of the kids. So she put on a short black dress—too short to sit in comfortably for the length of a play—and headed into Manhattan.

"It was good," Nicole said. "Long. But the performances were great. The lead was incredible." She didn't know if any of this was true, but it was Broadway. The actors had to be talented.

"That's great." He took a sip of his coffee. "What was it about?"

She stared at him and thought: Fuck.

She had no idea. She'd been so frantic to see Kate, and then so drunk on the memory of their evening together, that she'd forgotten to look up the show.

"Uhh," she stammered. Austin waited. "How do I describe it." She was stalling, but there were no slices of relevant information knocking around in her brain that she might eventually uncover. She knew nothing about the production.

"That memorable, huh?" Austin looked at her quizzically.

"No, it's just hard to describe."

"Aside from 'long'?"

"Yeah." She poured more coffee into her mug and willed the conversation to be over.

"You feeling okay?" It was a statement of suspicion more than concern.

"I'm just so tired," she said. "I got home late and then I couldn't fall asleep. I should really take a nap today."

Was this the play about the two sisters who almost starve to death on the American frontier? Or was it the musical about a rock band made up of vampires? It could have been anything. But she had to take a shot.

"It was a family drama," she guessed. "Kind of depressing. Lots of crying, lots of shouting. Not your thing." She hoped that would make him less likely to research it further.

He looked into her eyes as if trying to decode them. "Who'd you go with?" he asked.

"No one," she said. "It was a last-minute raffle. Single tickets. I'm going to go start some laundry. Henry's out of clean socks." Without waiting for him to respond, she opened the door to the basement and started down the stairs. "Let me know if there's anything you want washed," she called.

Downstairs, she leaned against the cool steel of the washing machine and tried to keep herself together. It was hard to know how much of an impression her bumbling had left on Austin. He might accept that she was scattered from being overtired. She really was a mess when she didn't get enough sleep.

She pressed her knuckles against the lid of the dryer, sending a bolt of pain up her arms. Who was she kidding. Austin was not an attentive husband, but he was a smart man. He had to know something was off.

A chill sliced through her as she seriously considered for the first time what a divorce might mean. Would he fight her for full custody of the kids? Would he do that to punish her? Would her unfaithfulness put her at an additional disadvantage? Did judges consider that sort of thing in a divorce? How would she even afford a lawyer? She had no money of her own. Austin transferred cash into her checking account every other week like an allowance, a feature of her life that felt like a bimonthly kick in the teeth. A fist of panic tightened around her throat.

She pictured herself seeing her kids only on weekends, spiraling into a "fun mom" who let them eat crap and watch R-rated movies they weren't ready for in a desperate attempt to curry favor. More likely, she would become a single mom five days a week, screeching at Henry and Sarah to do their homework or get ready for bed or eat their dinner, alienating her children with her wild swings of emotion.

She had to pull back, she decided, to allow whatever misgivings Austin might have a moment to cool. She had to be a constant presence at home, at least for a bit. Kate was going to have to wait.

36

I T TOOK HIM a while to notice, but it had been weeks since Gabe had any visitors during his library office hours. He appreciated the quiet time alone to get some work done—or to fret silently about his life—but even his regulars had dropped off. He tried to remember the last time Damian or Jaden came by.

He headed into the teachers' lounge to retrieve his lunch from the minifridge, a leftover chicken cutlet he'd covered in red sauce and a reusable silicone bag stuffed with baby carrots. Michael Lyman, his least favorite social studies teacher, was sitting at a round table in the center of the room eating a sandwich on whole-grain bread; trails of mayonnaise seeped out the sides. Across from him sat a ninth-grade global history teacher named Sophia, who ate the same microwavable vegan burrito every day.

"Hey, guys." Gabe sat down at the table and popped open his lunch container. The tin was metal so couldn't go in the microwave. He'd be eating his chicken cold.

"Hey," Sophia replied. Lyman nodded, then cast his focus back to his sandwich.

"Lyman, Damian Montrose is in your AP Government class, isn't he?"

"He is."

"Is anything going on with him?"

"Why?"

"I haven't seen him around in a while. He and Jaden Milles usually stop by my tutoring hours, but it's been a couple of weeks since I've seen them."

"Hm." Lyman took a bite of his sandwich. A glob of mayo slipped off the back and plunked onto the tinfoil he was using as a plate.

"I'm just wondering if something's up," Gabe continued.

"He's been to my class," Lyman said. The condescension in his voice made Gabe want to poke him with a fork.

"Okay, that's good. Still, it's unusual for them, disappearing like that."

Lyman chewed slowly, his jaw working side to side like a cow munching on fresh grass. He swallowed his food and took a sip of iced tea from a large plastic bottle.

"Well," he said finally, looking at Gabe with disdain. "Can you blame them?"

"Excuse me?"

"Maybe they want to keep their distance."

"Why would they want to do that?" Lyman was such a jerk. What was he talking about?

"Those kids look up to you." Lyman took another bite of his sandwich, then spoke with his mouth full. "They've got to be pretty disappointed."

"By what exactly?"

"I think you know," Lyman replied.

A heavy foreboding was taking shape in Gabe's mind, like a darkness clouding the edges of his vision. "No," he said. "I'd like you to tell me."

Lyman took another sip of his iced tea and swallowed. He was deliberately making Gabe wait.

"Both those boys are gay," Lyman said.

"I'm aware of that."

"And Damian's family is undocumented."

"Okay . . ."

Lyman looked resolute. "They had to be pretty disappointed to learn about your husband."

Gabe felt his face go cold.

"He wants to load Damian's parents onto a plane and send them back *where they came from*," Lyman said. "I don't think Damian appreciates that. Frankly, I think a lot of us are pretty disappointed."

Sophia put down her burrito and stared wide-eyed at the center of the table. Lyman dropped the crust of his sandwich onto the tinfoil and wrapped it into a lumpy, unrecyclable ball. "The kids have started talking about your husband's campaign," he said. "It's come up in AP Gov."

A chill crept down Gabe's neck. Damian was a kid Gabe respected, a kid he was rooting for, a kid who probably thought Gabe wanted him and his entire family deported.

Gabe had to fix this.

"What are they saying?" he asked.

"Like I told you, they're pretty disappointed."

GABE HOVERED NEAR the eleventh-grade lockers as a river of teenagers washed past. He hadn't been sure that news about Ethan would reach his students. It was a congressional primary in a different state, and these were teenagers only beginning to learn how to manage their own lives. But all of them lived so completely online, a few of them even read the news, and Ethan had a public profile now. It was probably inevitable; Gabe just hadn't wanted to see it.

He had never gone looking for a kid in the hallway before. If he wanted to check on a student, he'd usually send a note to their school email account, or he'd ask another teacher, maybe the guidance counselor. But this felt like an emergency.

Gabe spotted Damian, his thick brown hair sticking up at the back, like he hadn't brushed it when he got out of bed in the morning. He was drifting by himself through the crowd.

"Damian," Gabe called to him. "Can I talk to you for a second?"

"Why?"

His face was rigid and his tone, usually so eager, had a sharpness to it. The reception left Gabe flustered.

"Oh," Gabe said. "I just want to check in."

"I guess."

They moved to one side of the hallway so the scrum of students could sweep past them.

"Is everything okay, Damian?"

"Yeah."

"I just haven't seen you in a while. I wanted to make sure you're all right."

"Been busy."

"Okay. Anything going on?"

"Nope."

"Okay, that's fine. Is there anything you want to talk to me about?"

Damian tipped his chin upward as though he were readying for a fight.

"Nah."

Damian had always been so open, and Gabe couldn't think of how to draw him out. He couldn't just start talking about his politics and his marriage in a crowded hallway. He hadn't thought this through.

"I don't believe you, Damian. Something's going on."

"You calling me a liar?"

"No, of course not. But I can tell that something is bothering you."

"You're bothering me right now."

"Okay. So talk to me," Gabe said. A pair of juniors slowed and watched as they walked past.

"There's nothing to talk about."

"There is." Damian stared at him stone faced. "I think you've heard that my husband is running for Congress."

"Maybe."

"I want you to know that I don't agree with him on a lot of issues. On basically any issue, really."

"Sure."

"I'm serious. And I *really* don't agree with him on immigration."

"Whatever."

"No, not whatever. This is your home. You and your family deserve to stay here."

"Gee, thanks."

"I didn't mean it like that," Gabe pleaded. He felt himself getting desperate.

"Guess that was a question for you," Damian said.

"It wasn't! That's what I'm trying to tell you."

"I think I'm done here." Damian tried to step around Gabe back into the center of the hallway.

"Damian!" Gabe grabbed the kid by both arms. "You need to talk to me about this. Please!"

Damian looked down and Gabe's eyes followed, to where he was holding Damian's skinny biceps below the baggy sleeves of his T-shirt.

Gabe jerked away as if he'd grabbed a hot pan. He was never supposed to touch his students. He looked around and saw a dozen kids had stopped to gawk and were eyeing Gabe with suspicion.

"Let's keep it moving, everyone." Gabe clapped to hurry them along, hiding his panic behind a cloak of authority. "You, too, Damian. Sorry for holding you up. Everyone needs to get to class."

Damian shook his head in disapproval, then turned away silently, disappearing down the hall without looking back.

37

I BROUGHT LETTUCE." KATE had let herself into Gabe and Ethan's house and was headed toward the kitchen. Ethan was at a competitive local bingo night and wouldn't be home until late.

"Thanks." Gabe took the grocery bag from her hand. "I don't think I've eaten a salad in like a month."

"Are you giving my niece scurvy?"

"No. We eat clementines and baby carrots, but cleaning bits of lettuce out of the salad spinner makes me want to jump off the roof."

"Okay, that's excessive. How about I make the salad?"

"Love it." He handed the brown paper bag back to Kate. "I'm so burnt out on cooking. Can you believe we have to eat dinner every night?"

"Takeout is a beautiful thing."

"Tonight we're having chicken nuggets."

"Great. Who doesn't love chicken nuggets?"

"I can't wait for this campaign to be over," Gabe grumbled. "I'd like to have a husband again."

"You know," Kate said gently, "he's going to be around even less if he wins."

Gabe ripped open the nugget bag and sent chicken skittering across the counter.

"Right," he said. He seemed to have embraced a siege mentality of getting through the day rather than thinking about long-term strategy. He leaned down to pick up two golden circles of frozen chicken that had landed on the floor, then dropped them onto a baking sheet with the rest of the nuggets. He drenched them in olive oil and slid them around roughly like angry hockey pucks.

"How are you holding up?" Kate asked.

"I'm not great." He let the bottle of olive oil slam against the counter.

"If he wins, you guys will come up with systems," Kate assured him. "It will get better."

"No, no, it's not that. Well, it's not only that. I fucked up at school."

"You fucked up? How?"

"One of my favorite kids found out about Ethan and decided he hates me."

"That sucks."

"So I tried to talk to him." The pitch of Gabe's voice was rising. "It didn't go well."

"What happened?"

"I fucking grabbed him in a hallway full of kids!"

"You grabbed him?"

"Yeah." Gabe snatched a sponge from the sink and started wiping at the countertop like he was trying to drill through the granite. "This kid and his whole family are undocumented, and now he thinks I want to put them all on a plane and deport them. I wanted to explain myself, but he just wouldn't engage with me and I fucking lost it."

"It can't be that bad," Kate said. "It's not like you hit the kid. You didn't hit him, right?"

"Of course not! But we're never supposed to touch our students. If you grabbed your boss by the arm, how would that go?"

"It wouldn't be great."

"And your boss is not a child! I'm in such deep shit with my assistant principal. And I'm humiliated! I had a meltdown. On a fucking kid!"

"Aunt Kate." Chloe burst into the room.

"Yes, sweetie, hi." Kate snapped a smile on her face and hoped Chloe hadn't been listening.

"I'm going to make art," she declared. "I'm going to turn this into a caterpillar." She held up an egg carton. "This will be a paper airplane." She brandished a long piece of brown paper that must have been padding from some package. "And this is a hat." She plopped a green paper berry container on her head. She must have been looking for treasure in the recycling.

"Those look amazing. Can I have a hat like that?"

"You can have this one." Chloe removed the container from her head and handed it to Kate. She watched expectantly as Kate peeked inside for additional treasure, then placed the tiny basket on her head.

"I'm going to make my caterpillar." Chloe marched out of the room.

"You know what, I don't want to talk about this anymore." Gabe slid the tray of nuggets into the oven.

"But Gabe—"

"Truly. I am so sick of my life right now." He took off his glasses and rubbed the lenses furiously with a dish towel. "Can we please talk about something different? Tell me about you."

"I guess."

"Great." He put his glasses back on and took a deep breath. "How's work?"

"It's fine. The same, really."

"What about that Nicole thing? Is that still happening? I feel like I haven't heard about her in a while."

"It is still happening." Kate removed the romaine lettuce from the salad spinner in big handfuls and dropped them into a wooden bowl. She rarely talked to Gabe about Nicole. He was unable to move on from things that happened fifteen years ago. "You'd really love her," Kate said. "She's got such a dry sense of humor and is totally no bullshit. I still have a fruit carton on my head, don't I?" She reached up and removed her custom hat. "But the whole thing does give me flashbacks sometimes. I haven't heard from her in a few days, and given our history, I'm trying not to worry that she'll disappear without explanation, never to be heard from again."

"That sounds relaxing."

"Oh, it's fine. Ignore me. I'm just being paranoid. Usually, she's in touch all the time." It had been four days, Kate thought. Four days wasn't terrible.

"Have you texted her?"

"Yeah, I sent her a very cute video yesterday of a baby elephant interrupting a newscast. It's been, let me see." She pulled her phone from her pocket and glanced at it to check the time, which also allowed her to make sure she hadn't missed anything from Nicole. "It's been twenty-two hours. So that's less than a day. But in the span of twenty-two hours, you can find a few seconds to comment on an adorable baby elephant. Am I right?"

Gabe was quiet for a moment, watching her throw handfuls of walnuts and raisins onto a pile of romaine.

"I know this is annoying of me," he said, "so I'll say it once and then I'll move on. But the woman is *married*. I don't know anything about her life, but this isn't good for you. It's not healthy."

"I know. It's not great."

"This has been going on for months now."

"I've noticed."

"And it's fucked up! I want you to be dating a caring, single person who does not cheat on their partner."

Kate ripped the lettuce into smaller pieces than necessary so she'd have something to do with her hands. She did not need to be reminded that Nicole was married.

"It just makes me furious," he continued. "She is jerking you around just like she did the last time you dated. She's wasting your time."

It wasn't like the last time; in that he was mistaken. Nicole was available and open with her now. But she was married. Her wedding ring was a thin platinum band studded the whole way around with tiny diamonds. She never took it off. Sometimes, Kate felt it on her skin, a small roughness between them.

"Okay, lecture over," Gabe said. "I'll drop it."

"Thank you," she said sharply. The things they didn't want to discuss were like invisible boulders sitting between them in the kitchen. "Now let's talk about literally anything else."

IT HAD BEEN six days since Kate had any meaningful communication with Nicole, and she was sitting at her dining room table, hovering over a breakfast of black coffee and a peanut butter protein bar, trying not to think about it.

Since they'd gotten back in touch months ago, their communication had been frequent and regular, and Kate didn't want to read too much into this brief, if excruciating, period. Nicole had a life and she was entitled to be busy. Still, whenever Kate's phone buzzed, she lurched toward it, wondering if Nicole had texted. It made her feel more than a little ridiculous, and unfortunately, it happened a lot. Kate received easily two hundred emails and dozens of texts every day. If she wasn't looking at her phone when a message came in, there was enough time for a flicker of hope to build, and then explode, small bombs of disappointment detonating throughout her day.

She picked up her phone and texted Gabe.

Kate: Hi hi hi. Sending you a message so I don't send one to HER!

Gabe: Still nothing?

Kate: She responded to the baby elephant right after I left your house. She laughed but that was it.

Gabe: What the fuck??!

Okay, so this was making her feel worse. She didn't want Gabe to start trashing Nicole and decided it would be best not to text him about this in the future. If she used Gabe as her customary complaint line, he'd be even more opposed to her relationship than he already was.

Her relationship. She shouldn't call it that.

She stood up to get her computer from the kitchen counter. She would not sit around fretting about this like some teenager. There was work she could do, important work. That's how she would spend her time.

Brett Cooper had begun showing up at rallies for candidates around the country, casting himself as a kingmaker with national influence, part of a strategy to enhance the impression that he was the inevitable standard bearer for his party. While stumping for a congressional candidate in Indiana, Cooper projected on a large screen behind him the faces of anonymous brown-skinned men whom he claimed had been caught violating the law by his anti-voter-fraud task force. Kate and other reporters called his office for more information, but Cooper's spokesman wouldn't answer any questions about who the men were or what they were accused of doing wrong, furthering the impression that it was all just a bit of race-baiting, fearmongering theater.

It was a good story, revealing about Cooper's strategy and about the continued rightward drift of the election cycle. Kate knew it would be a better story if she did some digging, tried to find one of the men whose picture was being misused. Instead, she decided to bang it out because she needed something to focus on other than Nicole's frosty silence. She wrote her boss an email.

Hey Mark. I'll have Cooper for you tomorrow.

THE KITCHEN CABINETS were chirping while Gabe did the dishes.

Fang, Chloe's snake, never reappeared, probably concluding its time on earth in the beak of a hawk or flattened as extravagant suburban roadkill. Chloe had agitated for some kind of lizard to replace him, and because Gabe had no emotional reserves, he relented. He bought her a leopard gecko, which had creepy vacant eyes and a spotted pattern along its back that looked like it belonged on a pair of stiletto boots. Chloe named it Mr. Wizard. The gecko lived in her room, in a new tank with a more elaborate locking mechanism that Chloe was forbidden to touch. Gabe was responsible for opening the tank to feed Mr. Wizard his diet of crickets and salad.

And then the fucking crickets escaped! Gabe kept their sad plastic pen in the basement, but he'd brought it upstairs because Mr. Wizard needed some protein. While he was in the basement, Gabe had grabbed a carton of vanilla ice cream, a bag of frozen blueberries, and a box of chicken nuggets from the old freezer they kept plugged in by the washing machine for extra storage. He balanced his cargo carefully as he ascended the stairs, focusing on each step, one by one. But when he went to unload on the kitchen counter, the cricket container slipped. He knocked the top askew, just a fraction of an inch, before slamming it closed again, dropping all the frozen food on the floor in the process.

He wasn't fast enough. A handful of crickets lunged successfully for their freedom, and now, days later, they were still hanging out in his kitchen, chirping away. Their screeching echoed around the room. He had no idea where they were hiding or how to get rid of them, and he briefly considered burning down the house. But the internet said the bugs would die in a few days, he just had to wait them out.

He stared blankly at Chloe's pasta bowl as a *T. rex* wearing sunglasses drowned in soapy water. All around him, the crickets chirped.

THE BALLS OF Nicole's feet were throbbing. She'd run eleven miles the day before and thirteen miles the day before that. She hadn't worked her way up to it, and her knees were sore; her hips screamed. But she was out running again, deep into mile twelve, running loops in a park where she sometimes took the kids to play. The ground was damp that morning from an overnight rain and gentle green sprouts glistened on the trees.

When she wasn't running, when her body didn't hurt, she could feel the places on her skin where Kate's hands should be. Kate liked to brush her fingers up and down Nicole's arms, to trace the lines of her collarbone, to rest her palms on Nicole's back. Her body ached with missing her. So she ran. She hoped she could keep it up without breaking an ankle.

Nicole was trapped, back against the wall, with only terrible options before her. She was going to hurt someone. Her husband, who had been good to her. Kate, whom she adored. Her children. She was allowing her own dissatisfaction and poor decision-making to hurt her children. She ran faster.

Her lungs burned. She felt every footfall in her calves and her joints, and she deserved that discomfort, she thought.

As a chilly breeze licked Nicole's skin, bending the branches around her, her foot came down on a damp green leaf, and she slipped.

She slammed into the blacktop, which grated chunks of skin off her right arm and both her knees as she braced herself against the fall. She rolled onto her back to get her wounds off the ground, then sat up, moisture seeping into her spandex shorts. She examined her scrapes, wincing as she pulled specks of blacktop from the bloody gashes in her skin.

It was early on a Saturday morning and she was about two miles from home. She didn't have her cell phone because she hadn't trusted herself that day to be alone with the temptation. She would be walking back to the house.

She stood up to start her journey and took a few steps, adjusting to the sting, which felt like a hundred needles poking her when she bent and straightened her legs.

This new feeling, she thought, would do.

IT WAS DAY ten without word from Nicole, and Kate sat on her couch downloading the Meet Cute dating app.

She hadn't done much online dating. When she and Shirin met, looking for romance on the internet was a fairly new thing, new enough that people still mostly lied about it. So she went from not having tried it to being married. When she came back to New York, she downloaded a lesbian dating app called You Haul. (Its name was a play on Kate's favorite lesbian joke, which was about how quickly two women move in together: What do lesbians bring on a second date? A U-Haul!)

Over the course of a few months, Kate went on three dates. The first woman was reasonably cute, but so delicately soft-spoken that Kate found herself nearly dipping her hair into her wine as she tried to get close enough to hear. The second woman, who worked in PR, spent their fifty minutes together pitching Kate stories about her real estate clients. The third woman never showed up. Kate deleted the app.

But it had been more than a week without any real contact, and Kate was certain this was no accident of Nicole's busy life. In her less generous moments, Kate found herself screaming inside that *Nicole doesn't even have a job!* What could possibly be keeping her so occupied?

She knew this was unfair, that kids were the world's greatest time suck—but they were in school all day! Nicole could find a few minutes to say, "Hey, I'm really busy," or "Hey, I have the flu," or "Hey, my kids have chickenpox or strep throat or lice—but you're still sexy and I'll see you soon." Instead, there was an anguishing silence. Kate was a reporter at the *Herald Ledger*. *She* was busy.

The other possibility was that Austin had found out about them, in which case Kate might never hear from Nicole again. She didn't like to dwell on that scenario.

In Nicole's absence, Kate was finding it more difficult to get Austin off her mind. She googled him a few times, and considered doing a deep dive into whatever she could find about him on the internet. But the smiling headshot at the top of his search results always made her feel vaguely stalkerish, and she would quickly close her browser.

Kate had already sunk too much time into Nicole. She would disappear into their assignations for entire mornings or afternoons, and while she would work late into the evening to compensate, it really wasn't enough. An important part of her job was speed, and when she was in bed with Nicole at 11:30 a.m. on a Tuesday, she didn't see the news she should have jumped on; she didn't give her bosses the lightning responses they expected. An aggressive colleague, who had sharp elbows and a comb-over that fooled nobody, paused at Kate's desk to make note of her inadequacy. "I haven't seen your byline in the paper in a while," the competitive viper said. "You must be working on a big project." She was not working on a big project, and he knew it. Kate had to get her focus back. So she was filling out a Meet Cute profile while watching a TV detective explain how a serial killer hid bodies in beer kegs. She looked through the cheerful blue interface until she found the "women for women" tab. There was someone a little younger than her smiling in front of a shelf full of books and a potted plant, like she was trying to pick up women over Zoom. Kate scrolled to a woman who was standing on a boat holding a long, shiny fish. And there was an eager-looking couple, both with chin-length blond hair, looking to add a third.

She swiped no on the throuple—given her current circumstance, that was a strong no—and yes on the books and the boat. As she stood to get herself another glass of wine, she wondered if either of those people was actually single.

NICOLE SAT IN her bedroom in the dark, the raw skin of her knees tender against her sweatpants. When she'd curled into her favorite reading chair that evening, there had been a pale hint of sun still radiating through the window, but now, the sky was black. The only light in the room crept in from the hall. She liked it this way. She could see the dogwood tree in her yard clearly against the night sky as she thought about what a fucking mess she'd made of her life.

She hadn't been able to run for the past few days and her insides were restless, clawing around in her chest. She'd hoped that by cooling it with Kate, she might find her way to some answers. Instead, she was being additionally careless, no longer just with Austin but with Kate, as well. Nicole still had no idea what she was doing and—

A flash of white flooded her vision as the room grew suddenly bright. Too bright.

"There you go, babe," Austin said as she blinked and squinted. He'd popped his head into the room and flipped on the overhead lights without asking. He smiled, pleased with himself for being helpful.

"Turn that off!" she snapped at him. "I didn't want the light on."

"What is your problem?" He seemed shocked by her response, which, in fairness, had been excessive. "You can turn the light off yourself." He sighed at her as he walked out of the room.

The dogwood tree was hidden now by her reflection, and she didn't want to look at herself. She picked up her phone and typed a message to Kate.

Nicole: Hey. I'm so sorry I've been MIA. I've had to be home a lot more the last two weeks. There's been a lot going on. When can I see you?

Kate was professionally tethered to her phone, and usually, her responses were instantaneous. Nicole waited for what felt like a very long minute, then she texted again.

Nicole: I miss you.

She let her phone fall in her lap and stared at herself in the window. Her reflection wasn't quite sharp enough to see the newly formed lines in her forehead or the gray hairs she'd recently found in her curls. This trick of perception didn't make her look any younger, and she certainly didn't look less miserable. She wished she was still staring at the dogwood tree.

Nicole's phone buzzed against her thigh and she almost tossed it across the room, fumbling frantically to read the screen.

Kate: Can you come over tomorrow?

Relief flooded through her, like her overheated body had been cooled in the ocean.

Nicole: Yes. I drop the kids off at 8:20. I can be there by 8:55.

38

CURLED UP FACING Chloe in her narrow bed, Gabe rubbed her back slowly up and down until her eyelids grew heavy. In moments like these, he was struck that she could still have such tiny shoulder blades, that the cartilage of her ears could form such compact swirls. She seemed so big to him most of the time, fully a kid now, exploding with personality and chutzpah. But when she was still, she looked so small.

Her eyes had been closed for a few minutes and Gabe thought he was free to get up and go about his evening. But no. As soon as he removed her slender arm from around his neck, her eyes shot open.

"Don't leave, Abba."

She was close to sleep. So close! So he stayed. The muscles in his neck knit together into an elaborate cramp.

Finally, he was released from his adorable prison. He untangled himself, arranged the giraffe duvet neatly around his daughter, and headed downstairs to talk to Ethan, who had come home that night for dinner. Often when he came home for a meal, he would go back out again to hit one more event before collapsing into bed, but tonight he'd stayed in to make fundraising calls from the living room.

Gabe found his husband pacing the ash-gray carpet in his socks, a white button-down untucked and open to the V-neck shirt underneath.

"Hang on one sec," Ethan said into his headphones, then, directing his attention to Gabe, "I just need a few minutes to talk to Andrew."

"Take your time." Gabe dropped onto the couch and opened a crossword puzzle app on his phone. Five Across: An emperor also known as Octavian.

"No, but I want my support for the Blocking Wokeness Act out there as loudly as possible."

Oh, Jesus.

"Facebook and Instagram are fine, but how many people really pay attention to social media? Is it weird to cut an ad on somebody else's policy? Could we do that? Cooper's really got the right idea here, and I think it would get good traction."

Cooper has the right idea? Ethan had to be talking about Brett Cooper.

"One piece to highlight is what they're doing with large institutional investors. They won't be able to do business with any of the state's pension funds if they're engaging in shareholder activism with woke social causes."

Gabe stood up.

"They did it in Texas and it was very powerful. But is there a way to talk about institutional investors without putting everybody to sleep?"

Gabe crossed the room with long strides.

"Definitely into the stump speech."

Gabe rounded the corner and headed up to his bedroom, taking the stairs two at a time.

B Y THE TIME Ethan came up to join him, Gabe had been rehearsing an argument for twenty minutes and had worked himself into a froth of preemptive anger. He fired the first shot as soon as Ethan crossed the threshold of their bedroom.

"You know if Brett Cooper becomes president, he'll come after us, right?"

"Wait, what?" Ethan closed the door behind him. "Who's coming after us?"

"Brett Cooper. The Supreme Court. Congress. Republicans! If Brett Cooper becomes president, our family is going to be a target."

"Hon, I am really tired. Do we need to talk about this right now?"

"You know that Cooper would appoint Supreme Court justices who would get rid of gay marriage, right? I'm sure they'd love to bring back anti-sodomy laws, too."

"Gabe, I really don't think that's—"

"Maybe you can help them make that happen!"

"Okay, I guess we're doing this." Ethan took a breath and sat down on the bed to remove his socks. "What are we talking about here? What do you mean 'they'll come after us'?"

"It could mean anything. I have no idea how far these people will go, but they don't *approve of our lifestyle*," he hissed.

"Look, no one is going to come knocking on our door. I promise you." He took off his button-down shirt and dropped it on the floor with his socks. "There are very well-known conservative commentators who are gay. There are well-known conservative talk show hosts who are godparents to the kids of gay couples. There are some extremists out there, sure, but I haven't seen any significant group of conservatives say that gay people are bad and that they want to get rid of them. Even the ones who talk openly about repealing laws, they always make a distinction between gay marriage and gay people."

"How reassuring—they just want to invalidate our marriage! So I'll pay hundreds of thousands of dollars in taxes on your estate when you die. Or if I'm in the hospital on a fucking ventilator, you might not be allowed in the room. And I don't even want to think about what it could mean for us as parents." Gabe was careful to keep his voice at a whisper. He'd hate for Chloe to hear any of this. "When those assholes talk about 'repealing laws,' they are threatening us!"

"If repealing gay marriage became a party platform, that would be a problem for me. It would. But it is *not going to happen*." He hit each word separately for emphasis. "What is happening is individuals are voicing their opinion. And we don't get to pick the perfect party in this country. There are Republicans, there are Democrats, and other than that you are wasting your time. And I think conservative values, including conservative family values, are important. Marriage and two-parent households are good for society, and the more people who want to get married, the better.

"Gabe, I need you to trust that I understand the conservative movement better than you do," Ethan said. "I am steeped in this world every day, and I'm telling you we have nothing to worry about."

"But I don't think you understand the conservative movement at all!" Gabe cried out quietly. "You can't see that these people hate you."

"Gabe, it is almost eleven o'clock. We both have to get up early tomorrow and I am bone tired. I love you, but you are not going to convince me that I'm wrong tonight and I'm not going to convince you. So can we please, please go to sleep?"

He was right about that, at least. They were not going to convince each other. Not tonight. Probably not ever. Gabe felt bereft and exhausted, like a piece of him was breaking off and floating away. There was a distance between himself and Ethan he didn't recognize, and it sapped his energy to fight.

"Fine," Gabe said. He got in bed and turned toward the wall. He didn't remember the last time they'd gone to bed angry. "Good night."

The room was silent for a moment, until Gabe heard the click of the bedside lamp. He watched the curtains in front of him go black, then tint with grays and blues.

"Good night," Ethan said. He took his phone into the bathroom and closed the door.

39

KATE'S FLIGHT HOME was delayed, so she set herself up on a reasonably clean patch of gray carpet in the Atlanta airport, next to an outlet where she could charge her laptop and her phone. She pulled a strip of beef jerky from her *Ledger*-branded overnight bag, which, as an experienced and extremely efficient packer, she could stuff with three days' worth of gear.

As she scanned an app on her phone for a cooking show to watch, it buzzed with a message from Nicole.

Nicole: How was your trip?

Kate: Got what I need. At the airport now coming home.

Nicole: Good. I want to take you out this weekend! Does Catty Shack still exist?

Catty Shack was a lesbian bar on Fourth Avenue in Brooklyn where they had gone together in their twenties. The bar occupied a small two-story building, with room to dance on both floors and a small deck upstairs. This was back when Fourth Avenue was populated mainly by gas stations and parking lots, before they sprouted into condo buildings and restaurants with seasonal cocktails. After a few years, Catty Shack met the fate of most lesbian bars and shut down. Now, in New York City, a town of eight million people and the promised land for baby gays all over America, there were only three lesbian bars remaining, two in Manhattan and one in Brooklyn. Meanwhile, it would have been almost impossible to count the number of gay bars that catered to men. Maybe the imbalance had something to do with all the U-Hauls.

Kate: Long gone. If you want to go to a lesbian bar, how about Sandy's in the West Village?

Nicole: YES! When can we go??

Kate was surprised that Nicole wanted to go out like this. When she and Shirin lived in Mexico City, Kate had developed a—what was it exactly? A charged friendship. An inappropriate flirtation. Physically, nothing ever happened, but Kate knew she had crossed into a gray zone of betrayal.

The woman was named Romina, the chef at a restaurant Kate and Shirin loved that was near their apartment. It was tucked into an un-assuming brick town house, with just a diminutive bronze plaque out front engraved with the word "Sud." It was all clean lines and blond wood inside, with delicate flavor bombs served on matte-black plates. For a while, she and Shirin went there a few times a month for dinner. When things at home got tense, the air spiked with resentment, Kate started visiting the bar by herself, where she'd order a meal or sip a few glasses of wine. When the restaurant slowed down for the evening, Romina would often join her.

Romina would sometimes squeeze Kate's shoulder, or she'd slap Kate's knee when laughing especially hard. They would lean toward each other, allowing their bodies to pitch closer together as the night wore on. But Kate's disloyalty was really an emotional indiscretion, a breaking of confidence. She would rummage around in her marriage and dump out intimate details for Romina's examination, looking for validation that their unhappiness was not all Kate's fault, or hoping for the closeness that comes from sharing secrets. Kate told her that Shirin was exacting and unforgiving, that she never gave Kate the benefit of the doubt in any error, whether it was a broken dish ("Be more care-ful!") or an errand she forgot to run ("You think I should just do it because my job is less important?"). Kate mocked Shirin's shyness. She complained about their sex life.

She and Shirin would still eat at Sud together on occasion. Romina would come over to say hello, and Shirin would have no idea the details to which the woman was privy.

The end came suddenly, and Romina never explained why. One night, Kate arrived at the bar, and Romina just nodded at her coolly from the open kitchen. Kate hung around for more than two hours, but Romina never so much as came over to say hello.

Kate tried the bar again a few weeks later. Romina was there, but she greeted Kate with the same formality and indifference. After that, Kate stopped going to Sud alone and she tried to steer Shirin elsewhere when they went out as a pair. A few months later, Kate moved back to New York.

But when that crackle of possibility existed, Kate often thought about how she and Romina would execute the logistics of an affair. Romina could write her address on a bar napkin and they'd meet at her apartment. If Romina had a partner at home she'd never mentioned, they could meet at a hotel, arriving separately. They would have to stop sitting together at the restaurant. In the affair Kate imagined, anything in public beyond a trivial greeting could give them away.

Yet here was Nicole, suggesting that they go out dancing surrounded by lesbians.

Kate could see why, though. Gay bars offer something to queers that straight people don't need to go out looking for: a room where they are not an anomaly. If a straight couple goes dancing, their presence isn't a novelty. If they want to walk down the street holding hands, they aren't likely to be greeted with stares. For queer people, a gay bar is one of the only public spaces where their choice of partner is pretty much guaranteed to be unremarkable. It always made Kate smile to see older couples with matching wedding rings—the same filigree pattern or the same shade of rose gold—perched on stools at queer bars, holding hands, stroking each other's face, savoring a room where no one gives a shit.

Maybe Nicole just wanted to see that part of herself reflected all around her until it became blissfully ordinary. From what Kate had gathered, Nicole spent the last fourteen years living a very straight existence, married to a man, surrounded by straight people, assumed to be straight herself. Maybe she wanted a night where everyone would look at her and assume, for a change, that she wasn't.

"Customers traveling on Flight 2224 with service to New York LaGuardia, your gate has been changed. I repeat, we have a gate change." The travelers around Kate gave a collective grumble. "Your new gate will be B seventeen, Bravo seventeen. Please make your way to your new gate."

Kate packed up her chargers and her untouched beef jerky and made her way toward B17. Her flight was going to be at least two hours late, and the airport smelled stale from all the sad sandwich shops and recirculated air. None of this bothered Kate, because Nicole wanted to take a step forward.

40

NICOLE WAS NOT the oldest woman at the gay bar, but there were plenty of people on the dance floor who could, mathematically, have been her children.

There were some older butches with their salt-and-pepper hair cut short, but more of the patrons wore their hair long than the last time Nicole was in a place like this. Was there less pressure now to be visibly gay? Did young people not feel the need to broadcast their identity so publicly? She had no idea. What she did know was that all around her were dykes. Dykes!

Did they still call themselves that? Well, whatever they called themselves, there were women making out! And she could be one of them!

Nicole bought a bourbon for herself and a vodka soda with two limes for Kate, which were delivered to them in plastic cups. Drinks in hand, they wove through the crowded space, which had purple walls and a long black bar. They found a window seat where they could perch, overlooking the pedestrians and traffic on Christopher Street, but it was much more interesting to watch the people inside.

There was a jittery butch with short blond hair sitting at the bar, taking small sips in quick succession from a bottle of Miller Lite.

There was a very young woman with an undercut standing alone against the wall, shifting her hips from one side to the other, loosely casting her gaze around the room. She looked nervous, and Nicole wanted to run up and invite her to join them so she'd have someone to talk to. But the girl was maybe twenty-three, and an evening tucked under the wings of two forty-year-olds out on a date was probably not her goal.

A couple about Nicole's age wearing office attire were laughing together with their whole bodies. They looked like they were on a date that was going very well. They also appeared to be drunk.

There was a group of three, well, kids, really. They looked like they'd turned twenty-one last week, or like they'd presented the bouncer with fake IDs and a smile. Then again, maybe that's just how twenty-one-year-olds looked, which made Nicole feel like somebody's grandma. They wore crop tops and loose-fitting pants; two had on bright white sneakers and the third wore lace-up combat boots. They were all clustered together on the small dance floor, but two of them kept grazing their fingertips across each other's body and making wildly exaggerated eyes at each other. The third one looked around desperately for better options. They were singing along, each with a different level of commitment, to a pop song with heavy bass. Nicole had never heard it before, but it made her shoulders bounce reflexively with the beat.

She took a sip of her drink. Nicole hadn't had booze out of a disposable cup in years, and she wondered if the alcohol was leaching traces of plastic into her beverage. She turned her attention back to Kate.

"Come here often?" Nicole asked, a grin stretched across her face.

Kate laughed. "I do not," she said. "I go to lesbian bars maybe a couple times a year. I used to go more because Shirin liked to go dancing. But I prefer to devote myself exclusively to working too much." She raised her vodka soda to toast her poor life choices. "But it is nice to be in a place where you're surrounded by the family."

"You know, I thought for a long time about getting a tattoo that would tell the world: 'I'm bi!' Or 'I'm queer!' Or *something*!" Nicole said. "But I could never settle on what that should be. And it felt kind of desperate."

"What does a gay tattoo look like exactly?" Kate asked.

"I was thinking about an upside-down triangle."

"I've seen a few of those. But didn't the Nazis make gay people wear pink triangles in concentration camps?"

"They did. Which I learned in my research and was the reason I decided not to get one," Nicole said. "Then I thought about getting a gay pride flag, but it used to be just the colors of the rainbow and now it's also got the black and brown and pink and blue stripes— which is great! But what if I get that version, and then they add more stripes later and I've got some old, exclusionary pride flag tattooed on my arm?"

"Also, pride flags are everywhere now." Kate sipped her drink. "It could be on the arm of a gay, or in the window of a bank."

Nicole laughed and grabbed Kate's arm. "Exactly! Then I thought about getting a labrys."

"A what?"

"A labrys," she repeated more loudly over the music. "It's like a two-headed ax. It was a symbol of lesbian feminism in the seventies. But no one would have gotten the reference."

"Oh, absolutely no one. I still have no idea what you're talking about!"

Nicole slapped Kate's thigh. "Who asked you!"

"Also, you're not a lesbian."

"True," Nicole replied.

"So perhaps you should not get that tattoo," Kate offered. "But this should show people you aren't straight." She smiled and leaned in for a kiss. Their lips were open and their mouths slid together.

"That helps," Nicole said, smiling, as they pulled away. "You ready to dance with me?"

"Kate, right?" There was a woman standing in front of them, talking to them, a woman with short brown hair and yellow statement glasses, a woman Nicole had never seen before. Thank God she had never seen this woman before! But this woman knew Kate. Shit, Nicole thought. She knows Kate. Shit shit shit.

"Oh, hey." Kate shifted her body toward the interloper, but did not move to stand. "Shelly, this is Nicole. Nicole, Shelly."

"Nice to meet you," Nicole said, nodding. She squeezed her drink too hard and put a dent in the plastic cup, sending a tiny explosion of bourbon into the air. She didn't expect to be recognized at a gay bar. She'd thought it through, cataloged her acquaintances, and determined that if anyone surprised her here, they probably had just as much to hide as she did. But she hadn't considered that Kate might know someone. And of course she did. This didn't present such an obvious, razor-edged danger, but it wasn't good.

Shelly gave Nicole a single nod, then turned a practiced smile toward Kate. "I just wanted to say hi," she said. "Reconnect. Not every date is going to end in marriage, and that's okay, am I right? But I do have some clients whose projects I think you'd really be interested in. I'm an agent," she added, smiling at Nicole.

"Oh," Nicole said, wishing this networking could take place at any other time.

"I manage the speaking engagements of high-profile clients," she continued, though Nicole hadn't asked. "Major business executives, motivational speakers, and"—she made a gun with her finger and pointed it at Kate—"politicians."

"What do you do?" Shelly turned back to Nicole.

Fuck this woman.

Nicole stared back with steady eyes. "I'm a housewife," she said.

"Oh," Shelly replied. Her shock registered in a flicker of rapid blinks. Was she surprised that Nicole admitted she was a stay-at-home mom, or that Kate was on a date with somebody else's wife?

"How great!" Shelly said with too much enthusiasm. "So." She turned back to Kate. "I'll leave you ladies to it, but Kate, I'd love to set up a coffee or a video call sometime to put a few people on your radar."

"Sure," Kate said. "Send me an email and we'll find a time. It was nice to see you."

"Hey, same to you. And it was nice to meet you," Shelly said to Nicole.

Nicole pulled her lips into a tight smile as Shelly turned and melted back into the crowd.

"Housewife was a bold move," Kate said.

"Well, it's true." Nicole thought for a moment about whether they should leave, if that intrusion should be taken as a warning about the risks of coming here. But she needed to be this part of herself, out in public, at least for tonight.

Nicole knocked back the rest of her bourbon. She stood up and put her legs on either side of Kate's right thigh. "I want to dance with you."

IT WAS ALMOST 2:00 a.m. when Nicole eased the side door of her house closed behind her. She would feel like useless garbage in the morning, but it was worth it. She punched the date of her wedding into a keypad by the door to engage the house's overnight alarm.

She headed through the mudroom and into her kitchen, where she planned to drink at least two glasses of water before going to bed. Her pinky toes ached from her pointed boots and her lips felt puffy and sore. She turned on the light.

On the marble counter near the sink, she was greeted by a plate of double-chocolate sandwich cookies, perfectly textured on the outside with a layer of dark cream in the middle. Her favorite. A yellow sticky note, written in Austin's tidy hand, was attached to the plate: "We made you a little something. Hope you had fun!"

She couldn't remember the last time Austin had made a dessert un-prompted. He would break out his standing mixer just twice a year, to make the kids elaborate birthday cakes covered in superheroes or horses made of fondant. It was never a surprise. He would discuss these projects for weeks in advance, calling attention to all the work he planned to do. The cakes would elicit coos of jealousy from their guests (*"Your husband made that?"*) but this skill, as he utilized it, wasn't practical. It was a party trick.

Nicole pushed almost an entire cookie into her mouth and chewed miserably.

Austin knew that something wasn't right.

21

KATE WOKE UP alone. Of course she did. Her bed was bathed in a brilliant morning light that made her feel as though someone were pressing their thumbs into her eyeballs. With one hand gripping her forehead, she looked at her phone. Nicole had texted just after 1:00 a.m.

Nicole: Didn't want to wake you. I'd better see you again SOON. Xo

Kate dragged herself to the front door, which had apparently been unlocked since the middle of the night. She flipped the dead bolt, then went to the kitchen in search of dry toast and some ibuprofen, which she kept above the sink next to the water glasses.

Forty minutes and a protein bar later, she was showered, dressed, and on her way to the office. It was a warm day, so she took the train down to Thirty-Fourth Street, then walked east across midtown Manhattan. She used to love the newsroom on a Saturday. There was just a skeleton crew there on weekends, a few editors from each of the major news desks—National, Metro, and International. The Politics editors worked constantly during election season, but they mainly worked from home on Saturdays and Sundays, so she had that corner of the newsroom to herself. People didn't wander by to chat. There were none of the distractions of home. Being in the office when it was quiet allowed her to tear through her work.

Before she had gone abroad as an international correspondent, she'd usually come in at least once every weekend. She'd get a charge out of spending Saturday or Sunday, or both, writing an extra story or digging through a pile of documents. It left her feeling ahead of the game for the coming week, invigorated, like she had her life under control. She knew this had been true, but she couldn't get that feeling back. Now she went in on weekends mostly because she didn't know what else to do.

She sat at her desk, opened her laptop, and navigated to the *Ledger*'s internal publishing system, where stories were written, edited, and then put on the website. She had finished the necessary reporting for a story about a new political action committee that was using its mysterious funding to buy enormous chunks of TV advertising in purple states. She was ready to write it, but she couldn't bring herself to start.

Instead, she went to the back end of the Politics section so she could see what other reporters had filed. This was an old habit she'd carried from department to department. It was considered fairly rude to read someone else's article uninvited before publication, with their unpolished thoughts and baggy ledes, like you were seeing someone in a state of partial undress. So she did it on "Read Only" to avoid leaving fingerprints. She wanted to know what her closest colleagues were working on—they were also her closest competitors—and it was fun to get an early peek at pieces other desks were going to publish.

Some of her favorite stories to snoop on were advance obituaries, which were written for major public figures, often years or even decades before they died. Once a renowned individual reached a certain age or hit a patch of poor health, the Obits desk wanted to be prepared. Artists, world leaders, athletes—it was fascinating to read these summations, designed to be read at the end of a life, while the subject was still kicking around, probably off somewhere having breakfast. It felt like seeing into the future. Reading movie reviews in advance was fun, too.

Kate also liked to see which reporters routinely got heavy edits and whose copy was mostly left alone. She was edited lightly, and she pushed back hard if anyone tried to slice up her work.

She scanned the list of stories on the Politics dashboard, which were labeled with a number that signified the date it would publish, or 00 if the piece hadn't yet been scheduled. The number was followed by a word or two that signaled the subject matter.

29Florida That's a story about Florida that would publish on the 29th.
00Donate Must be an article about donations that didn't have a run date yet.
00SenateFight A piece about a battle in the Senate. No date scheduled.
00Keller

Keller. That had to be Ethan.

Kate instinctively moved her cursor over the story—and then she stopped.

She was not supposed to be involved in the coverage, and she hadn't been. That rule made sense to her. Absolutely. She could not cover Ethan with any reasonable expectation of objectivity or fairness. It was an unconditional conflict of interest.

But she was going to read this story when it came out, of course, so what was the harm in reading it now?

She wasn't really supposed to. She knew this. She wasn't supposed to know about any of his upcoming coverage. But great reporters were not great rule followers. She had been to innumerable goodbye toasts for retiring colleagues who were praised for believing the word "no" meant "find another way." Reporters spend their professional lives ferreting out information they're not supposed to have.

As long as she didn't do anything to stick her thumb on the scale of Ethan's race, reading the story would be harmless. It would be fine. But she would open the article in "Read Only," just in case.

Ethan Keller, who is running for Congress in New Jersey, likes to say that he is an unusual Republican candidate. He was once an aide to a powerful New York Democrat, Willard Keyes, who was forced from his position as attorney general after he was accused of taking bribes. Keller, 43, is also gay, running for office in an election cycle where much of his party has focused on social issues in an effort to motivate voters.

This background has garnered Keller an unusual amount of national attention for a first-time congressional candidate.

What has received significantly less attention are parts of his past he has chosen not to reveal.

When he was 28, while driving under the influence of drugs and alcohol, Keller was in a car accident that nearly took a woman's life.

Shit.

Erin Mitchell was just 22 when Keller ran a red light and plowed into the driver's side of Mitchell's car, a Ledger investigation has found. The accident left her in the hospital for weeks and in a wheelchair for months. She suffered from organ damage and had so much internal bleeding she nearly died on the way to the hospital, according to her brother, Brian Mitchell. She still walks with a limp today.

"That wreck really messed her up," Mr. Mitchell said. "That guy," he continued of Keller, "was high and drunk and he almost killed her."

Shortly after the accident, Keller checked himself into a drug and alcohol rehabilitation center in New Canaan, Connecticut.

Ms. Mitchell declined repeated requests to comment for this article.

Keller's decision to conceal this part of his history raises questions about how forthcoming he would be as a member of Congress and about the kind of campaign he is running today.

An editor had inserted a note in the story: *WE WILL ADD KELLER'S RESPONSE HERE. REPORTERS WILL REACH OUT TO HIM FOR COMMENT ONCE THE STORY IS READY TO GO.*

So Ethan didn't know about the article yet. Kate quietly closed her laptop and rose from her chair.

She crossed the newsroom toward the elevators, careful not to let her rising panic quicken her pace. She punched the brass elevator button repeatedly with her knuckle.

Once outside, she walked over to Lexington Avenue, then headed north. When she reached a safe distance from the office, she turned onto a side street and stood with her back to a sandwich shop that had a forbidding metal gate pulled down over its storefront. She took a careful look in both directions and called Ethan.

"Yo!" he said.

"We are not having this conversation."

"Okay," he replied slowly.

"Are you alone?" she asked.

"I can be. Give me a second." There was a shuffling on his end of the line. "Okay, I'm alone. What's up?"

"I am breaking the letter of some rules here, but not their spirit," she said, as much to herself as to him. "We have had this conversation before, and I am going to say the exact same thing to you I've already said. Nothing is different."

"Okay," he said again, drawing out each syllable.

"You need to get out ahead of any story that could come out about you," she said. "Just as we've discussed. You need to get ahead of this."

"Uh-huh." He was silent for a few beats, long enough that she began to wonder if they'd been disconnected. "How quickly do you think we need to move?" he asked, the tone of his voice rising just a hint.

"Tomorrow would be good. Like I've said before, you need to get your story out as soon as possible. So no time like the present."

"Tomorrow sounds good to me," he answered. "You know, I listened to you the last time we had this conversation. We made a video where I talked about my addiction and the accident, and we paired that with a plan I have to steer more federal dollars to addiction treatment. I don't think the video has been edited yet, but we are planning to post it on all our social media—"

"Stop," she said. "I don't want to know any details. I am not involved in your campaign. I'm not involved in the coverage. And I did not tell you anything I haven't told you before."

"Of course you didn't," he said. "I was going to invite you over for dinner tonight, but it seems like it might be a late one for me. I'm sure Gabe and Chloe would still love to see you."

"I might be working tonight," she said. "I'll text Gabe if I can get myself to New Jersey."

"Keyes used to love a Sunday press conference," Ethan said.

"What? What are you talking about?"

"When I worked for Keyes, he used to love making announcements on Sundays. There was less news to compete with, so even boring pressers with minimal substance could get a little pickup." He chuckled at the memory. "It was a pain in the ass working Sundays all the time, but it made a difference. The man got a lot of extra press that way. Tomorrow is Sunday, and I have been moved to follow in his footsteps."

"He was an effective motherfucker, that guy," she said. "Too bad about the envelopes full of cash."

Ethan laughed. "I'm going to go make some phone calls now."

"You enjoy your Saturday!" Kate said with exaggerated perk.

"I'm not going to thank you," he said.

"Don't," she replied, and hung up.

HE GOT IT done. At seven the next morning, a slickly produced atonement video was on the internet. Ethan, looking penitent, speaking directly into the camera. Ethan, walking in some grass with Chloe and Gabe, the three of them a daisy chain connected by Chloe's hands. Ethan, standing alone again, pledging to increase the number of rehab beds available in the country.

"If you need help, like I did, please don't wait," he said. "It changed my life. Don't let anyone tell you that you can't change yours."

The video was spreading quickly online, accumulating views.

Whoever managed his social media accounts—and it certainly wasn't Ethan, who had neither the interest nor the aptitude—posted that he would be a guest that day on a highly rated conservative morning show, hosted by a woman named Chauncy and a man named Todd, who had icebergs for teeth and cheerful smiles. They liked to remind their viewers that the earth's climate had gone through warm cycles before and that Judeo-Christian values underpinned American society.

Kate watched the show on her couch with a mug of black coffee. Ethan wore a dark suit and a somber red tie. (He never wore blue ties anymore. His campaign manager didn't want photographs of him wearing the color of the Democratic Party available to run alongside stories about his political past.) And he was good. Contrite without being pathetic. Passionate, but not yelly. It helped that the questions were true softballs. "How would your experience make you a better representative for your district?" Todd asked, wrinkling his brow with concern for the little people.

It was working. Ethan had cast himself as a changed man owning up to a past that would help him improve the lives of others. It made him a more interesting story. It made him more human, less of a politician.

The *Ledger* article was published around lunchtime. Much of the language remained the same, but its power had been diluted almost to nothing, a bucket of warm water dumped in the Hudson River. Gone was any mention of a "*Ledger* investigation" or the implications of concealment. The morning's events had rendered it something meager, a follow-up to the announcement of a savvy politician who was recasting a significant liability as a personal strength. The *Ledger*'s story had a lot more detail than its competitors; it had the woman's name and her brother on the record. But it would do Ethan no harm.

Kate closed her laptop. She wondered what Nicole was doing at that moment, if she was shepherding her children from one activity to another, or if she was reading the story about Ethan, too.

Kate went to the photo app on her phone. She'd taken a few pictures at the bar on Friday night. There were a couple of Nicole out on the dance floor, her arms raised in the air while she sang along to the music, making up the words she didn't know. The flash was too bright and her arms were blurry, moving too quickly for the camera to capture precisely in the dark. Kate had also taken some unflattering selfies of the two of them together, pictures that emphasized their chins and made their faces look oddly pear shaped.

Nicole had better selfie skills. She'd snatched Kate's phone, held it above them, and snapped another photo. That shot was Kate's favorite: Nicole laughing with her mouth wide open, Kate's face nuzzling her neck. Alone in her apartment, Kate smiled as she flipped from Nicole dancing through the selfies and back again. In all those photos, even the chin-centered ones, it was clear how much fun they were having. She selected the best picture of them together and texted it to Nicole.

Kate: I had a great time Friday night. Looks like you did, too!

42

"**M**OM, CAN I play Candy Cart on your phone?" Henry asked.

Austin was playing golf with a group of clients and coworkers, so Nicole was left to chauffeur both kids to their weekend activities. She had reached the stage of parenthood where swim lessons and dance classes and baseball practice and piano lessons and soccer teams all collided into one metastasizing car ride, during which she ferried the children from one obligation to the next and always had the pleasure of being late. Austin had scheduled his golf game for the peak of the Sunday crunch. He said it couldn't be avoided.

So Henry was stuck sitting next to his mother on a damp bench that afternoon watching his sister practice dunking her head underwater. When it was Sarah's turn to jump in, she spread her limbs out wide and launched herself as far as she could in a joyful belly flop. Henry was unmoved by the exuberant display. He just wanted to mess around on his mom's phone.

"We brought your new library books," Nicole responded. "Why don't you read *Robo's Adventure*? You love that series."

"Yeah, but it's so hot in here," Henry said, slumping dramatically against the wall. He had a point. Sarah's swim classes were held at an indoor pool, and the air was thick and damp; it was like visiting a sauna while wearing jeans and tennis shoes. They had gone to the library just the day before and left with a stack of graphic novels, in part so that Nicole could be the one to look at her phone while stuck on the sidelines of Sunday's activities.

"How much longer do we have?" he asked.

"Twenty minutes."

"That's so long!" He slumped further, his back nearly flat against the bench.

Nicole sighed, lacking the energy to debate who was more deserving of digital distraction.

"Try using your manners, please," she said, defeated.

He sat up on the bench with his back straight.

"Can I play Candy Cart on your phone, please, Mom?"

"You may." She handed it over.

He hunched over the phone and punched in her passcode. He learned it. She changed it. He learned the new one. She changed it again. The cycle continued. So she gave up on trying to keep the code a secret.

Henry was immediately subsumed by a world of brightly colored targets and prizes shaped like lollipops and candy bars. Nicole watched Sarah, who had befriended another kid in her swim class, a boy with yellow swim trunks and a man bun. That child collected friends wherever she went.

Sarah instructed her new friend to watch her and then jumped into the pool again, completely submerging herself for a second or two. She popped back up and squealed with delight as she scrambled toward the side of the pool, her arms and legs splashing extravagantly.

"I thought you went to a Yankee game on Friday," Henry said.

"What was that, honey?" Nicole replied, putting a hand on his back. "Yeah, I did. Why do you ask?"

"This doesn't look like a Yankee game." He turned the screen of her phone toward her. There she was, laughing in a dark room, women dancing together all around her—and there was Kate, pressing her face into Nicole's neck.

No, it did not look like a Yankee game.

And with it was a text from Kate: *I had a great time Friday night. Looks like you did, too!*

"Oh," she said, her mind careening from one excuse to the next. "That was after the game. We went dancing. I love dancing, don't you? Doesn't that look like fun?"

"You went after the game?" Henry was unconvinced. Nicole was a morning person who did not like to stay up late, and he could smell her deceit like blood in the water. There was nothing more delicious to an eight-year-old than catching their grown-up in a lie. "You weren't tired after the baseball game?"

"I was a little tired, but dancing sounded like so much fun that I decided to go."

"Who is that?" His eyes narrowed as he pointed at the screen.

"That's my friend."

Calm, she told herself. Stay calm.

"Why are you snuggling like that?"

Oh fuck.

"What, honey?" she stalled. "She's just giving me a hug. Don't you ever hug your friends?"

"No. If you went dancing, why didn't you go with Daddy?"

"It's not that I didn't want to go with Daddy."

"Daddy likes dancing," Henry said.

"I know, sweetie." Nicole kept her eyes on Sarah. She hoped that if she didn't look directly at him, Henry wouldn't see the panic exploding across her face. "I'll go dancing with Daddy next time."

A FTER SWIM CLASS, Nicole drove the kids back home, then forced them to walk with her to their next destination. Poppy, one of Sarah's classmates, was turning six, and the invitation to her birthday party promised there would be beer for the adults. Nicole could feel her brain pressing against the inside of her skull, and she was afraid to look her son in the eye. She hoped a drink or two would calm her.

They walked in a row down their narrow suburban sidewalk, pinned between the street and a procession of lawns that were pristine or tidy, shaggy or densely overgrown. Sarah was at the back and she stopped roughly every twenty-five feet to examine a bug, or to pick up a stick and use it to whack at a tree. Then she would sprint to catch up, her fluffy yellow party dress shooting out around her. Henry positioned himself just behind his mother and committed to a steady, theatrical whine over the fact that they weren't taking the car. Nicole had never been so happy to hear it. Normally, she ignored Henry when he fussed at her like this, but she didn't want to leave him alone with his thoughts, so she responded to his many rhetorical questions with lectures on carbon emissions and walkable urban planning.

After a fifteen-minute journey, they turned onto the lush, velvety lawn of Poppy's house. Poppy was a kindergartner with one giant grown-up tooth at the front of her mouth, which was rarely made visible behind her customary frown.

They swung around the house, which had pale gray siding and blue trim, and headed for the backyard. It was longer than it was wide, with a table by the back porch and a swing set on the far end of the grass. A piñata in the shape of a white horse had been attached to a bungee cord and thrown over a tree branch. About two dozen children were lined up behind it, jumping up and down, thirsting for the horse's candy insides. Sarah bolted toward her friends. Henry ran in the same direction, toward the candy. Nicole went to the picnic table to look for beer.

She replayed the conversation with Henry in her mind. Dancing after a baseball game was possible, if not a regular occurrence for a woman who liked to be in bed by 10:00 p.m. But what exactly had she said? The panic she'd felt on the pool deck made her memory cloudy, a scene she was watching through a fog of apprehension and concern. She could see in her mind's eye Sarah rocketing into the water just as Henry asked the first question, but what had she said in response? The overall message was plausible, wasn't it? She did like to dance. But would he believe she went around snuggling her friends? Did she even want him to think that? Would he start trying to snuggle with kids in his math class? He had to know something was off.

Nicole found a turquoise cooler the size of a coffee table that contained a good assortment of pilsners, hard seltzers, and IPAs. She picked a double IPA with a purple zombie on the can and cracked it open.

THWACK!

She turned to see Poppy smacking at the piñata. She had what looked

like a repurposed cloth headband over her eyes. Was that a Swiffer handle she was using to hit the piñata? My God, they were going to be
here all day.

Nicole took a big sip of her beer. It was only slightly cooler than
the late-spring air around her, which gave the hops a sour taste in her
mouth. She took another sip anyway.

THWACK!

"Hi, Nicole."

She turned and found Gabe Alter standing in front of her, a can of
pilsner in his hand. He looked very much like he did on TV, with a
long, handsome face, tortoiseshell glasses, and neatly trimmed brown
curls. He gave her the barest hint of a smile.

"It's been a long time," he said.

"Gabe! Oh my God, it's been forever!" She tried to pretend it was
excitement, not hysteria, that was making her voice so high pitched.
"What are you doing here?"

"Our daughter, Chloe, takes swim classes nearby and she's in Poppy's
group," he said. "Chloe's the one with a lightning bolt on her T-shirt."
He pointed toward the cluster of feral children, at a girl who looked like
Kate.

"Not to sound creepy, but I know that's her. As a registered voter
in the town of Wickham, I think your husband is stalking me. I see his
ads everywhere."

THWACK!

Nicole and Gabe stood facing each other.

"Is it working?" Gabe asked her.

"Is what working?"

"The stalking. All the ads. Are they convincing you? If you don't
mind my asking."

"Oh, no, no, no, no, no. No way."

THWACK!

Well, shit, she thought. That sounded bad.

"I just mean I wouldn't vote for any Republican right now. Ethan
seems great, of course, but it wouldn't matter who he was. I just wouldn't

vote for that party." She couldn't tell if she was making things better or worse.

Gabe nodded. He wasn't smiling.

"I mean, I'm from Cincinnati. I know lots of conservatives, lots of liberals. We're all just people, right? It's just politics. But the party today, I mean, my God, it's just bananas. Everyone running is a lunatic."

Worse. She was making things worse.

"Not Ethan, of course. You know what I'm saying," she scrambled, trying to right herself. "I think my husband's going to vote for him. I mean, he is. He's excited about Ethan."

Gabe paused for a moment, watching her.

"Got it," he said. What was he looking at? Did she have something on her face?

She wasn't sure what else to say.

"So," Gabe said. "Where *is* your husband?"

Nicole froze.

It was not an unusual question. People asked her this in different ways every day. But his tone was unmistakable, laced with accusation. She looked at him. His eyes were slightly narrowed, his thin lips drawn together. He waited. He watched. And it was clear to her: He knew.

What was he trying to tell her? That he thought poorly of her? That he had power over her? What he did was threaten her family. She clenched her teeth and felt a sharp pain shoot down the right side of her jaw.

"He's not here," she said, turning toward the line of bloodthirsty children. She and Gabe stood side by side looking straight ahead. "The kids and I are going to meet up with him after this."

How dare he. How *dare* he! He didn't know anything about her marriage. She wanted to crush her beer can into the side of his pretty face.

She could lose her children over this. She sucked down a quarter of her beer without stopping to breathe. Her eyes started to water and she blinked to smother her tears. She had no idea how to get her hands back on the wheel.

She glanced quickly at Gabe, who stood in the grass looking calm and self-satisfied. She wondered what it would be like to hit him, how much it would hurt, bone against bone. Nicole felt like she was outside her body, watching the seams of her life come apart.

But Gabe's life was gray and complicated, too. Plenty of people would disagree with the choices he was making. She was hardly a model of righteous principles these days, but Gabe was propping up policies that would destroy the environment and make it easier for belligerent teenagers to buy guns—even though he believed in none of it. He'd drenched his principles in kerosene and set them on fire, but he felt fine judging her. He felt just fine.

You know what? she thought. Fuck this guy.

"And how's the campaign going for you?" she asked. Her demeanor should be pleasant, she reminded herself. Friendly, even.

"It's going," he said. "Campaigns are stressful, of course, but Ethan has been very considerate. He's doing everything he can to make this as easy as possible on Chloe and me. Family always comes first."

"I'm sure that's true," she replied. "I have to tell you, I was a little surprised to learn you were a Republican. Is that bad to say?"

She heard him sigh.

"It's not bad," he said. "But I'm not, actually. I'm just married to one. Like you are, presumably."

"Wow," she said. "That must be complicated. I mean, my husband and I, we vote differently for sure, but our votes cancel each other out. If he were running for office, that'd be a whole other thing.

"It must be hard for you," she continued. "I don't know how you feel about abortion or immigration, but I guess people must make assumptions—just like I did! Sorry about that."

THWACK! The Swiffer knocked a clump of pink streamers from the piñata's tail.

"It's fine."

Nicole took another sip from her zombie can and wiped a residue of beer from her upper lip. It was a boozy IPA and she was drinking too fast, but it was so much easier to be angry than terrified. "You know, I feel like if my husband were running for office, and I was supporting him, I'd be standing behind all the stuff he believes in that I don't."

THWACK!

"It wouldn't matter what I thought or how I voted," she said. "A campaign is so much more important than any of that."

THWACK!

"It's admirable to stand by your husband, I guess. It must mean a lot to him," she mused. "But I don't know how you do it. I'd need a fistful of Ativan to help me sleep at night."

THWACK THWACK THWACK! A kid with a long braid down her back broke the one-hit rule, lopping away at her target.

"But!" Nicole said brightly, smiling toward the children. "That's just how it would be for me and my family. And you never know what goes on in someone else's marriage. Don't you think?"

CRACK! The horse's backside went flying off and candy sprayed onto the grass. Henry, using the advantage of his size, had knocked the thing in half. Children hurled themselves into a writhing pile on the ground where the lollipops and chocolates had fallen.

"Is that right," Gabe said quietly as they watched the most aggressive kids charge the candy. "But I think I *do* know what's going on in your marriage. And if I were you"—his volume shot up—"I would *watch it.*"

A woman behind Gabe who was munching on a tiny bag of pretzels turned to look at him.

"You need to back off, Nicole. Let's not pretend you're making polite conversation here, okay?"

He was yelling at her. Yelling at her in the middle of a child's birthday party. Nicole hadn't expected him to fly so completely off the handle.

She had made a mistake.

"I don't know what your problem is," Gabe shouted, "but I suggest that you leave me out of it!"

Suddenly, by her side, there was Henry, his shaggy curls falling across his forehead. He had candy clutched in his fists and was staring daggers at Gabe.

"Honey." Nicole put one foot in front of Henry so she could block him with her torso. "Please just give me a minute, okay?" He shook his head and wove one of his arms through hers, locking them together by the elbows.

Gabe looked at Henry, with his smooth cheeks and untied shoes, and took a step back. He looked around the party at the adults who were awkwardly watching them, surveilling while avoiding eye contact. One woman took out her cell phone and started recording him.

"Excuse me," Gabe said. "We were just leaving." He walked toward Chloe, who was kneeling in the grass counting her candy.

Nicole kissed the top of Henry's head and breathed in the scent of his shampoo.

"Why was that person yelling at you?" Henry asked.

"I don't know, honey," she said. "I think he had too much to drink. But he's leaving now and I'm totally fine. Why don't you go back and play?"

"No," Henry said. "I'll stay here until he leaves."

43

NICOLE HURRIED THE kids into the house, turned on the TV, and threw the remote on the couch. By the time Henry and Sarah leapt onto the sofa—too tantalized by the prospect of cartoons to notice their mother's unusual, wordless behavior—Nicole was already halfway up the stairs. She marched straight to her bathroom and pulled the door closed behind her.

She called Kate.

"Well, hi," Kate said flirtatiously.

"You told Gabe!" Nicole hissed.

"What?"

"You told Gabe about us!"

"Oh, uh—" Kate was clearly flustered. "I did, yeah. He's family, though. He's not going to tell anyone. Wait, how do you know that?"

"He confronted me at a fucking birthday party for a six-year-old!"

"What? What do you mean he confronted you? What did he say?"

"He said, 'Hm, where's your husband?'" Nicole mimicked Gabe's voice in a way that made him sound ridiculous. "Where's your husband? Where's your husband!" She was racing around the bathroom, her heels thumping on the marble.

"He asked, 'Where's your husband?'"

"He was not asking if Austin was off getting a piece of cake, if that's what you mean. He was telling me he knew, Kate," she snapped. "Trust me, the conversation devolved pretty quickly after that. He screamed at me in the middle of this party! He's out of his goddamn mind."

"Jesus. Look, Gabe is under a lot of pressure and he is not at his best, but he's not going to go tell Austin—or anyone. But I will talk to him. I am so sorry."

"I can't believe you fucking told someone."

"I'm sorry!" Kate sounded wounded. "I needed to talk to somebody about us, and I trust him."

"Did you tell anyone else?" Nicole saw herself in the bathroom mirror. She'd been tugging at her curls and had left them frizzy and tangled.

"Just Gabe and Ethan."

"Christ."

"They're not going to tell anyone, okay? But I will talk to them."

"Mom?" Henry called from outside the bathroom door.

"Shit!" Nicole's voice came out a high-pitched squeak and she hung up the phone. She opened the door with a smile on her face that felt like it might crack her cheekbones. Henry stood in front of her, his eyebrows scrunched together in a way that reminded her of Austin.

"Hi, honey!" she nearly shouted.

"Who were you talking to?"

"No one! I was just talking to myself."

"You were yelling."

"Was I? Jeez, I didn't notice." She tried to sound cheerful as she ground her teeth to dust.

"Did someone tattle?"

"What do you mean, honey?"

"You said someone told. Were they not supposed to?"

"I think you must have misheard me." Shit shit shit shit shit. She pulled him toward her by the shoulders and hugged him against her chest. "Do you need something, honey? Are you hungry?"

"Yeah, I'm hungry. Can I have a sandwich?"

"Sure, sweetie. You go back and watch TV and I'll be right down. I just need one more minute."

"Okay." He looked back at her, as if trying to figure out what was wrong with her face, then went on his way.

Frantic, Nicole texted Kate.

Nicole: SHIT!!!!!!! Henry heard me!

ETHAN WALKED INTO the house at 6:36 p.m., just in time for their weekly dinner.

"I'm sorry I couldn't get here earlier," he called as the front door closed behind him. He generally tried to contribute by setting the table, but his success rate was middling. He'd be going back out later that night to hit one more event.

"Reporters have been showing up at Erin Mitchell's house," Ethan said. Gabe heard him drop his leather shoulder bag on the floor and walk toward the dining room, where the rest of the family was already seated. "She got in touch with the campaign office this morning desperate for help getting the press to go away, so I put out a statement asking people to give her privacy. Not that it's going to do anything." He was looking down at his phone, typing with his thumbs as he walked into the room. "Why did the *Herald Ledger* print her name? What is wrong with the mainstream media? All they did was make her a target. Now there are swarms of reporters rummaging around in her life to see how badly I ruined it."

He stuffed his phone in his pocket and put a smile on his face. "Anyway, let's have dinner." When his eyes landed on Gabe, the corners of his mouth fell.

"What's wrong?" he asked.

"Nothing," Gabe said sharply.

"Huh," Ethan replied. "Hi, honey," he said, bending down in front of Chloe's chair.

"Hi, Daddy." She allowed herself to flop into his chest when he pulled her in for a hug. She reached into her green silicone bowl for a baby carrot. "You want one?"

"Sure, honey, I'd love one. Thank you." He popped it into his mouth, then stood and kissed Gabe on the top of the head. "Hi," he said as he chewed. Ethan took his seat across from Chloe. Gabe sat between them at the head of the table.

"So!" Ethan cracked open a can of Diet Coke. "Chloe, what was something fun you did today?"

"I don't know."

"Just tell me one thing you liked doing."

"I watched TV."

"Okay. Thank you for telling me. Gabe, how was your day?"

"Uneven," Gabe snapped.

"We went to Poppy's birthday party and I only got eight pieces of candy from the piñata," Chloe complained.

"I'm sorry, honey," Ethan said. "Did you get to hit it?"

"Just one time. Then a big kid broke it when I was at the back of the line and everyone else took all the candy!"

"That's too bad. Gabe, what happened to you today? Did you get any candy from the piñata?"

Gabe glared at him.

"Okay, not funny. Can you tell me what happened?"

"I met your sister's friend," Gabe said.

"Kate has friends?" Ethan quipped.

"Daddy, Aunt Kate has friends!" Chloe was horrified. "I'm her friend."

"Of course you are, sweetie, and of course Aunt Kate has friends. That was a bad joke."

"The one she's been spending a lot of time with recently," Gabe said. He was cutting his chicken fingers into tiny pieces instead of eating them.

"Oh. Wow," Ethan said, intrigued. "What was she like?"

"Blunt," Gabe replied.

"What does blunt mean?" Chloe was making her food into a tower, chicken on the bottom, toast in the middle, carrots on the top. Gabe decided he didn't have the emotional energy to care.

"It means someone who is very honest," Ethan answered. "Sometimes a little too honest."

"No, no, not too honest," Gabe jumped in. Chloe could be an enthusiastic fibber, and this kind of nuance was not helpful. "But there are ways to say things that are more considerate of other people's feelings."

"What did she say to you?" Ethan's forehead crinkled.

"She said what everyone else has been thinking about me since you started running for office."

"Okay. And what was that?"

"She basically asked how I sleep at night."

"What?" Ethan's voice cracked with outrage. He glanced at Chloe, who was deeply engrossed in her carrot tower, but she was always listening. "Because you're supporting me? What a . . . B-I-T-C-H."

"What's a B-I-T-C-A?" Chloe asked.

"Nothing, honey, don't worry about it," Ethan said.

"B-I-T," she repeated slowly. "That spells bite."

"It's nothing, honey," Ethan pleaded. "I shouldn't have said it."

Gabe took a sip of his water. "I may have asked where her husband was."

"Like in a totally natural, neutral kind of way?" Ethan looked like he was bracing for impact.

"Not really, no."

"Oh, Gabe, no," Ethan said. "I mean, whatever she said to you does not sound great. But the husband stuff, that's not ours to talk about."

"I'm aware of that. It was not my finest moment." Gabe's knife squeaked against his plate as he sliced the last of his chicken fingers. "But you know what?" he added. "She's got a point."

"What?" A flicker of exasperation puncturing Ethan's expression. "What does that even mean?"

"I'm supporting you, so I'm supporting all your policies, all your beliefs. I have to live with that."

"Come on." Ethan rolled his eyes, clearly aggravated. "The moral superiority is getting a little old, don't you think?"

"Who's old?" Chloe asked, elbowing her way back into the conversation.

"No one, honey," Ethan said.

"Excuse me?" Gabe demanded.

"You're excused," Chloe assured him.

"I'm condescending to you now, is that it?"

"In that moment, yeah, you were," Ethan said. "Do you really think half the country is immoral? Or is it just that they're not as smart as you?"

"You know what, I've had enough." Gabe stood up from the table. Everything he touched that day had exploded in his hands, and he did not trust himself to have this conversation. He needed a few minutes alone without looking at Ethan's face. He would have liked to storm out of the house, to shackle Ethan to the evening's childcare duties so he couldn't leave for his next event. But Gabe didn't want Chloe to worry, so he settled for an escape into the kitchen.

"I'm finished with my dinner," he said, though he hadn't taken a single bite. "The kitchen is a mess and I'm going to clean it." Chloe started to get out of her chair. "You're not done, miss. Please sit down and eat some of your chicken."

"Gabe, I'm sorry—" Ethan started.

"It's fine," he said, though it did not feel fine. He wanted the conversation to be over. "Stay with her, please. I need a minute." Gabe picked up his plate and pushed through the swinging door into the kitchen. He turned on the faucet and let the water run while he sank to the floor.

45

Kate,

I need you to come into the office today. Let's meet in the Politics conference room at 11am.

Best,

Mark

BEST." MARK WAS never that formal. Something was up.

Fuck.

She hadn't done anything wrong, she reminded herself. She had told Ethan he needed to get his side of the story out there—how many times before? Twice? Three times? She wasn't sure, but she had said it repeatedly. And she hadn't gone any further than that. She did not cross that line.

John Keyes, a journalist and the cousin of Willard Keyes, had been fired from his post as a national TV anchor shortly after Willard resigned from office. But he had really reached his tentacles into that scandal and tried to make it go away. In close coordination with his cousin, John had tried to wave other journalists away from the accusations, and he disparaged the motives of whistleblowers and legislators leading the charge.

John deserved to get fired for what he'd done. But that was different. She had given Ethan some advice, sure, but she didn't try to influence other reporters. She wasn't involved in the coverage.

And when she'd called Ethan, the video was already done. He was already doing it! He had a plan, and even without her phone call, it might have been executed ahead of the story. It probably would have been.

She knew, however, that she could tell her bosses none of this. Not everyone would agree with her interpretation, that she had not actually provided him with an unfair advantage. Preventing that kind of interference was precisely the reason she was not to know what coverage was coming. For intervening in that way, she could be fired.

K ATE FELT LIKE she was wobbling into the newsroom carrying another person on her back. There was a tightness between her shoulder blades and she was aware of each movement required to take a step—lift your foot, slide it forward, place it down, lift your other foot, slide it forward, place it down.

She landed in front of Mark's desk at 10:58 a.m.

"Morning," she said with practiced ease, a skill she'd sharpened over years of tense phone calls and meetings with sources who couldn't know they made her nervous.

He looked up from his computer. Not a muscle in his face shifted when he saw her.

"Hi," he said. His tone was flat, a sheet of ice, as he pulled himself out of his chair. "Follow me."

He led her across the newsroom and up a flight of stairs. He walked quickly, taking full advantage of his long legs, and tall as Kate was, she didn't try to keep the same pace; it would have required an undignified scamper. So she watched him disappear into a conference room from a few yards away, and she followed.

"Oh, hi, Diego, Peter," she said. Mark let her pass through the door, then closed it behind her. He dropped into a chair next to Diego Sandoval from the Policies and Ethics department, a small team that oversaw delicate issues and controversies, both in the news report and among the journalists.

At the head of the table was Peter Toussaint, an assistant managing editor, a title that came without clearly defined duties but with a rank at the very top of the institution; it meant he had power. Peter had a booming voice and some sort of human resources job Kate did not completely understand.

"Kate," Peter said.

"What's going on?" she asked, trying to sound breezy and casual.

"We need to talk about the Keller story," he said.

"Okay," she said. "What about it?"

"What'd you think of it?"

"It was good," she said. "It had a lot more detail than the competition. But why are we talking about this? That coverage is off limits to me."

The three men looked at her without speaking and silence thickened the air. They were waiting for her to say more, like they had laid out a trap and hoped she would fumble into it.

"Can someone please tell me what's going on?" She looked at Mark, who pursed his lips and dropped his eyes to the scuffed wooden table in front of them.

"You opened the file, Kate," Diego said.

Breathe, she reminded herself. Breathe.

"Yeah," she said. "So what? I read the story. But I didn't touch it, you know that. I am not involved in that coverage."

"But did you change the trajectory of the story?" Peter asked.

"What? Of course I didn't. I'm going to go in and rewrite somebody else's lede and hope they don't notice? You know I didn't touch that piece."

"That's not what I asked," Peter said. "Did Keller have any inside knowledge of that story?"

Kate pulled her body back ever so slightly, as if the question were a heavy object that landed on her chest. She looked at Peter, then at Mark.

"Are you serious?" she asked. "Of course not! I didn't tell him anything about it. You've got to be kidding me. I would like to keep my job, you know."

The three men watched her silently, her hands splayed open on the surface of the table, steadying herself against them.

"Hang on," she said. "You think I read that story on Saturday, and then by Sunday morning, Ethan had that slick video ready to go and all those appearances lined up? How could that possibly happen?"

"Maybe he asked you to look at the story," Mark said.

"This is crazy," she replied. "He did not ask me to look, okay? And if he had, I would have said no."

Keep breathing. Keep breathing.

"You were not supposed to be involved in the coverage in any way," Diego said.

"And I wasn't! I was not involved in that story, or any other story about him. I'm not in the planning meetings, I have no idea what's going on. If there's a story list somewhere, I don't know where it is and I don't know what's on it."

"But you read that story before publication," Diego said. "Whether or not you did anything with that information, it put you in a position where you could have."

"What could I have possibly done with it?"

"You could have told Keller about it," Peter said.

"But I didn't!"

"That doesn't matter!" Mark snapped. He looked at her.

"How can that not matter?" she barked back.

"Kate," Diego said, "it matters. We have no proof, at this point, that you communicated with Keller about the story, but we will be conducting an investigation."

"Proof? Did you go through my email?"

"We did, yes," Peter said.

"Jesus." She shook her head then leaned forward in her chair. "I did not tell him about the story."

"Kate, the appearance of impropriety can be just as damaging to the institution as impropriety itself," Diego said.

"You should not have looked at that file—period," Peter said, rhythmically stabbing at the table with his pointer finger. "You should consider yourself on leave while we conduct the investigation."

"This is unbelievable," she said as she stood up from her chair. "But fine. Have somebody call me when you come to your senses." She yanked open the door and walked out before they had a chance to respond.

Her eyes burned as she crossed the newsroom, but she would not allow herself to cry in the office. She would preserve the dignity she had left.

46

GABE WAS SITTING on the couch rereading *Mrs. Dalloway* in the company of a terrible headache. He was massaging his left temple with his fingertips, waiting for the three ibuprofen he'd taken to kick in, when he heard Ethan open the front door.

"Hey," Gabe called from the living room.

"Hey, angel." Ethan sat down beside him, giving Gabe a quick kiss. "Chloe's got to be asleep by now, right?"

"The party was still going until about a half hour ago, but she's finally out," Gabe said. Things between them felt strained, and Gabe was relieved that Ethan was home at a reasonable hour, so they could spend some amount of time together before going to bed. "How was your day?" he asked.

"Long." Ethan untied his shoes and let them drop to the carpet. "But a pretty major thing happened this afternoon."

"Oh yeah?" Gabe wedged his thumb into the book to keep his page. He had to finish it for a discussion with his student advisory group, and he was close to the end, where Septimus hears his wife talking to Dr. Holmes on the staircase.

"You're not going to like how this sounds," Ethan continued. "But this is a huge opportunity."

Gabe installed his bookmark, a slip of paper Chloe had decorated with an orange monster, and let the novel fall closed on his lap.

"Okay," he said. "This sounds exciting, I think? Tell me what's going on."

"I had a meeting with Andrew. We're trying to figure out what our final push is going to be, how we're going to spend the money we've been raising and what we're going to do in the last couple of weeks to get me over the finish line here. But we've got a problem. We ran another poll and the hard right of the party still doesn't believe I'm a real conservative. They think I'm an impostor. Did you see that ad where Caruso calls me a RINO?"

"I try not to watch attack ads about my husband."

"Totally makes sense." He squeezed Gabe's knee. "Well, it's an issue. So I need an endorsement that will make those voters feel comfortable pulling the lever for me."

Gabe waited.

"Brett Cooper has been trying to raise his national profile."

Gabe blinked. Brett Cooper?

"He's been making endorsements all over the country, and he's looking to get involved here in New Jersey. He wants to be seen as someone with wide influence, broad appeal."

Brett Cooper. Gabe tossed the book onto their polished wooden coffee table with too much force. It slid across the top and fell to the floor on the opposite side.

Ethan took a breath and powered through. "He's going to endorse somebody in this race. And if it's not me, I'm toast. So our offices have been in touch. He and I talked today, and he made his decision. I've got his support."

Gabe looked straight ahead and tried to inhale into his diaphragm. Ethan kept talking while Gabe counted silently to twenty.

"We're going to start with a cross-endorsement, probably tomorrow, and then we'll do a joint appearance next week. It's a big deal that we were able to convince him. Caruso is a much more natural fit because they're both to my right. But Cooper knows I've got the momentum and the fundraising support, and I think he wants to be seen backing a variety of successful conservative candidates. There are James Carusos running all over the country, but what I offer is unique."

Gabe had stopped counting. He could feel acid building in his throat. His mouth was watering.

"So that gives me some power," Ethan continued. "I bring something to him, too, so I'm not going into this purely as a supplicant." He rose to his feet and began pacing the living room in his red-white-and-blue-striped socks, too much energy pulsing through his body to keep still.

Gabe tented his fingers across his forehead. His eyes were fixed on a purple stain on their ash-gray carpet, a slice of color where a frozen blueberry had once tumbled out of Chloe's mouth.

"It will help him with moderates to be seen supporting me. It will show them he's open-minded about certain things and that he's not always going to take the extreme position.

"This is the piece we've been missing." His speech-giving hand was slapping around in the air. "He can help me with exactly the voters I need. They trust Cooper, and if he says they can trust me, then—"

"No," Gabe said into his hands. His voice sounded unfamiliar, guttural.

"What?" Drawn back from his speechmaking, Ethan snapped his head toward his husband.

Gabe kept his eyes trained on the blueberry stain. He had not foreseen this. Somehow, he had not foreseen this.

He and Ethan disagreed on many things, things that seemed as obvious to Gabe as gravity and sunlight. But he accepted that. He accepted it because Ethan was a gentle father and a generous husband. Ethan was his person. He didn't understand how they'd found themselves so far apart on so many issues. And yet, he knew Ethan, every part of him, and Gabe trusted that Ethan wouldn't go too far.

But this—this was too far. And he had not foreseen it.

"I know how you feel about Cooper," Ethan said. "He's not my favorite, either. But this is a really big deal for me."

Gabe took a breath and raised his head from his hands.

"How could you do this?" he asked.

"I thought you might be kind of relieved, actually. If Cooper was going to position himself as the person to repeal gay marriage, he wouldn't want to work with me."

"You thought I might be *relieved*? Cooper is using you!" Gabe bellowed, raising his hands in the air. "And tomorrow, if he thinks it's to his advantage to become the spokesman for firebombing gay marriage, he'll do it. Remember, gay *people* and gay *marriage* are different!"

"Gabe," Ethan said. "Whoever Cooper supports is going to win. Would you rather he endorse Caruso? That man is a maniac! You can't want him going to Washington because I'm afraid to get my hands dirty. You know how powerful Cooper is. There are a lot of people who don't particularly want to vote for a gay former Democrat, but if Cooper tells them to, they will. They trust him."

"Well, they're fucking idiots!" Gabe launched off the sofa. "Never mind the fact that you want to do something that will help this man, that will help that racist, hateful shitbag—"

"Chloe is sleeping," Ethan reminded him.

"Not only are you going to be helping this man," Gabe shouted, "but you will be taking our family's reputation and shitting all over it!"

"This is a practical decision—"

"You will be taking *my* name and shitting all over it!" They paused for a moment and looked at one another, each of them stunned by turns in the conversation. "All these people who read stories about you or see *my* face in *your* campaign ads—to them I'm just the gay Republican's faggot husband. It doesn't matter that I don't agree with any of the shit you're trying to sell them. I don't exist anymore! I'm just an extension of the worst parts of you!"

Ethan stood quietly, his eyes level on his husband.

"If you're supporting Cooper and he's supporting you, then we're all part of his hateful bullshit."

Ethan lowered himself slowly onto the couch.

"Gabe, this is politics," he said. "I'm just making an appearance with the man. I'm not going to go work for him. I'm not adjusting my platform. If he were to become president—"

"God for-fucking-bid!" Gabe cried.

"I agree, actually. But if he does win, I'd never join his administration. This isn't going to change what I'll do when I'm in office. It's just going to help me pick up some votes that, otherwise, I won't get. And if he is the party's nominee for president, I'm going to have to endorse him eventually anyway. So I should do it now, when, frankly, there's some benefit to it."

Gabe was standing, his face buried again in his hands. He didn't want to watch these words come out of Ethan's mouth.

"I don't love being associated with the guy, either," Ethan continued. "But it could really change the race, and I can't be precious about that."

Gabe felt like his skin was peeling away, exposing parts of him that were pink and raw underneath. He was a progressive. He was a proud gay man. He was a public-school teacher. Who would he be now?

"You're going to do it," Gabe said, the words brittle in his mouth. "No matter what I say, you're going to do it."

"Can we not think about it like that, please? I would like your support."

"But you don't need my approval. So you're just going to have to do without them both."

★ ★ ★

BRETT COOPER SUPPORTS KELLER FOR NJ SEAT

BRETT COOPER ENDORSES FIRST-TIME CANDIDATE WITH UNEXPECTED RÉSUMÉ

COOPER SAYS YAY GAY! ENDORSES KELLER

Gabe sat in his classroom, his left hand like a vise around his temples, his right hand gripping his phone. He read article after article, each providing him the same information with marginally different packaging and tone. Brett Cooper had endorsed Ethan, and Ethan had endorsed him back. It all happened on social media.

Cooper posted first, on all his platforms:

Ethan Keller is a FIGHTER and a WINNER—just the kind of conservative the Republican Party needs! He has my support. Wouldn't want to be a Dem in his way!! AMERICA FOR THE WIN!

Ethan's campaign posted a screenshot of the endorsement and added its own message on top:

Honored to have your support @CooperAmerican! You're an inspirational leader and a true conservative. You've got my vote!

Honored. Honored! The word felt like glass in his throat. How could Ethan say he was honored? How could he allow someone to say it on his behalf? Cooper, who tried to put people in jail for minor errors on their voter registration forms. Cooper, who said immigrants from Muslim countries were destroying the fabric of our Christian nation. Cooper, who cast doubt on perfectly legitimate elections whenever he didn't like the result. Cooper, who said teachers who taught books with gay characters should be fired. This loathsome, duplicitous, narrow-minded bigot—this was an endorsement Ethan was honored to receive.

Gabe dropped his phone on his fake-wooden desk and took off his glasses to rub the bridge of his nose. He could feel himself unraveling. He didn't know how to explain his husband anymore. He didn't know how to explain himself.

He looked at the comments under Ethan's Instagram post.

Ok. If Cooper says to vote for @EKeller4Congress, I'll do it.

What happened to you as a child @EKeller4Congress to make you hate yourself so much??

How are gay republicans even a thing?

@EKeller4Congress is a strong conservative who will help us take back our country! I believe Cooper!!

It was hot in his classroom, with slices of warm afternoon light cutting across the gray metal desks. The air was motionless and heavy. A bead of sweat crawled down his neck. He needed to be outside.

He stood, pulled his backpack over one shoulder, and stuffed his headphones into his ears. Clutching his phone in one hand, he took a breath and started talking. He hoped his colleagues would believe he was calmly chatting on the phone on his way out the door, rather than muttering to himself as he decompensated in the hall.

He opened his classroom door and powered down the hallway, red lockers standing sentry on either side. He kept up a fictional conversation as he walked, creating an imaginary menu and an accompanying grocery list. Really, he just named whatever ingredients wafted into the house fire of his brain. He passed a colleague, a science teacher with whom he was on polite terms. Gabe raised a hand in greeting, his eyes on the linoleum-tile floor, as he bolted past.

Dear Ms. Keller,

We are writing to inform you that the investigation into your conduct is complete. Investigators have determined that you violated the company's Ethics Policy by apprising yourself of coverage, in advance of its publication, on a topic from which you had been explicitly barred due to a conflict of interest.

You will be reassigned from the Politics desk to the Obituaries desk. The Obituaries editor, in concert with the Policies and Ethics department, will determine the details of your new assignment and inform you when a decision has been made. In the meantime, you will remain on leave from The Herald Ledger.

You will be demoted from Domestic Correspondent to Reporter and your compensation will be adjusted accordingly.

Respectfully,

Peter Toussaint
Assistant Managing Editor

Diego Sandoval
Editor, Policies & Ethics

48

NICOLE WAS STARTING to settle into the possibility that Henry had moved on from her night of illicit dancing, that it had receded into the crevices of his mind that swallowed up all things boring and adult, like the need to brush his teeth or occasionally change his socks. Perhaps she wouldn't need to address it further. She started to smile at her son again without panic behind her eyes.

She was wrong.

"Does Daddy know you went dancing without him?" Henry asked. He and Sarah were in the back seat of her SUV on their way to school, late as usual. Mercifully, Austin wasn't there.

"Mommy went dancing?" Sarah said.

Shit. Shit shit shit shit shit.

"Yeah," Henry said. "She went with her friend. Mommy, what's your friend's name?"

"Sorry, honey, I couldn't hear you." She had absolutely heard him.

"Why didn't I get to go dancing?" Sarah whined.

"Oh, sweetie, this was a place for grown-ups." Nicole tried to strangle her voice into a composed tone. "Kids aren't allowed."

"Why not?" she asked.

"That's a good question," Nicole stalled.

"Did Daddy go dancing, too?" Sarah asked.

"No, it was just me. Daddy was home watching you guys, so he couldn't come with me. Who would have taken care of you?"

"Does Daddy know?" Henry asked.

"What, sweetheart?" Nicole looked at him in the rearview mirror.

"Does Daddy know?"

"Of course Daddy knows," she said. Shit shit shit shit shit.

"Does he know your friend?"

"Can I go dancing with you, Mommy?" Sarah asked.

"Definitely, honey! Let's do that." Her words were wispy and thin.

"I'm a great dancer, Mommy. Watch me!" Sarah wiggled and shook as much as her booster seat would allow.

"That's great, sweetheart," Nicole said, but she wasn't watching. She was looking at Henry, who was gazing out the window, now back in his own world, probably thinking about Candy Cart. But the damage was done.

S HE TUCKED IN the kids one at a time and then sat down in her bedroom reading chair, folding herself on top of some sweatpants and her pajamas from the night before.

Henry could sense her deception, and she knew he would pick at it until he had proof. He was a rule-bound child, eager to monitor the behavior of his classmates and his sister, but there was special glory for an eight-year-old in ratting out his own mother.

He'd caught her lying before, like when she told him he couldn't play with her phone because it was running out of batteries, then left it sitting on the kitchen counter long enough for him to peek and see that it was fully charged. Or when he found a bar of dark chocolate in her purse after she told him there wasn't any dessert in the house. When he figured out the tooth fairy wasn't real, he was thrilled. He jumped on his bed, pointed at her, and yelled, "I knew it! I knew it!"

He was only eight, she reminded herself. His focus was still immediate and narrow, and he was much more concerned with computer games and his Rubik's Cube than he was with the intricacies of her personal life. He was only just beginning to realize that she was a person at all.

But he was only eight, and he was not yet at a point where he might shield his mother from her own falsehoods. The world was still too black and white for that. She could never ask him to keep things from his father. It would be a terrible lesson for a child, and she wouldn't put him in that position. It would backfire anyway, heightening the issue in his mind.

She pictured him announcing to Austin that he'd been excluded from her dance party, marching up to his father and asking if he knew Mommy's friend. Henry might do this privately, but more likely, he'd want to gauge the reaction of one adult against another. It could come at any moment, at the dinner table or during bedtime, or the next morning while Austin was having breakfast.

Austin didn't deserve that. He didn't deserve any of this. Nicole had to tell him before Henry did.

She tried running through the conversation in her mind, but she couldn't get past the first sentence: that she hadn't gone to a baseball game like she'd told him. She went blank beyond that point, as though she was trying to envision a physical impossibility, like she was going to sit down in her bedroom chair and have it take flight. She didn't have the basic building blocks to get there.

She looked around her bedroom and wondered how different her life would be in an hour. Austin had a charger by the bed next to some black-framed reading glasses. Would they be gone tomorrow? Would she miss them? Her side of the bed was a mess. A stack of books and old magazines threatening to tip over, surrounded by a phalanx of used tissues. If he moved out, would her clutter slowly take over the bedroom, then creep through the rest of the house like mold?

It occurred to her that she could use this moment to tidy up, at least throw away her dirty tissues. But that would be too ordinary a thing to do, a sign of disrespect for the conversation that was to come.

At 9:30 p.m., she forced herself out of her chair, checked that the kids were sleeping, and went downstairs.

AUSTIN WAS SITTING at the dining room table in front of his laptop, a finger of bourbon in a glass beside him. She came to a stop on the opposite end of the table and gripped the back of a chair. He kept typing and didn't look up.

"Austin," she said. "I need to tell you something."

"Okay. Let me just send this email," he said, muttering out the rest of it. "Thank you for your help and hard work on this. Regards. Austin.

"Okay." He left the laptop open and looked at her expectantly. "What's up?"

"We just need to talk." She kept her eyes locked on the table.

"Okay," he said slowly.

She didn't respond. He closed his laptop and took a sip of his bourbon.

"What do we need to talk about?" he asked.

"I need to tell you something."

"You mentioned that," he replied. "What's going on?"

"When I said I went to a Yankee game last weekend"—she paused—"I actually didn't."

"Uh-huh." He crossed his arms over his chest. The sky blue of his button-down shirt made his crystalline eyes pop. "Where did you go?"

"Dancing," she said. The word quivered ever so slightly as it came out of her mouth. "I went dancing."

"Who did you go dancing with?"

"I've reconnected with someone," she said.

"You've reconnected with someone, and you went dancing." He looked uneasy. "What the hell are you talking about? What does it mean you reconnected with someone?"

She tightened her grip on the back of the chair, noticing how the smooth wooden bar across the top didn't dig into her palms no matter how hard she pressed.

"Nicole," he said again. "What is going on? You're making it sound like you cheated on me or something."

He said it as though it sounded ridiculous. Absurd. But she didn't answer.

"Nicole," he repeated forcefully. "Why aren't you saying anything? You didn't fucking cheat on me, did you?"

She looked down.

"Nicole!" he shouted.

"I did."

He stared at her, frozen in place. The only movement she could discern was his eyelids blinking rapidly.

"How many times?" It came out like a growl.

"It doesn't matter," she said.

"Don't you fucking tell me what doesn't matter. How. Many. Times?"

"More than once."

He stood up. He had seventy pounds and eight inches on her. His lips were contorted and open, baring his top front teeth, which had begun to tint with yellow as he aged.

"What the fuck is wrong with you?" he demanded, as though he expected an answer. "How could you do this to us? To our family? What do you think this is going to do to our family?"

"I'm sorry," she said. Her voice wavered. "I am so, so sorry. I know that's not enough, but I am sorry. You didn't deserve this."

"Who is it?"

"No one you know."

"Who?" he barked, slamming his hand on the table. She jumped. She wondered if he might hit her and how much it would hurt. She felt an instinctual, animal fear in her belly.

"Kate Keller," she said. "You've never met her."

He paused and stared at her, a look of confusion trickling down his face.

"Kate Keller?" he repeated. "Kate?"

"Yes."

"Kate who drank too much after college?"

"Yes."

"Kate," he repeated quietly to himself. "Kate."

Nicole watched him. She held her breath and waited for her life to crack in half.

"Jesus," he said, shaking his head. He exhaled. His shoulders relaxed. Did he sound—relieved?

"You scared the shit out of me!" he said.

"I'm sorry?"

"Shit, Nicole, you don't think you could've led with that?"

She stood without moving, trying to puzzle out what he could possibly mean.

"I'm going for a walk," he said, sliding his phone into his pocket and turning toward the front door. "I'll be back."

GABE FELT HYSTERICAL all evening. He and Chloe walked in the door at 5:15 p.m., and he immediately dropped her in front of the television, in flagrant violation of their no-TV-during-the-week rule, so he could scroll through his phone and not answer any questions. He ordered pizza for dinner, which they ate in silence in front of a show about a talking penguin family. The primary was only three weeks away and Ethan wasn't going to be home until late.

When Chloe was tucked into bed for the night, Gabe tried calling Kate. Straight to voice mail. He went to text her but saw her notifications were turned off. He didn't think there was anyone else he could handle talking to. He served himself a glass of scotch that was more than double what he usually poured, but this was an emergency. He sank onto the couch.

Publicly, Gabe had been a blank slate. A Google search of his name brought up only his social media accounts and an article he'd written for the Skidmore alumni magazine about teaching at an arts high school. And even those things were buried. Most of what Google surfaced was about two other guys named Gabe Alter, one a plastic surgeon in Miami and the other an art gallery owner in Los Angeles.

All of that had been completely subsumed, not only by his husband's beliefs, but by that fascist shitbag Brett Cooper. Gabe's online presence instantly became a series of articles about what Cooper stood to gain from Ethan's voters—and oh, by the way, Ethan is married to a guy named Gabe Alter, who must be a shitbag, too.

He did not think immigrants should be sent back to "where they came from."

He thought voting should be made easier, not harder.

He thought affirmative action was good and necessary.

He did not think that America was a Christian nation. He was fuck-ing Jewish!

And he thought that Brett Cooper was a bigot who made every-thing he touched turn to shit.

But no one knew any of this. The entire world, even his students, thought he was a completely different person. He felt helpless, like he was drowning in someone else's life.

He picked up his phone and looked at Instagram, feeling the muscles in his neck start to twitch. At the top of his feed was a new picture posted by Ethan's campaign: a photograph of Ethan and Brett Cooper together in some unfamiliar office, smiling. Cooper had one arm over Ethan's shoulder. Both men were giving a thumbs-up.

Gabe moaned like he'd been punched in the stomach. It was a nightmare. This was a nightmare.

He finished his scotch and went to the kitchen to get another.

NICOLE SAT ON the couch watching old episodes of *Criminal Masterminds*. She wanted no romance. She wanted no loose ends. She just wanted voices in the room with her while she waited for Aus-tin to come back.

Midway through her fourth episode, which involved a fraternity haz-ing ritual gone wrong, she heard his key in the door. She turned off the TV and shot to her feet. When she reached the front vestibule, he was pulling off his tennis shoes.

"Where'd you go?" she asked, because she didn't know what else to say.

"I walked into town," he said. "Got a couple drinks."

He looked up at her, his face wrapped in an expression she did not understand. It reminded her of the exasperated look he gave their chil-dren when they were caught in a lie about eating candy or watching television.

He put his hands in his pockets and took a few steps toward her. Would he throw her out of the house? Would he be the one to leave? Or would he fight for them, insist they go to therapy?

He sighed. "We're okay," he said.

Huh?

"We're okay?" She could not have heard him right.

"Look, I don't like this. I don't like that you did it," he said. "But I know things have been hard for you for a while now. And people do crazy shit sometimes."

She stared at him.

"But you told me about it," he continued. "It's not like you're trying to leave me for this woman. I guess this is an itch you have that I can't scratch. So I'm going to need a little time. But we will be okay."

What was happening?

"Do not go behind my back again," he said, louder now. "But we can figure this out."

Her mind was blank. She waited for relief to wash through her, but she felt only confusion.

"I—" she started. "I'm sorry. I'm trying to understand. You're . . . okay with this?"

"I said I don't like it. But I'd like it a lot less if it was a guy, I'll tell you that much."

"If it was a guy"—she spoke almost in a whisper—"what would you do?"

"I'd fucking kill him," he said, stepping back. "I'd kill *him* and I'd divorce *you*. It wasn't a guy, though, right? You're telling me the truth?"

"I am," she said.

"Good. Don't you ever fucking cheat on me with a guy. Do you understand me? That would be completely different."

She looked at him, his planted feet, his clenched jaw. He was angry again. This was the thing that made him angry.

"Are you fucking kidding me?" she said.

"Excuse me?" He drew back as if she'd slapped him.

"How would that be different, exactly?" she demanded.

"Are you yelling at *me*?"

"What do you think happens when I fuck a woman? You think it doesn't count because there's no dick involved?" The words were flying out of her mouth. "Do you think that part of me isn't real?"

"You're unbelievable. I'm your husband! If you were gay, you wouldn't have married me!"

"This is insane." She grabbed her phone off the sofa and came back to the front door for her shoes and purse. "I'm going out."

"What?" He spread out his arms like he'd been suddenly knocked off balance. "You're not going anywhere."

"Oh, I am," she said. "I need some space. I'll be home tomorrow."

"Where are you going? To Kate's?"

"I haven't decided," she said, opening the door. "Sarah has swim class at ten a.m. Don't be late." She slammed the door closed behind her.

She got in her car, backed out of the driveway, and raced down the street. She had lied about one thing: She knew she was on her way to Kate's. She had nowhere else to go.

WITH THE LAST few sips of his third generous scotch swishing around in his glass, Gabe opened up Instagram. The screen gave a little wobble before coming into focus.

He went into his mentions, which had become a shouting match between furious strangers. A queer website had published a long story about Ethan and tagged Gabe in a post about the article. The head-line read: "This Is the Gay Republican Brett Cooper Has Endorsed. WHY?!?!?!"

@sirlouis212: Look at these self-hating queens. Wonder what terrible things happened to them as children to make them this way

@greatmerica776: This just shows how closed minded THE LEFT is in this country! I like Keller. And Brett Cooper is an American hero!!!

@eddiebatman: Your out of your godamn mind!! Cooper is a human dumpster fire! Anyone he endorses can rot in hell.

@jonfam740: Fucking faggots are fucking disgusting

@querrrjj: It's one thing to hate yourself, but THEIR self-hatred is going to mess up MY life! Go die in a closet & leave the rest of us alone.

@bookluvv2: This guy and his husband are absolute morons. They're just being used and they're too stupid to notice!!

Fuck these people, Gabe thought.

@docholmes44: God, I feel bad for their kid. She'd be better off with ANYONE else.

Gabe stared at his phone for a long moment, feeling his pulse throb in his left temple. He hit reply, and started writing back: *Fuck you,* he wrote. He hit post.

@proflife4: They're celebrating an endorsement from one of the most dangerous people in the country! And the husband is a history teacher!! What is wrong with HIM???

@gabealterteach: Cooper didn't endorse me! I think he's the worst!

@jerseygirl07712: What is a gay Republican exactly? How is that a thing?

@gabealterteach: Beats me—I'm a lefty pinko! Viva la revolución!

@daveyblue212: How do they live with themselves? I hope they die miserable and alone. People like this just make the world a shittier place.

@gabealterteach: Fuck you! Fuck you fuck you fuck you

It was a tiny act of self-preservation, but the replies felt good. He knocked back the last of his drink and prepped for a selfie, fluffing the front of his hair, flashing a grin and a peace sign. He took the picture. Were his eyes sort of bloodshot? Whatever, he looked cute. He would post the selfie on Instagram with a manifesto underneath:

Married people can disagree, kids! I love my husband, but his politics are gross and Brett Cooper is the antichrist! He's a race-baiting fascist asshole and I hate him—thanks, byeee!

Post.

He felt a jolt of liberation. For the first time in months, his public image wasn't a forced reflection of his husband. This time, Gabe had told the world what he actually believed. It was petty, sure, but it felt good.

He switched his phone to Do Not Disturb to block incoming messages and notifications until morning. He needed to wall it all off, at least for a few hours. He dropped his silent phone in his pocket and went to brush his teeth.

KATE HAD HAD too much to drink. But what did it matter? Tomorrow was another empty day, in which she would rattle around her apartment with nothing to do.

She'd been spending her time watching a succession of multiseason TV shows, ordering in Szechuan food she would only pick at and deliveries of wine two bottles at a time. (The liquor store had a delivery minimum.) It had been a while since she'd gone outside.

She hadn't told anybody yet what had happened to her at work. Ethan would feel terrible, and she wasn't ready to deal with someone else's emotions. She didn't want to call Gabe because she'd have to explain what she'd done, and she wasn't ready for that, either. She thought about calling Nicole, but she couldn't trust her with this. They hadn't spoken since Nicole flipped out at her for confiding in her brother and his husband, and Kate thought there was at least a fifty–fifty chance she would disappear again.

The only person Kate wanted to tell was her mother. But she was unavailable.

She went to the bathroom and squirted a bit too much electric-blue paste on her toothbrush as she scrolled through her email. Along with the usual campaign schedules and press releases, she'd gotten a note from another reporter on the Politics desk, Samantha Fennig. Where had Kate been this week? And something was up with Mark—did Kate know what was going on? Samantha felt like she couldn't get a straight answer. There was no email from the Obituaries desk with details on Kate's new position.

Obits was exile. It was where reporters were put out to pasture when they got old or where journalists still in their prime were sent when they fucked up but didn't cross the line into a fireable offense, like sleeping with an underling. It was intended to send a message, to humiliate.

She opened Instagram while she finished brushing her teeth. She scrolled mindlessly past a Dalmatian standing on its hind legs push-ing a baby stroller and a chef making the world's most elaborate mac and cheese using a quail's egg and Ossetra caviar. Then into her feed popped Gabe's face, grinning and visibly drunk, with droopy, reddened eyes and flushed cheeks, posted by—Patrick Luo? Patrick was a cable news anchor who sometimes invited Kate to be a guest on his show. He had taken a screenshot of something Gabe posted on Instagram and added some helpful context: *Read this explosive post from the husband of a Republican congressional candidate who just received Brett Cooper's endorse-ment. Wonder what this will do to the campaign . . .*

It had been liked 19,541 times in just the last half hour.

"He's a race-baiting fascist asshole and I hate him—thanks, byeee!"

Holy shit.

Kate tried calling Gabe, but it went straight to voice mail. She tried again, and got the same.

Kate: *GABE! CALL ME! CALL ME NOW!*

Kate: *CALL ME CALL ME CALL ME*

But it was too late. Neither she nor Gabe could undo this.

By morning, this headline would drown out everything else about Ethan. And the story she had thrown her body in front of, about his drinking and his drugs and his accident, all of that would be forgotten.

HER LIFE WAS exploding all around her, and Nicole could not find a place to park.

She'd driven her SUV into the city, flying over the George Washington Bridge as Manhattan twinkled and flexed against the night sky. Now she was on the Upper West Side in the middle of the night circling endlessly for a spot that did not exist. The mundane frustration of it felt like a middle finger from the universe, absurdly incongruous with the immensity of her evening. She finally rolled past a garage that was tucked into the bottom of a glassy condo building and swerved inside.

As she walked from her car, she considered calling Kate to let her know she was coming, but she didn't want to explain over the phone why she was showing up unannounced in the middle of the night. She shoved her hands into the pockets of her sweatpants and sped up.

When she arrived at Kate's building, it was just after midnight and the tree-lined street was quiet. She pressed the buzzer for Kate's apartment.

Buzz. Buzz buzz buzz.

No answer.

Buzzzzzzzzzzzzzzzzz.

She took out her phone and called Kate. *Buzzzzzzzzzzzz.*

Kate answered the phone. "Hi," she said.

"I'm downstairs."

"So that's you leaning on my buzzer?"

"Will you let me in, please?" Nicole sounded more frantic than she would have liked.

"I'm on my way right now," Kate said. The door released a flat, high-pitched tone as the latch clicked open. Nicole pushed her way inside.

Kate was standing at her front door in a faded T-shirt and a pair of gray sweatpants, a grease stain on her right leg. Her hair was oily. Her eyes looked heavy. She pulled the door open to let Nicole inside.

"What's going on?" she asked. "Are you okay?"

Nicole walked past her and dropped onto the couch, allowing her purse to clunk to the floor.

"I told Austin," Nicole said.

"You told Austin?" Kate repeated. "You told him what exactly?"

"I told him about us," Nicole said. "Henry saw that selfie of us you sent last weekend."

"Oh, shit," Kate muttered.

"He had a lot of questions, questions I apparently did a shitty job answering. I've spent all week trying not to throw up on myself every time he talks. He was going to say something to Austin eventually, so I decided it was better for it to come from me than from an eight-year-old. I owe Austin that much, at least."

"Jesus," Kate said. "I'm so sorry, I never meant to force your hand. Honestly, I didn't think you were close to telling him. I really hadn't even considered it."

Nicole paused and looked at her. She hadn't even considered it.

"Well, I did," Nicole said.

"Did he kick you out of the house?" Kate crossed from her position by the door and sat down on the sofa next to Nicole. She put a hand on Nicole's knee.

"I left," Nicole said. "I just couldn't fucking believe him."

"What'd he say?"

"He didn't care."

"He what?" Kate asked, her face rumpled with confusion.

"He said he didn't *like it*, but he wasn't all that upset—because you're a fucking woman!" Nicole pushed herself to her feet and started pacing in front of the couch. "When he thought for a minute that I had fucked another man, he was fucking livid. Fucking *livid*! Then I told him it was you, and he took himself out for a couple drinks, came back, and he was kind of all right! He said: 'We're okay.'" She mimicked Austin's deep voice. "The fuck we're okay! He said, 'I don't like it, but I'd like it a lot less if it was a guy, I'll tell you that!' I mean, what the *fuck*!"

"You're kidding," Kate said.

"Do I sound like I'm fucking kidding?"

"I didn't mean that literally. I just can't believe it."

"You know what?" Nicole stopped and turned to face her. "I can. He's a fucking misogynist. Is it not really sex if there's no dick involved? Or maybe it's because he's a man, so no woman could possibly replace him. It's not like it's news to him that I'm not straight. He just doesn't take it seriously.

"Honestly," Nicole continued, falling back down onto the couch. "I don't think I've ever felt like my choices mattered less. What I do, or what I want—it's like it has no effect on my life. I could throw a can of gas and a match on my front porch and nothing would burn. I'd still have to go inside and make fucking sandwiches."

Nicole dropped her face into her hands. She kept expecting herself to cry, but it hadn't happened yet. She felt Kate's hand traveling up and down the length of her back.

"Well, you're here now," Kate said, standing up from the couch. "Let me get you a drink."

"I don't want a drink." Nicole grabbed Kate by the wrist, then stood up and slid a hand under her shirt. "I want you."

49

WAKE UP! GABE! Wake up!"

A wave of nausea passed through Gabe's body, a sensation that was not improved as Ethan shook him awake by the shoulders. Gabe's throbbing head felt disconnected from the rest of him, as if it were floating a few inches above their upholstered linen headboard. He was both still drunk and already hungover.

"Gabe!" Ethan was whisper-shouting. It was dark in their bedroom. What time was it? "Gabe! You need to delete your post right now!"

"Huh?"

"Your Instagram post!" Ethan held Gabe's phone in front of his nose. "Delete it!"

Gabe took the phone from Ethan's hand.

1:17am

Hi @gabealterteach This is Patrick Luo from GSNN. We'd love to have you on the show to talk about your husband and Brett Cooper.

Missed call: Kate

Missed call: Kate

Missed call: Kate

@gabealterteach I'm a reporter with News10Today and we're do-ing a segment on you. Care to comment on your Instagram post?

Kate: *GABE! CALL ME! CALL ME NOW!*

HAHAHAHAHAH @gabealterteach had a fucking meltdown HA-HAHAHAHA

Kate: *CALL ME CALL ME CALL ME*

Is THIS the kind of family you want representing you in Congress? Vote @JamesCarusoCongress the only REAL conservative in this race!

Hi @gabealterteach I'm reaching out from The Herald Ledger. Do you have time for a phone call?

HAHAHAHAHAHAHAHA @gabealterteach
HAHAHAHAHAHAAAAAAAAAA

Gabe's Instagram post had gone viral. He sat up in bed like the house was on fire.

"Holy shit. I'm so sorry, I'll delete my whole account right now."

Ethan stood up and started pacing the room, his dress shoes landing softly on the carpet. "Fuck," he mumbled to himself.

Gabe poked frantically at the screen until he'd navigated to his account settings and found a bright blue tab underneath the words "de-leting your account is permanent." He jabbed it with his pointer finger until his account was gone.

Gabe tossed his phone across the bed. "Okay. It's done. All my posts are deleted. I am so, so sorry."

Ethan launched toward him, his hands spread open in desperation. "What were you thinking, Gabe? Shit!"

"I'm sorry!"

"This is a fucking disaster."

"I get it." Gabe tried to keep his voice down so he wouldn't wake Chloe. His temples felt like they might explode.

"Do you, though?" Ethan turned away and started pacing the room. "I can't think of anything more destructive you could have done here!"

"It was a mistake."

"Bullshit! You sabotaged me on purpose."

"It was a mistake!" Gabe threw the covers off and rose out of bed. "Have you never made a mistake when you were drinking? Oh, that's right, I guess you haven't."

"Fuck you, Gabe."

"No, fuck you!"

"Why did you ever say yes to this campaign?" Ethan was at full volume now. "You've never actually wanted to support me in any of this."

"What the hell was I supposed to do?" Gabe yelled back. "How could I have said no? You put me in an impossible position."

"I can't believe you would be this selfish."

"*I'm* selfish?" Gabe pointed at himself repeatedly as though he were trying to puncture his own chest. "I can't think of anything more selfish than what you've done. You've put yourself before Chloe, before our family—you're never fucking here! And what could be more selfish than putting us all in the spotlight like this? To be picked over and shat on by strangers and the media and fucking homophobes."

"I'm trying to do something important."

"It's important for *you*, and it's terrible for your family. Fuck, it's terrible for the country!"

They were standing in the dark on opposite sides of their king-size bed. Ethan shook his head slowly and squared his shoulders toward his husband.

"Since the moment this campaign started, you've been walking around looking like you want to throw up," he said darkly. "Like you're disgusted with what I'm doing."

"What you're doing is disgusting!"

"Like you're disgusted with *me*. Sometimes I catch you looking at me like I'm some piece of shit stuck on the bottom of your shoe. Do you think that feels good?"

"I—"

"You do not have a monopoly on the higher ground here, and I—"

"Abba?" Chloe was standing in the doorway in striped pajamas, hugging a stuffed turtle named Turtle. Oh God, how long had she been there?

"Let's get you back to bed, honey." Gabe crossed the room in five long strides and scooped Chloe up in his arms. She dropped her head onto his right shoulder and sandwiched Turtle between their torsos. Ethan started walking toward them, but Gabe held up one hand to stop him. "I'll go."

"Abba?" she asked as he carried her down the hall. "Why were you fighting?"

"Grown-ups fight sometimes, honey," Gabe whispered. "But there's nothing to worry about. Daddy and I love each other very much."

"You were yelling," she said in a slow, sleepy drawl.

He placed her gently in bed, pulled the blanket up to her chin, and surrounded her on both sides with a small flock of stuffed animals—a tiger, a pigeon, two bears, and a dog. He lay down beside her, his feet dangling over the edge of the bed.

"We were yelling, honey, and we shouldn't have done that. I'm sorry we woke you up. But there's nothing to worry about." He ran his hand gently over her chestnut hair. "Close your eyes now, sweetie."

As he lay in her bed waiting for the stillness of sleep to settle over her, he thought about what Ethan had said. Gabe had been angry these past few months. He'd been humiliated. But he couldn't imagine Ethan looking at him with disgust. It would be crushing. He felt ill.

When Chloe's breath was rising and falling in slow, even waves, he kissed her soft hair and walked quietly back to his own bedroom. There, he found Ethan sitting at the foot of the bed in a white T-shirt and boxers, his pillow laid out beside him.

They watched each other silently for a moment before Ethan asked, "Should I sleep downstairs?"

Gabe felt his body recoil. He was mortified by what he'd said on Instagram, and he felt indignant at how Ethan had responded; Gabe had so clearly made a mistake. But things would only be worse without his husband nearby. Gabe was emotionally wrung out, and what he wanted most was to crawl into Ethan's arms and let the rest of it melt away.

"No," he said. "No, please don't. Stay with me."

Ethan nodded. He walked over to his side of the bed, put his pillow back in place, and crawled under the covers. Gabe got in, too, and wrapped his arms around his husband.

50

WHEN KATE OPENED her eyes, Nicole was already dressed. Of course she was. She was sitting on the edge of the bed stroking Kate's arm, and Kate felt a ripple of cold sadness. All this woman had ever done, Kate thought, was leave.

"Hey," Nicole said. She smiled and leaned over with a kiss.

"Morning." Kate sat up and covered herself with the sheet. "Time to get going, I guess."

"I don't want my kids to worry," Nicole said. "I didn't say goodbye to them last night. They'll wake up soon and I won't be there. But Sarah has swim class and I'm going to take her, like I always do."

"Makes sense." Kate bobbed her head in a single, shallow nod.

"Who knows what Austin will tell them," Nicole said. Kate didn't feel she should respond to that.

"I'm going to ask him to move out."

"Okay." Kate nodded again. "Wow."

"I've been lying here all night thinking about this, and if I'm honest with myself, I've probably been waiting for an excuse."

"Maybe," Kate replied. "I don't know if you were waiting for this one so much as you went out and found it."

"Yeah. That's fair. He and I have been like roommates who don't particularly like each other for so long. That doesn't make me any less of an asshole, though. He did not deserve this." She closed her eyes for a moment and turned toward the floor. But she pulled herself back quickly.

"On the bright side"—she picked up Kate's hand—"I guess this means I get to see a lot more of you."

Kate's back stiffened. "Does it?"

"Yeah, of course. If you want it to." Nicole squeezed Kate's fingers. "Presumably he'll have a couple nights a week with the kids. I could be here then. Maybe I could be here a lot."

Kate twisted a bit of the sheet in her free hand. It had always been a risk to be involved with Nicole, but trying to date her in the middle of a divorce would be flagrantly self-destructive, like filling her pockets with stones and walking into a river.

"Honestly," Kate said, "I'm not sure that's a good idea."

"It's pretty bad timing, I admit," Nicole said. "But we've never had good timing, have we?"

"*Timing* was never our problem." Kate hit the word harder than she'd intended. "I'm sorry, but this seems like a bad idea."

Nicole pulled her hands away. "I don't think I understand. It wasn't a bad idea before, but now it's a problem? I'm just saying I want to spend more time with you."

"You don't need a girlfriend to divorce your husband," Kate snapped. "If that's even what you're going to do. I can't get deeper into this thinking we're moving in one direction, and then—who knows!" She pulled her knees up to her chest and wrapped her arms around them. "I can't do it, Nicole. I can't."

Nicole stared, and her mouth fell slightly open.

"You need to figure this out on your own," Kate continued. "I don't think you know what you want out of this—I don't think either of us does. It's only been a few months, and we have a messed-up history that's a part of this whether we want it to be or not.

"If you do actually leave him"—her voice was more gentle now—"you're going to have to completely rebuild your life. You're about to fall off a cliff here, and you've got to be worried about your kids and yourself, and that's it. You don't need a whole messy side thing with an ex you're fucking."

Nicole stood up. "What are you trying to do?" she asked.

Kate rose from the bed, feeling her nakedness like something sharp. She grabbed a shirt from the floor and threw it over her head.

"I'm not trying to do anything to you," she said, pulling on yesterday's sweatpants. Dressed now, she turned to face Nicole. "All the shit that happened between us in our twenties, do you realize what that was like for me? It was like being told over and over and over that I was not enough to hold your interest. I can't be casually dating you while you decide what to do about your marriage. I just can't."

Nicole's lips were set in a jagged grimace, and for a while, she said nothing. The silence felt like a heavy board pressing into Kate's chest.

"I feel like I've been tricked." Nicole's voice was sharp. "I just walked out on my husband and now you're—"

"Yeah, and you were looking for an excuse."

"So what is this?" Nicole asked. "Is this some kind of revenge?"

"Nicole, stop."

"That garbage between us was almost twenty years ago!"

"Yeah, it was garbage, wasn't it?"

They stared at one another across Kate's bedroom. The morning light cast a soft, speckled brightness across the room. A tear started to roll down Nicole's face, but she caught it and forced it away with the palm of her hand.

Kate crossed her arms and squeezed them against her chest. "I think we both need you to go home."

51

A **PHOTOGRAPHER JUMPED OUT** from behind the neighbor's bushes while Gabe was hauling a large recycling bin to the curb. Gabe held his arm over his face and darted back into the garage, abandoning the town-issued container in the driveway, where it would never be collected. Fucking perfect, he thought. Now he would be immortalized wearing a T-shirt with a hole under the armpit, a pair of old gym shorts, and his gardening Crocs.

Gabe's indiscretion was more than a distraction; he had become the center of the story—his politics, his biography, his dislike of Cooper—and the divisions within their household were seen as a stand-in for the angry discord in the country, dissected in countless high-minded think pieces and trashy blog posts. The conservative op-ed page of a major national paper wrote an opinion piece declaring that his use of the word "antichrist" showed the godlessness of the left and the immutable disdain liberals held for religion. The authors seemed unconcerned about the fact that Gabe was a congregant at his local synagogue, though he only went for the high holidays. He became the butt of jokes on late-night TV, where millionaire comedians with floppy hair suggested he take a Valium and find a divorce lawyer. And always, there was that same hideous selfie, his eyes and his smile drooping in a way that made clear he was drunk.

This, he realized, would be his Google search until the day he died. Gabe felt hounded and humiliated. He began commuting to school in a baseball cap and sunglasses.

Andrew crafted an apology and, with Gabe's approval, slapped his name on it. It said that Gabe was sorry, that as a man of faith himself, he was ashamed of his choice of words. He said he was not at his finest when he'd written that Instagram post—the assumption was that people could read between the lines without his publicly admitting he'd been shitfaced. It also said that, yes, he and Ethan sometimes disagreed about politics, a discord that existed within many families, but that he supported his husband 100 percent. Andrew tried to spin it so that Gabe's loyalty despite their differences was a reflection of Ethan's great character. Who knew if anyone would believe a word of it. Gabe thought Andrew's framing of them as a family rather than as spouses was more than a little homophobic, as if they were siblings who bickered during Thanksgiving dinner, but he was so racked with guilt that he agreed to the statement without a single change. It was fine. Put his name on whatever. Andrew drew up a companion statement on Ethan's behalf that contained similar brotherly language about familial debates and leaned into his message of independence.

A few days later, Andrew instructed Gabe to join Ethan at a train station to greet commuters on their way home. Andrew wanted to show unity, and Gabe accepted this as part of his penance.

"Ethan Keller for Congress," Gabe said with dead eyes, offering flyers to suburbanites who almost uniformly rushed past him toward their homes or their families or their televisions, like he was simultaneously invisible and annoying. "Ethan Keller will make an incredible congressman. Vote for Ethan Keller."

"Who's that?" said a man in gray slacks as he grabbed a glossy flyer that was printed with Ethan's face, some policy positions, and an American flag.

"That's Ethan Keller," Gabe said, enlivened that someone had unexpectedly spoken to him. "He's running for Congress."

"Oh! That's the gay guy whose husband hates him," the man said, pointing at Ethan's smiling face. "That shit was hilarious."

Gabe didn't share this anecdote with anybody.

Ethan, too, was feeling the strain of public embarrassment. He was short with Gabe and less engaged at home, though it was hard to tell really since he was out of the house even more now, campaigning with every second he could find. But after their initial fight on the night of Gabe's catastrophically public meltdown, Ethan never brought it up again. He didn't blame Gabe for his diminishing lead, which was clearly Gabe's fault, and never demanded they relitigate what he'd done. Gabe considered this to be a tremendous kindness.

"A LTER!" GABE WAS standing by the coffee machine in the teachers' lounge and he jumped a foot in the air when he heard his name. Someone had clapped him on the shoulder and caused him to spill lukewarm coffee down the leg of his khaki pants.

"Whoops, sorry, man," Lyman said, stepping back to avoid the coffee that had pooled on the floor. "I've been looking for you!"

"Oh." Whatever was coming next, Gabe was not interested. He dabbed ineffectively at his pants with a paper towel.

"That's right," Lyman said, putting his hands on his hips like he was ready to give a rousing speech to the football team their arts school did not have. "I want to tell you something."

Gabe stared at him. Lyman was waiting for Gabe to speak, to ask the great man for his thoughts. Gabe said nothing.

"I want to say," Lyman finally continued, "that I'm proud of you."

Gabe felt himself glower at his coworker.

"I'm proud of you, and I think we're all proud of you."

This fucking guy. Was Lyman the single most pompous man on earth?

"Keller deserved it," Lyman said. "He deserved to be called out. That took balls, man."

Gabe was not a violent person, but in that moment, he thought he really might shove Lyman against the copy machine. *Keller* deserved it? He wasn't Ethan anymore, the partner his colleagues asked after with polite disinterest, Gabe's co-parent, his husband. He'd become *Keller*, a public figure, devoid of humanity, undeserving of grace. He was an issue now, not a person.

"We're still married, you know."

"Sure," Lyman said, continuing to smile at him like a proud coach. "Then it took even more balls!"

"No!" Gabe roared to his husband's defense. "No, no, no, no, no. He didn't deserve this! I fucked up, okay? I fucked up, and you know how Ethan has responded? He has responded with kindness and generosity, because he is a good man!"

Gabe was yelling. He was yelling at his coworker in the teachers' lounge. Four additional colleagues were present, and they had stopped what they were doing to stare at him.

"I'd appreciate it if you would never bring this up to me again," Gabe said at a lower volume. He excused himself and walked out of the room before he did something that would get him fired.

52

KATE'S PRIVATE SHAME went public in the pages of *Vanity Fair*. A jealous colleague must have called their media columnist, a woman whose work Kate had always enjoyed for its juicy scoops and behind-the-scenes details.

Kate braced herself against her kitchen counter as she read the article on her phone.

Gay Republican Candidate Leaves Career of Star Reporter as Casualty

By Naomi Schmidt

At the peak of a contentious and closely watched campaign season, one of The Herald Ledger's star political reporters was quietly reassigned to the much less prestigious Obituaries desk last week. There was no announcement, just an abrupt transfer and a quick reshuffling of duties. Journalists around the newsroom were left wondering why.

The answer appears to be that Kate Keller—an award-winning journalist and a regular talking head on cable news—may have coordinated with the campaign of her brother, Ethan Keller, who is running for Congress in New Jersey.

"Shit," Kate said aloud to her empty apartment.

Journalistic ethics are designed to keep personal opinions and bias out of news coverage as much as possible. To that end, newsrooms have rules that prohibit reporters from accepting gifts—expensive meals, for example, plane tickets or designer goods—and bar things like trading stocks in companies they cover.

Perhaps at the very top of the list are rules that say reporters—along with editors, photographers, researchers and anyone else in a newsroom—cannot be involved in any coverage if they are personally connected to the story's subject. A journalist cannot be expected to write a neutral story about, say, a member of their own family.

As a reporter covering the midterms, Kate Keller would be barred from any stories, or even any discussions, about her candidate brother.

Rules like these are in place in virtually every newsroom around the country, and violating them would be a serious offense.

People at The Ledger say that's just what she did.

"This is journalism 101," a Ledger employee said. "She shouldn't have been anywhere near that campaign."

Fucking coward, Kate thought. If you're going to trash somebody in public, you should at least put your name to it.

Ethan Keller, who is gay and a former Democrat, is running as a Republican—a surprising candidacy in such a hyper-partisan environment, and in an election cycle that has focused so much on social issues.

Then came another surprise: He was endorsed by Georgia Governor Brett Cooper, a conservative firebrand and a major force in the Republican Party. That nod won the first-time candidate a second look from some conservative voters.

But Ethan Keller's husband, Gabriel Alter, wasn't so happy about that.

Alter, who is a registered Democrat, recently insulted both Cooper—whom he called "the antichrist"—and his husband's political views on Instagram.

"I love my husband, but his politics are gross and Brett Cooper is the antichrist," Alter wrote. "Thanks, byeee!"

It's unclear how Kate Keller coordinated with the campaign, and The Ledger said it wouldn't comment on personnel matters. But apparently, it was enough to warrant a demotion.

"It doesn't even matter what she did," another reporter said. "Any kind of coordination makes us all look compromised. It's embarrassing."

Kate had read enough. She put down her phone and realized that her old life was gone.

BUZZZZZZZZZZZZZZ BUZZ BUZZ Buzz Buzzzzzzzzzzz. Someone was leaning on Kate's intercom. She ignored it. It could be a reporter looking for a quote.

A text message chimed on her phone. It was Ethan.

Brother Ethan: You home? I'm downstairs. Let me in?

She hoisted herself off the couch, which had all but fused with the back of her thighs, and walked to the buzzer. She pushed the brass button to let Ethan in the building, left her front door ajar, and returned to the sofa and her stupid cooking show. The contestants had been instructed to make gourmet meals out of jerky and Spam, which they were frantically speckling with caviar and bone marrow.

"Jesus, Kate." Ethan let the door slam closed behind him. "Where the hell have you been?"

"Nice to see you, too," she said. "I've been exactly here doing exactly this for days. What's your problem?"

"My problem is you scared us!" He was brandishing a white paper bag in her direction, shaking it in his fist. "We've been texting and calling and you haven't responded, and then we see that article and what the hell were we supposed to think?"

"I didn't want to talk about it," she said.

"Fuck!" Ethan paced in front of the TV. "I have made such a mess of everyone's life. Will you turn that off, please?"

Kate hadn't seen him this worked up in years. She sat up a little straighter and hit the power button on the TV remote.

"I want you to know that I fucked up and I'm sorry. I should never have let you do this for me. I keep letting people do things for me— you, Gabe. Neither of you wanted any part of this, but I sucked you in anyway." He was yelling, striding quickly from one end of the living room to the other on his long legs. "Fuck!"

"I am an adult, Ethan. I made this decision. You didn't know how much trouble I'd be in if I got caught."

"Not exactly, but I knew you were walking a fine line. I shouldn't have let you do it."

"Stop it," she said. "You didn't let me do anything. Don't give yourself so much credit. Now will you stop pacing, please? You're making me nauseous." He stopped and turned to face her. He looked stricken. "That's enough of this shit," she told him. "Sit down."

He sat, folding his body onto her couch. "I'm sorry," he said to the floor. "I am responsible for this."

"No. You're not. You didn't ask me to do this. I knew the rules and I decided not to follow them. I did this."

"I'm sorry," he said.

"Stop! Stop apologizing. Look, this isn't the best way to go out, but it was my choice. And to be honest, I don't know if I'm going to miss it. I've been sitting around here for days feeling sorry for myself, but when news happens, I think, Thank God that's not my problem! Breaking news and responding to news—that was my actual job." Kate paused and shrugged her shoulders. "I guess it was the life I thought I should have."

Ethan nodded, and they were quiet for a moment.

"Do you think you forced yourself to make a change?" he asked.

"Could be," she said. "I never would have had the guts to quit."

He tossed her the paper bag he'd been holding, which landed against her thigh with a crinkle. "I brought you a bagel," he said. "Poppy with scallion cream cheese." Kate had a tendency to skip meals when she was upset. She smelled the warm poppy seeds and realized she was hungry.

"You didn't bring this from New Jersey, did you?" she asked.

"No. I wouldn't want you to throw me out. It's from Jacob's Bagels."

"Then you can stay." She didn't quite crack a smile, but she was closer than she'd been in days.

"I'm sorry," Ethan said, quietly this time.

"Stop apologizing."

"Maybe one day," he said. "Now will you eat something, please? You look like shit."

53

I T WAS PRIMARY night.

Gabe was in a suite at the Sheraton in Kymptonville with Ethan, a few campaign staffers, and Chloe, who was up way past her bedtime. She had gone from a delightful credit to their parenting skills to a hyperactive gremlin in a green dress, who was jumping up and down on the sofa, demanding the grown-ups build a fort with her out of cushions. He wished Kate were there to help keep Chloe occupied, but she had decided not to come. She worried that joining them to watch returns come in might antagonize her bosses. After Chloe threw a cushion at Andrew "by accident," Gabe gave up on childcare and let her watch a show on his phone about superhero cats.

The TV was tuned to GSNN, which would announce when the race was called. Ethan sat in a brown upholstered chair, which Chloe had declared the color of poop. Robin was perched at a cheap wooden table hunched over her computer screen, her phone clutched in her right hand. Andrew paced the room frantically, manifesting the tension felt by everyone else present, except for Chloe, who was curled up on the couch with Gabe enjoying her feline superheroes. A handful of other staff members circulated in and out of the room, running back and forth between the suite and a small ballroom downstairs where a crowd of volunteers and supporters waited for results.

In the weeks leading up to the primary, Ethan's campaign conducted snapshot polls, which showed James Caruso munching away at Ethan's narrow lead, until just days before the vote, when it became too close to call. Cooper hadn't withdrawn his endorsement, but they never made the joint appearance they'd planned. He never said Ethan's name publicly again.

Gabe, Ethan, and Chloe had all gone to vote together. Chloe stood with Ethan, watching him fill out the bubble next to his own name. Gabe was not a registered Republican, so he couldn't vote in Ethan's primary. Instead, he voted for the Democrat it would be easiest for Ethan to defeat.

Things could still break Ethan's way, Andrew insisted. Caruso read to conservatives as more reliable, but he scared moderates and came across as stern and a scold. Ethan had the charisma and, until three weeks before the primary, the momentum. He had knocked on every door he could find, shook every available hand. But it was done now. The polls were closed, and there was nothing left to do but wait.

At 9:07 p.m., the results came in.

"Another race has been decided," said a handsome GSNN anchor with silver hair. "The Associated Press has called New Jersey's Fourth District."

Ethan reached his left hand toward the couch. Gabe took it and squeezed.

It would be his fault if Ethan lost. But if he won, Gabe would be trapped in this hell for years. Or forever! He was in the eye of the hurricane now, deep in the quiet, just waiting for the roof to be torn off. He pressed down on Ethan's hand and held his breath.

"The race has been called for James Caruso," the news anchor said. "James Caruso will proceed to the general election."

Ethan frowned and nodded once.

"This was a hotly contested race that garnered a lot of national coverage," the anchor added. "Caruso's opponent, a former Democrat named Ethan Keller, received an unusual amount of attention and a high-profile endorsement from Governor Brett Cooper of Georgia, who has become something of a kingmaker tonight. But that doesn't appear to have been enough."

Gabe found himself spinning with remorse and sadness, elation and relief. He wanted to crawl toward Ethan and beg forgiveness. He wanted to jump on the couch and holler in celebration. He wouldn't have blamed Ethan for pulling his hand away or storming across the room, but he kept their palms pressed together. Gabe leaned over and kissed the cool gold of his husband's wedding ring.

Ethan grabbed the remote and switched off the TV. He got to his feet, still holding on to Gabe. Gabe gently disentangled himself from Chloe and stood beside him.

"We fought a good fight, everybody," Ethan said. "I hope you're all as proud as I am of the work we've done here, the ideas we shared, and the campaign we've run." He extended his right hand to Andrew, who shook it. "Let's go downstairs and finish this thing."

54

NICOLE HEARD AUSTIN'S key turn in the front door. She wasn't sure what the protocol was for that, at what point he should start knocking or ringing the bell. Or would that be too weird for the kids, an aggressive reminder of their parents' rupture? They still lived here with her five days a week, but they were at school that afternoon. Austin had come by to collect more clothing for them; it was November and they needed warmer pajamas and extra sweatshirts to keep at his place. She walked into the front hall to greet him, her arms crossed in front of her chest.

"Hey," she said.

"Hey." He cleared his throat and cast his eyes around the vestibule, as if looking for things she might already have changed. Nicole was staying in their old house, at least for a while, to give the kids a sense of stability. "After I'm done here, I'd like to pick the kids up from school. I thought I'd take them with me to vote," he said. "I'll bring them back in time for dinner."

"Sure, that's a nice idea." She had the kids from Sunday evenings through school drop off on Fridays, so this was technically her night, but she and Austin were trying to be flexible about that. He didn't always want to go so long without seeing the kids, and she sometimes wanted them for weekends. That part was working out so far. "Tell them who I'm voting for, too, please," she added.

"Yep."

"Who are you voting for, anyway?" Nicole asked.

"The independent without a chance," he told her. "I can't make myself vote for Caruso."

"Fair. How's the house?"

"I'm out of practice putting a place together, but it's coming along," he said.

Austin had a good eye, but Nicole had decorated every home they'd lived in for fourteen years. "You'll get there," she assured him.

It was a strange feeling, becoming unfamiliar with his daily life. They'd spent years slowly forgetting how to speak to one another, sliding further and further apart. But they had still been bound by proximity and the mundane tasks of their shared existence. Today, she didn't know if he'd gone into the office or where he'd be for dinner. He was wearing a shirt she'd never seen before. It unsettled her more than it made her sad.

"I'll just go up and pack," he said as he started for the stairs.

"Hey. Can I ask you something?"

"Okay." He crossed his arms.

"I don't want to fight about this. I just want to understand something."

"Okay." He looked down at the floor, as if he could hear her better if he couldn't see her face.

"You were so upset when you thought it was a man," she said. "Why did it bother you less when it was a woman?"

A long moment passed, in which his body stayed rigid and still. When he first moved out, she'd put this question aside. She had more urgent things to deal with, like custody arrangements and how she was going to find a good lawyer. Things felt calmer now, and she still wanted an answer. She couldn't let it go.

"If it was a guy"—his words dripped out slowly—"I thought it would have been him against me, and maybe that would mean I hadn't been enough. If it was a woman, that was something I just couldn't give you. It wasn't about something I was supposed to do that I failed at." He shook his head, still speaking to the floor. "It was dumb to feel that way. It's not better that you were looking for something I can't give. Now I wonder, if it was a guy, maybe I would have had a better chance at winning you back."

He still didn't get it. She didn't leave him for a woman, she left him for herself. But rather than the bubbling rage she was accustomed to when he misunderstood her so completely, she felt only a distant sadness, as though something terrible had happened to a person she used to know.

It wasn't worth explaining to him why he was wrong. Their marriage was over, and it didn't matter anymore what he understood.

"I see," she said. "That's helpful. Thank you."

55

BRETT COOPER'S WIFE was divorcing him, and she was ready to burn some bridges.

Felicity Cooper had given up her career as a well-compensated corporate lawyer to support her husband's ascent to higher office, and she'd been rewarded for this sacrifice with her own marginalization and, eventually, her husband's infidelity. A tell-all was in order, one that would be published in time for the presidential election. She and her publisher found a ghostwriter with relevant experience, both personal and professional, and who could work fast on deadline. They found Kate.

Reporters at the *Herald Ledger* were not allowed to ghostwrite. It was considered unjournalistic because the author's ultimate goal was to serve not readers or the truth, but an individual who was cutting them a check. So Kate quit. She thought this could be her new chapter, or at a minimum, that it was worth being paid more than two years' salary for a single project she was asked to complete in five months. She would have time after that to figure out what was next.

Felicity appreciated that Kate had seen up close how hard a campaign could be on a family. They talked sometimes about Ethan, who had parlayed his political connections into a new job, working in-house at a financial firm where he was paid more for working slightly less. He had no plans to run again; it had been too hard on Gabe. Felicity wasn't convinced that plan would stick, but Kate was.

One thing she and Felicity did not discuss, however, was Kate's romantic life. Felicity didn't care that her ghostwriter was gay, but she would not appreciate that Kate was dating a woman who had left her husband after a monthslong affair.

Kate was seeing Nicole again.

She hadn't planned this, but when Nicole called a few months into her separation and asked if they could have lunch, Kate was curious. And she missed her. It was early days and they were moving slowly, going out on actual dates. Gabe, in particular, was not enthusiastic about this turn of events, but even he admitted that things between them seemed healthier this time, though that bar was low.

Nicole had signed a joint custody agreement and enrolled her kids in an after-school program five days a week, and she was working as an assistant interior designer at a small firm in Manhattan. She was still trying to find her own way, but she wasn't lost anymore. The real difference wasn't the job or the childcare, but the fact that she was no longer trapped in someone else's shadow. She had lost herself in Austin's life, as Gabe had lost himself in Ethan's. That was Felicity's problem, too, that she'd disappeared into her husband's public profile. Kate told her that, and she was hired.

Kate spent more than a hundred hours with Felicity, going for long walks and suburban bike rides, sitting in the floral and beige living room she had shared with Brett in Atlanta. Kate met Felicity's friends, interviewed her parents, spoke with her college-age children, filled a pile of notebooks, and recorded weeks' worth of interviews. It was time to write.

She sat at her dining room table with a new computer in front of her—she had relinquished her old laptop to the *Ledger* when she quit. Kate took a sip of her strong black coffee and she began:

Brett and I were sitting at the dining room table on a thick summer evening when he made an announcement that would change both of our lives.

Honey, he said. I want to be president.

Oh, I thought, my face gone cold. Oh no . . .

ACKNOWLEDGMENTS

I COULD NEVER ADEQUATELY thank all the people who helped me get this book onto the page and out into the world, but here's trying:

Thank you to Brettne Bloom for your generosity and your guidance. To Rachel Kahan for your vision and steady hand, and for your comment bubbles that made me laugh out loud. To the team at William Morrow: Liate Stehlik, Eliza Rosenberry, Kelly Rudolph, Jennifer Hart, Rachel Berquist, Alexandra Bessette, Andrea Molitor, Lisa Glover, and Marie Rossi. To DJ Kim and the Book Group. To Jabin Ali, Ellie Game, Indigo Griffiths, and Maud Davies at the Borough Press.

To my readers, who helped make this book immeasurably better: Alexandra Alter, Lauren Groff, Ali Shapiro, Elisabeth Egan, Anahid Nersessian, Brian Faas, Anika Chapin, and Emma Graves Fitzsimmons. To my cheerleaders, Sarah Maslin Nir and Rachel Fein.

To my father, Timothy Harris, whose insight as an author and a reader was invaluable. To my mother, Sharon Harris, the toughest person I know, who believes I can do anything. To my brother, Joseph Harris, who spent countless hours on the phone with me talking about this book. Thank you to my kids, Isaac and Charles. You are my heart.

Most of all, thank you to my wife, Kelly Kleinert. You gave me the space to do this when we had two full-time jobs and two full-time kids. You kept me going. You kept me laughing. I am the luckiest.

ABOUT THE AUTHOR

Elizabeth Harris is an award-winning reporter at the *New York Times*, where she covers books and the publishing industry. *How to Sleep at Night* is her first novel. She lives in New York City with her wife and kids.